IF WE WERE US

IF WE WERE US

K. L. WALTHER

sourcebooks
fire

Copyright © 2020 by K. L. Walther
Cover and internal design © 2020 by Sourcebooks
Cover art © Kat Goodloe
Internal design by Ashley Holstrom

Sourcebooks and the colophon are registered trademarks of Sourcebooks.

Published by Sourcebooks Fire, an imprint of Sourcebooks
P.O. Box 4410, Naperville, Illinois 60567-4410
(630) 961-3900
sourcebooks.com

Library of Congress Cataloging-in-Publication Data

Names: Walther, K.L., author.
Title: If we were us / K.L. Walther.
Description: Naperville, IL : Sourcebooks Fire, [2020] | Audience: Ages
    14-18. | Audience: Grades 10-12. | Summary: Sage Morgan and Charlie
    Carmichael prove to everyone at Bexley School that their close
    friendship does not hide a romance when new student Nick Morrissey and
    Charlie's twin brother, Nick, stir things up.
Identifiers: LCCN 2019058943 | (hardcover)
Subjects: CYAC: Best friends--Fiction. | Friendship--Fiction. | Dating
    (Social customs)--Fiction. | Twins--Fiction. | Brothers--Fiction. |
    Gays--Fiction. | Boarding schools--Fiction. | Schools--Fiction.
Classification: LCC PZ7.1.W362 If 2020 | DDC [Fic]--dc23
LC record available at https://lccn.loc.gov/2019058943

Printed and bound in the United States of America.
LSC 10 9 8 7 6 5 4 3 2 1

To my parents:
Mom, for all those long walks
and hours at the command center.
And Dad, since without you and the
yearbooks, Bexley would cease to exist.

CHAPTER 1
SAGE

THERE WERE CIGARETTES WEDGED IN THE cracks of my windowsill, and my mom noticed right away. "Those aren't mine!" I blurted when she held up two of them, tips browned and singed. This was a given, because I'd lived in this room for all of ten minutes. My sheets weren't even on the bed yet.

She frowned and shook her head. "Use an ashtray next time."

"Maybe it's in here," my dad joked, pulling out one of my desk drawers. I was surprised the cleaning crew hadn't caught the butts. My mom had opened the window because the smell of Clorox was so strong.

"Who lived here last year?" she asked.

"Schuyler Cole," I said, and couldn't help but laugh as she dug out another stub. I almost told her to stop, since I kind of wanted to show the girls later. Up on the third floor, my friend Reese had already texted us that her room's last occupant left her prom dress hanging in the closet.

Not a night to remember? I'd written back.

"Schuyler Cole..." my mom mused. "Isn't she...?"

"Yeah, Charlie's ex."

She nodded. "Will he be coming by to say hello later? And help, since we all know how much you *love* unpacking?"

"We wish." I smiled. "He's still in rehearsal." Charlie had gotten a weeklong head start here at Bexley, moving into school early for the musical's "preseason." This year's show was *Into the Woods*, and he was playing none other than Prince Charming.

My mom sighed. "What about Nicky?"

I shook my head. "Soccer."

"Andrea," my dad said, chuckling. "We don't need the extra labor. This is Sage's senior year. We've got this."

I smiled. My parents were divorced, but I loved that they always moved me in together. "Oh, that's a relief." I faked a yawn. "Because I'm a little woozy from this smell." I flopped down on my mattress and shut my eyes. "Please wake me when the people from Pottery Barn Teen arrive for the photo shoot."

◇◇◇◇◇◇◇◇◇◇◇◇◇◇◇◇◇

I went to boarding school, but I didn't grow up *thinking* I'd go to boarding school. When I was in third grade, I'd fantasized about someday wearing blue and white at Darien High School's football games and maybe being voted homecoming queen. But all that had gone out the window in eighth grade. Holding court from the back of the bus, Charlie told me he couldn't come over and binge on ice cream and Netflix because he needed to go home and work on his Bexley application. "Mom wants Nick and me to start them today," he'd explained. "She doesn't want us to get behind."

"Wait, Bexley?" I'd said. "*The* Bexley School? Like where Kitsey went? You guys are going to go?"

"Well, yeah." Charlie shrugged. "We all go. My grandfather, my dad, Kitsey... Of course, Nicky and I are gonna go."

So naturally, I started my own application as soon as I'd gotten home and finished an episode of *Gossip Girl* and a bowl of Ben & Jerry's Half Baked. If Charlie was going to Bexley, then I was too. I wasn't going to let us be separated.

I smiled as I tacked a picture of us up over my bed. One of me wearing Charlie's spare hockey jersey with black paint under my eyes and standing on his skates as he danced us around outside the locker room. It went next to a fifth-grade snapshot, taken after our school's production of *Charlie and the Chocolate Factory*. We both held huge flower bouquets.

My parents were gone, my mom en route back to Connecticut and my dad to New York, and the girls and I were about to head over to the Pearson Arts Center for Move-In Day's school meeting. "Okay, enough pictures," Reese said, and waved her phone around. "Jennie sent the scouting report."

"Oh, yes!" Nina hopped up from my desk chair. "Anyone British?"

I laughed. "You're not still hung up on Jamie, are you?"

Nina blushed. "Listen, he was *really* nice."

"But he had that *posh* girlfriend back home, Miss Davies," Reese reminded her, nodding her head toward my door. Nina and I followed her out of the room, down the hall and stairs, and once outside, we were swept up in the sea of students. Bexley had rolled out the welcome wagon: the auditorium had our black-and-blue school flags streaming down from the windows, and odds were, Headmaster Griswold, with his retro handlebar mustache, was greeting people as they passed through the front doors. It was the same way every year, and though I'd been so excited on the drive here, I suddenly felt something in me deflate, like I was secretly hoping that this time would be different.

But all signs pointed to same old, same old.

"Okay, Jennie's list," I prompted as we walked, arms linked. Jennie Chu was our fourth musketeer, and as student council president, she'd scored a lineup of this year's postgraduate guys. They were the new kids in the senior class, and most of them came to Bexley for sports after graduating from their own high schools. They were known to everyone as the PGs. Nina's beloved Jamie had been a soccer PG last year.

Reese scanned her phone. "No Brits," she concluded. "But there're two football guys, both from Texas, a lax bro from Long Island..." She glanced up and smirked at me. "Sage, you're *so* lucky."

"Why?" I asked. "Is Shawn Mendes here this year?"

My friend shook her head. "No, but someone named Luke Morrissey is, and you'll get to meet him very soon."

Luke Morrissey, I thought. *Why does that ring a bell?*

"Oh my god," Nina said. "You're going to sit next to each other at the meeting. Morgan and Morrissey. Alphabetical order!"

"I recognize his name for some reason," I said. "What's he here for?"

"Cross-country," Reese answered. "He's from someplace in Michigan called Grosse Pointe."

"It's right outside Detroit," Nina informed us after consulting Google Maps on her phone. She looked at me.

I shrugged. "Grosse Pointe sounds kind of familiar."

But why?

"Find his Insta," Reese said. That was her answer to everything. Instagram.

I laughed. "Okay, no. I don't want to know that his family has a goldendoodle named Waffle before we actually meet."

She raised an eyebrow. "Waffle?"

"Yeah! How cute would that be?"

"So cu—" Nina started, but then the mob of students surged forward, so we surged with it, getting torn apart by the time we made it into the PAC's lobby. A thousand voices bounced off the white walls as I elbowed my way through a horde of junior boys in striped polo shirts, suddenly excited to find my new auditorium seat.

Because after nearly getting tripped up in the balloons out front, I'd figured out who Luke Morrissey was. A conversation in May with Charlie had started: "My aunt Caroline called last night and said the kid who babysits my cousins is coming to Bexley next year. The one Tater Tot is in love with..."

◇◇◇◇◇◇◇◇◇◇◇◇◇◇◇◇◇◇

"You're the Carmichael twins' cousins' babysitter!" I exclaimed the second I turned into my row, and at that, a head turned...

An *adorable* head.

But an adorable head that also looked like I'd just slapped him in the face. I saw his cheeks heat, and when I dropped into my seat next to him, he reached up and ran a hand through his jet-black hair. ("The kind of hair you want to run your hands through," I'd tell the girls later). His eyes darted around behind tortoiseshell glasses. "Uh, pardon?" he asked.

"You're the Carmichael twins' cousins' babysitter," I repeated.

"Or Luke." The guy nodded. "I go by Luke too. Less of a mouthful."

I smiled and held out my hand. "I'm Sage."

We shook. "Nice to meet you," Luke said, and then he was quiet. Not awkward-quiet, but definitely shy-quiet.

That didn't faze me.

"So, why are you at Bexley?" I asked, even though I already knew he ran cross-country. I also wanted to pinch myself at how enthusiastic I sounded. *But at least Charlie isn't here.* "You and Charlie freak people out," Nick once told me. "You guys are like sunshine on steroids."

"Oh," Luke said. "My indecision."

I blinked. "What?"

Luke smirked, and I felt a flutter in my chest. "My indecision."

My eyebrows knitted together. "You *aren't* here for cross-country?"

"No." He shook his head. "I mean yes, I *do* run cross-country, but that's not why I'm here. I graduated from my high school last year, but with zero idea what I wanted to do for college." He hesitated. "This, uh, also might sound stupid, but I didn't feel ready for it."

"Well, no offense," I said with a laugh, "but you certainly don't *look* ready for it."

Luke smiled and rolled his eyes. "Yes, I'm aware I look fourteen. My sister, Becca, who *is* fourteen, looks older than I do."

"Did you apply anywhere else? Or just here?"

"No, also Lawrenceville, Taft, and Kent. But this was my first choice."

I nodded. "So you've met Charlie and Nick?"

Another head shake. "Not yet. You know them well?"

"You could say that." I grinned. "We took baths together back in the day."

"What're they like?"

"Oh, well, Charlie's the best!" I said, but then the PAC's lights dimmed, and the giant projection screen lowered in front of the stage's blue velvet curtain. I smiled and got comfortable in my seat. *This* was the reason for the stampede inside; it was tradition for the student council to emcee school meetings, and they always made an *entrance* for the very first one.

"Get ready," I whispered to Luke. "You're going to *love* this."

This was a ten-minute video of Bexley meets *The Office*, and I wanted to nominate it for an Emmy. The skit was a mock student council meeting, with each member playing up their title. President Jennie was banging the oval-shaped Harkness table in frustration over how Bexley was a good school, but this year, it was their job to make it a *great* one!

"I appreciate Jennie's passion," VP Samir Khan said in a confessional, "but in order to make this a great school, she needs to support my ideas for a stronger peer tutoring system, instead of just focusing on the athletic and theater departments..."

Then the camera panned to a shot of Jennie in the library, with the redheaded Carmichael twins waiting on her hand and foot. "You're really tense, Madam President," Nick, in his hockey jersey, told Jennie as he massaged her shoulders.

"Oh, Nick, I *know*. Feel free to dig in *harder*..." She sighed happily as Charlie held up a chocolate from the enormous box on his lap. He was decked out in his Prince Charming costume and totally grinning. ("That boy could set off fireworks with his smile," my mom always said.)

"And this one, dearest Jen, has a raspberry *cream* filling." He took a slow, seductive bite of the candy and licked his lips before popping the rest into Jennie's mouth.

"That's them," I whispered to Luke.

Luke nodded, but didn't say anything. He just watched, and then listened as Jennie came onstage and welcomed everyone to the new school year before introducing the rest of her cabinet. "And last but not least, this is your Arts Representative, Charlie Carmichael," she told us. "His favorite color is blue, he loves Cool Ranch Doritos, and before you ask, *no*, he is not a paid model for Vineyard Vines!"

Out of the corner of my eye, I saw Luke lean forward in his seat.

◇◇◇◇◇◇◇◇◇◇◇◇◇◇◇◇◇◇

"Come have dinner with me," I said after the lights went up. "I want you to meet my friends." Charlie especially, but he, Nick, and Jennie wouldn't be around. Student council always ate with Headmaster Griswold and the deans across the street in town the first night.

On Bexley's dime, he'd texted me. I'm getting a steak.

"Okay, sure," Luke agreed, following me out of our row. "That'd be great."

"So, there are two different dining halls," I explained once we made it outside. "Leighton is the bigger one, and it's for all the underclassmen. And Addison is the smaller one. That's where we're going now. It's seniors only."

"Right." Luke nodded. "That's the building next to my dorm. Where do you live?"

"Down that way," I said, gesturing behind us. "Simmons. The senior girls' dorm."

Luke whistled. "Seems like a hike."

"It is, but I have a bike." My sweet mountain bike, recently demoted from hilly woodland trails to Bexley's cobblestone streets. *Stinger*, Nick had named it two summers ago, an homage to the bike's screaming black-and-yellow paint job.

Eva Alpert was holding the door open for us when we got to Addison. "Hi, Sage!"

"Hey, Eva." I smiled, and introduced Luke. "This is Luke. He's a PG."

And we basically watched Eva melt right there in the doorway. "Oh, gr—uh, awesome to meet you," she said, twirling a curl around her finger. "You're gonna love it here." I caught her eyes travel from Luke's head to his toes.

Stop it, I wanted to say, already feeling territorial. I took Luke's arm and led him inside.

"I feel slightly violated," he whispered once we stood in the long line for food. It snaked across the black-and-white tile floor. I spotted Reese's sleek dark braids several heads in front of us. She could command a room.

"That's Eva Alpert for you," I whispered back. "She's nice but is always like that with guys." I laughed. "And you're *totally* her type." I thought of Jeremy Tanaka, Nick's freshman-year roommate. Eva dated him for a while last year, and he wasn't nearly as good-looking as Luke, but they weren't dissimilar, both having the artsy-intellectual cute vibe going for them.

"Oh, that's too bad," Luke replied, tucking his hands in his pockets.

I raised an eyebrow. "She's not *your* type, I'm guessing?"

Luke smirked and shook his head. "Not exactly, no."

"Good, because she once called Charlie an overrated actor." I glanced around to make sure no one was eavesdropping. "But I think that's really because she's jealous of Greer Mortimer."

"Why would she be jealous of Greer Mortimer?"

"Because Greer's gotten to make out with Charlie for three musicals in a row. They're always a couple, and Eva's always a villain. She's The Witch this year."

"Charlie's Eva's type too?"

I smiled. "Charlie is *everyone's* type."

<hr />

Charlie finally made his way up Simmons' front pathway a little before 9:00 p.m. He was wearing a light blue checked button-down, sleeves rolled up to the elbows, a pair of navy chinos, and his usual Sperrys with the black-and-green ribbon belt I'd given him last Christmas.

"The Prince!" Reese waved him over to the patio, and five seconds later he was in the hammock with me. I hugged him tight, smelling his familiar Irish Spring soap as he slid an arm around me. It felt like we hadn't seen each other in eons, because the Carmichaels spent the whole summer on Martha's Vineyard. I'd gone out to visit for a couple of weeks in July, but still.

"This is only a drive-by," Charlie said. "I have to get back to the house soon. The festivities are almost afoot."

We laughed. Charlie was a prefect in one of the underclassmen dorms, Daggett House, and had to lead a bunch of bonding activities tonight. We've cranked the heat in the common room so we can do hot yoga, he'd joked via text earlier.

"Well, you just missed Luke," Reese said as I ran a hand through Charlie's red-gold hair.

"Luke?" Charlie asked, leaning forward a little.

"Luke Morrissey," Nina said. "The PG who lives down the street from your cousins." We'd gotten all the details over spaghetti.

"Yeah, I've known the Hoppers forever," Luke told us. "Adelaide, Tate, and Banks, they're tons of fun."

"We've been hanging out with him all day," Reese added. "He left like ten minutes ago." She shrugged. "Mandatory house meeting."

"But you *have* to meet him, Charlie," I said. "He's the coolest." I looked at the girls, requesting backup. "Right?"

I knew they would agree with me; we'd all fallen in love at dinner. "Alphabetical order for the win," Nina had whispered as Luke explained why he was doing a PG year ("I'm calling it my 'victory lap' of high school!").

"Definitely," Jennie agreed. "So nice and interesting. And well-traveled! He just got back from Tokyo. His mom is Japanese, so he's been there a few times."

"He also has this killer sense of humor," I said. "Bone-dry sarcasm."

"Sounds like he'll have you fighting over him in no time," Charlie deadpanned, and then stood. "I better jet. Time for karaoke with the guys."

"You said you were baking cookies," Nina replied.

"I thought it was mani-pedis," Reese said.

I stood too. "And I was told hot yoga."

Charlie winked. "Yeah, a major agenda."

"See you tomorrow!" the girls chorused as he took my hand. I'd walk him halfway home to catch up. We said "hey" to a few other seniors sitting in the front lawn's Adirondack chairs, and they started whispering after Charlie gave them a friendly smile.

But it slipped away once we reached the chapel, and I felt him lean against me. "Tired?" I asked.

He sighed. "Waiting for my second wind."

I wrapped my arms around his waist. "You happy to be back, though?"

Oddly, he dodged the question. "You guys seem seriously obsessed with this new guy," he said instead. "Should I be worried?"

"Charlie, I met him..." I paused so I could check my nonexistent watch, "a little over four hours ago. I'm not *seriously* obsessed." I smiled. "Just obsessed."

"Well, at least you're honest."

I laughed. "I can't wait for you to meet him."

"So you've said."

"Ugh, shut up! He's going to be your new best friend."

"I don't need a new best friend," Charlie said. "I've got you." He held up his phone to show me at least a dozen missed texts. "Plus all these people."

I punched him in the arm. "You're so full of it."

He smiled. "I should go."

"Yeah, okay," I sighed. "Love you."

"I'm aware," he chirped, already starting to walk away.

I rolled my eyes, and started to turn back toward Simmons, but Charlie's voice stopped me, shouting out into the night: "And I love you, Sagey Baby!"

I laughed and shook my head.

Yes, I told myself, pretending I didn't just see his shoulders slump. *He's happy to be back.*

CHAPTER 2
CHARLIE

MY ROOM SMELLED LIKE DEATH WHEN I WOKE up. My phone screamed at 6:00 a.m., time to meet Sage for our morning run. I climbed out of bed and threw on a T-shirt and shorts before lacing up my sneakers.

"So how'd it go?" Sage asked as we headed toward the Kingdom of Far, Far Away—the nickname for the farthest athletic fields from main campus, inspired by the greatest sequel ever made: *Shrek 2.* "Did you puke?"

"Yes," I told her. "All my sins have officially been purged." Last night after the standard Name-Year-Hometown icebreaker, the main event in Daggett had been a sickeningly professional chicken nugget-eating contest. I'd made it to the semis, but this sophomore named Dhiraj Bagaria ended up winning; he'd eaten sixty without breaking a sweat.

Sage cracked up after I told her the full story. "I can't believe it." She shook her head. "I thought Paddy would win for sure."

"Well," I replied, "had he been going at full speed, he probably would've." Paddy Clarke was another Dag prefect, and never sat down at dinner without a minimum of *three* plates.

Sage turned and smirked at me, her hazel eyes shining. "I think Paddy needs a girlfriend."

"Why? You interested?" I asked, half-wanting to add, *Because he is!*

And like I knew she would, Sage just laughed, something she always did when we talked about stuff like this. Sometimes I baited her: "If you were the Bexley Bachelorette, which four guys would make it to hometowns?" but today, I didn't push things. Instead, I followed suit when she picked up her pace, and then we ran in silence for a stretch, whipping by pine trees.

"Are we still on for Pandora's today?" I asked once we'd slowed back down, turning off the fields and onto Ludlow Lane. Every year on the first day of classes, a *totally grueling* half day, Sage and I went to Pandora's Café across from campus for lunch.

"Of course." Sage nodded, and as I began to mentally page through the Bible-length menu, I heard her add, "I was also thinking of inviting Luke, if that's okay with you."

My immediate response was to pretend I'd never heard the name. "Luke who?" I asked, aloof.

But I had to fight a laugh when Sage responded by reaching over and shoving me.

◇◇◇◇◇◇◇◇◇◇◇◇◇◇◇◇◇◇◇◇

Mom cried when she and Dad had dropped Nick and me off last week for preseason. The two of us were in different dorms, so we'd gone our separate ways with one parent to execute "Operation Move-In" before all meeting in The Meadow to say goodbye. "I just can't believe it," she whispered, managing to wrap both Nick and me in a single hug. "I can't believe my twins are *seniors.*" Dad on the other hand, couldn't stop smiling. "This is it," he'd told us. "I remember being where you are..." He clapped me on the back. "Make it count."

To be perfectly melodramatic, the Bexley School was in my blood. It had been up and running since 1816, and from then on, the boarding school had dealt with generations of Carmichaels wreaking havoc across its campus. Great-Granddad hid his homemade moonshine under a floorboard in Mortimer House during Prohibition, while Granddad was responsible for "The Great Daggett House Fire of 1956," and Dad nearly slept through graduation in the 80s. The latest diploma belonged to my sister, Kitsey. Nick and I always knew we would apply to Bexley, and then *go* to Bexley. It was how things were done in our family.

So here we were, back for round four, and as clichéd as it sounds, it was never hard to separate the new students from the returning students on the first day. Freshmen were dressed like their moms picked out their outfits (afraid of breaking dress code) and turtled with their backpacks while they ran across campus as if they were on some mad Easter-egg hunt. "No, sweetie, all math classes are in the Carmichael Science Center," I overheard Mrs. Leveson telling one girl, and I laughed to myself; Granddad thought of the CSC as his penance for burning down half of Daggett.

I spent my free period in Knowles Basement, Bexley's student center. It was an open floor plan, all glass and warm woods, and the only closed-off spaces were the newspaper and yearbook offices at one end and the Tuck Shop at the other. I'd met up there with

Dove earlier this morning during teacher consultation for a snack, and unsurprisingly, the place had been packed, its line twisting and turning. I'd draped an arm around her and pretended to fall asleep while we waited to pay. She giggled and buried her face in my shoulder, and I'd noticed her perfume smelled like sugar cookies and that it didn't take much to make her laugh.

But now class was in session, so the basement had pretty much emptied out. I set up camp on one of the black couches near Tuck's end zone, facing a floor-to-ceiling window in the corner. My usual setup. Sometimes I studied, sometimes I watched Netflix, and sometimes I took naps. Today was one of the nap days. I collapsed onto the couch and stretched out on my back, wishing I hadn't forgotten my headphones in my room. There was no choice but to be carried away by the *click-clack* of people's laptop keyboards.

A voice woke me up ten, possibly forty-five, minutes later. Some kid was talking nearby, and even though I couldn't see him—the back of my couch put me in stealth mode—I put it together that he was on the phone.

I wasn't an eavesdropper, but this kid had a nice voice, so I lay there listening. "Yeah, I guess I slept okay," he said. "It was just different. You can hear *everything*. People walking up and down the hall, and the toilets flushing..." He sighed. "No, Mom, do *not* send Bec's noise machine. I've been here one night. I'm sure I'll get used to it."

No! I wanted to shout. *Have her send the noise machine! You will* want *the noise machine!* Because I had one, and it was a game-changer. I'd gotten it sophomore year, when Paddy and I ended up with a shitty room assignment: second floor, right next to the bathroom. Paddy had been skeptical at first, but by night three, he'd changed his tune. We also found that combining it with our big box fans was even more effective. We called it *The Vortex*.

"Classes were fine," the guy continued. "Today's a half day, so we go to all of them. It turns out my chemistry teacher knows exactly where we live. She used to teach at..."

What year is he? I wondered. He was obviously new but sounded older than a freshman. Plus, he hadn't mentioned getting lost yet. *Maybe a new sophomore?* That was pretty common at Bexley, for your class to multiply your second year. Most of the recruits were New England kids who'd gone to day schools that capped off at ninth grade. In fact, if Nana (Dad's mother) had *any* influence over Mom, Nick and I probably would've been in that boat. Dad had gone to private school his whole life, but Mom was public all the way. "Part of the reason we live in Connecticut," she told Nana, "is because of the school system. It's important to Jay and me that our children experience both." So we did, and Darien's hockey coach had been less than excited when he found out we were going elsewhere for high school.

"And," the new sophomore added, "I think you'd really like my math teacher, Mrs. Shepherd. She reminds me of..."

Smooth, I thought. His voice was smooth, but also subtle, with this coolness to it. It made me want to close my eyes and risk drifting off to sleep again. Not because his voice was boring or anything, but because it was...well, soothing. I felt strangely relaxed listening to this random kid tell his mom about his day, a day that wasn't even half over.

"But English was a *total* CFS," he said, now in a tone with a little more urgency. What did CFS mean? "That class I was put in? It's the English department's equivalent of 'Rocks for Jocks.' It's the class for..."

And that's when it dawned on me. I knew exactly what he was talking about: Bexley's Senior Writing Seminar, always with a roster heavily skewed toward PG guys, a demographic that was *remarkably* athletically inclined. It wasn't hard to connect the dots, and when I did, I smiled to myself.

I wasn't eavesdropping on a new sophomore.

"No, Mom, you don't need to do anything. It's handled."

So, this is him, I mused. *This is Tater Tot's future husband.* "I'm going to *marry* him, Charlie," my six-going-on-sixteen-year-old cousin had informed me last Thanksgiving. "And you can't object!"

"Yes," Tate's beloved went on. "I went to the registrar and asked to be put in a different one."

Which one?

"The only class that worked with my schedule was Frontier Literature. Fingers crossed *Huck Finn* isn't on the syllabus."

I smirked. *It is.*

"I should go, though. I have history in fifteen minutes." He paused, then laughed. "No, I haven't gotten lost yet. This girl I met yesterday gave me a tour after dinner last night, and I annotated my campus map." Another chuckle. "Yeah, you know me."

Sage, I realized. She had been a tour guide since freshman year, usually the admissions office's first call. It was one of the things I loved most about her, how bright and friendly she was—sunshine in human form.

I heard him sigh, getting ready to embark on his journey to history. "Uh-huh, talk later. I love—oh, no, I haven't met them yet."

Patience, young Padawan, I thought. *Patience.*

"Yeah, I know, but I think they've been busy. They're a pretty big deal here."

Well, yes.

"But I'm meeting Charlie today."

Yeah, you are, I thought, because after all, it was my duty to make sure he was good enough for Tate. She deserved only the best.

◇◇◇◇◇◇◇◇◇◇◇◇◇◇◇

The Meadow was where we'd rendezvous. All the brick sophomore-junior houses and a few academic buildings overlooked the green space, which was perpetually flooded with students. It was the universal shortcut to literally anyplace on campus, and when the weather was nice, girls spread out blankets and did homework, while Nick and I and some of our friends played a round of campus golf. Today was no different. It was at least eighty degrees and sunny, pockets of people all over. "Hey, Charlie!" Quinn Bailey, my ex-girlfriend who didn't really *get* that she was my ex-girlfriend, shouted from over by Wexler Hall's front steps. It looked like she was restringing her lacrosse stick. I waved at her, feeling people's eyes on me. Yeah, The Meadow was, without a doubt, Bexley's center stage.

So I did what I did best.

I put on a show.

"Fiancée!" I called when I zeroed in on Sage, her long, wavy blond hair in its usual ponytail. I broke into a cheesy slow-motion run. She flashed me a smile, and, a blink later, she was heading toward me, her lack of speed right on point.

"My intended!" she called back. When we were little, she and I always said that we would get married someday. We'd spent an entire afternoon planning our wedding, agreeing on a coconut-flavored cake and a honeymoon in Hawaii. Even today, we still talked about it (lately I'd been pitching a Bermuda honeymoon). The idea always made my parents smile.

As soon as we met in the middle, I picked her up and spun her around.

"Come meet Luke." Sage tugged my sleeve.

Luke.

"Lead the way." I draped an arm around her shoulders as we walked.

Sage took a deep breath and then kicked things off, exclaiming: "Luke Morrissey, meet Charlie Carmichael, my best friend since *birth*!"

He was young-looking, but tall. Classic black Ray-Bans matching his floppy black hair. Thin, dark blue button-down, Bermuda shorts, and Adidas Sambas. His feet looked a little pigeon-toed.

Here he is, I thought, and realized it had been two seconds too long when I felt Sage nudge me.

Do something.

I took a page out of Nick's book, extending a fist for him to bump. "Nice to meet you," I said. "Sage literally hasn't shut up about you."

Luke glanced at my fist before bumping it back with his own,

so fast that I didn't even feel his knuckles touch mine. "You too."
He reached up to adjust his sunglasses. It sort of seemed like he
wanted to say something else, but he didn't.

"Well!" Sage clapped her hands together. "I'm starving! Off to
Pandora's we go!"

◇◇◇◇◇◇◇◇◇◇◇◇◇◇◇◇◇◇◇

"So, Morrissey," I said after we ordered, "what's the reasoning
behind your victory lap of high school?" (That's what I'd call it if I
had to do a PG year.)

Next to Sage, Luke unrolled his utensils from his napkin and
told me what I already knew. "He's not sure what he wants to do
for college," Aunt Caro explained back in the spring. "I suggested
he do a PG year, so he could gain some new experiences, and take
time to figure things out. You'll look out for him, won't you?"

"A.k.a. you aren't satisfied with your test scores?" I asked
without even thinking about it. Sage nailed my shin under the table.

Luke looked at me, and suddenly I needed to shift around in
my seat. Something was creeping up my spine.

I tried to backtrack, stuff sort of spilling out. "I'm sorry. It's just
Nick, my twin. Well, those tests weren't his thing. He's committed
to Yale for hockey, and we were all worried he would have to do a
PG year somewhere so he could get his score up. Luckily he beat
the ACT back in May."

And, I kicked myself, *I'm sure he'd be amped to know you told
someone that. It's only been his biggest source of stress for the past year!*

Luke nodded.

"Do you have any idea where you're going to apply now?" I asked, wondering if Pandora's had switched light bulb brands or something. I could feel the rays searing my skin.

Luke stirred his iced tea. "Not yet. I have a meeting at the college counseling office tomorrow."

I nodded. "Oh, good idea—" I stopped speaking when my phone vibrated on the tabletop.

Sage laughed. "All right, tell us who's first in line."

"First in line?" Luke sounded amusedly concerned.

Sage shot me a sweet smile before turning to Luke. "First in line this term. Charlie dates girls and then boots them after only a few weeks."

I rolled my eyes. "Sure, call me King Henry..."

"The Eighth," Luke quickly supplied as Sage said, "You do! Catherine Howe is *still* in mourning from your *whirlwind* two weeks together!"

"Listen," I told Luke. "She likes to embellish."

Sage shook her head. "Who is it?"

I sighed. "Dove McKenzie."

"Who's that?" Luke asked.

"A junior." Sage refocused on me. "She's Rapunzel in *Into the Woods*, right?"

"*Oui*," I said.

"Ah," Luke said over Sage's snort. "Mixing business with pleasure...a bold choice."

When he cocked his head, it took me a second to get with the program. Sage burst into laughter, but I just reached for my Coke. "Touché, Morrissey," I heard myself say. "Touché."

I was right; he was pigeon-toed.

Not in a super noticeable way, but just slightly—and it was kind of adorable. His feet were all I could look at as we crossed back onto campus. I did my best to ignore the flicker I felt every time he took a step.

It wasn't working.

Luke cleared his throat. "So, what's Mr. Magnusson like?"

My head snapped up, right as Sage bumped into me, per usual. One of life's greatest challenges for her was walking in a straight line. She was a zigzagger all the way. "Mr. Magnusson?" I turned to look at him.

He nodded, and we made eye contact. He wasn't wearing his sunglasses anymore, and I made a mental note to *never* tell Nina I agreed with her—his eyes were pretty incredible. A deep brown, like the juniper berries on the Vineyard.

"Yeah," Luke said. "Mr. Magnusson. What's he like? All the registrar said was that I was in for an *experience*."

Sage and I laughed. "Mr. Magnusson is a Bexley School treasure," I quoted Dad. "He's been here forever, but nobody knows how old he is…"

"Our best guess is seventy-seven," Sage said.

"Right," I agreed, because Gus Magnusson *had* to be pushing eighty. He'd been Kitsey's English teacher her freshman year, *and* Dad's back in the day. "Ah, Charles Carmichael," he said when I walked into his classroom early this morning. "I knew your journey would eventually lead you here." He'd given me this serious look. "If the pattern holds, *you* are the smartest Carmichael yet."

Luke's eyes were wide when Sage and I finished speaking. "He seriously grades papers drunk?"

I shrugged. "It's really only a rumor, but yeah, I think so. My sister keeps in touch with him, and he sent her a crate of all his favorite alcohol when she graduated college."

"Hard liquor?" he asked.

"Hard liquor," I confirmed. "Whiskey, gin, tequila, and *a lot* of vodka."

"Wow, too bad he isn't my housemaster," Luke said as someone called Sage's name, causing her to smile and zigzag away from us. "That would make it perfect."

I raised an eyebrow. *What would make* what *perfect?*

"This is my stop." He nodded his chin at the dorm. "Gatsby's house."

A tremor went through me. *Did Sage tell him? Or did he seriously just think of that?* Brooks was easily the largest dorm on campus and didn't look a thing like any of the other buildings. Bexley was mostly Greco-Roman brick, but Brooks was sandy-colored stone, with three floors, two serious turrets on each end, multiple chimneys, and a sprawling terrace out front. It was a total monstrosity, one I had called *Gatsby's Mansion* since reading the book as a freshman.

Luke hid his hands in his pockets. "I should probably go. I have practice in a half hour."

I nodded. "Yeah, me too. Rehearsal in"—I checked my phone—"ten minutes."

He laughed, and I felt one corner of my mouth tug up. When

he laughed, it was like his whole body was laughing. "Well, I guess I'll see you—"

"At dinner?" I asked.

Luke gave me a questioning look. "Aren't you having dinner with Sparrow?"

My stomach dropped. *Oh...right.* Dove and I'd made plans for tonight.

But I shrugged and said, "Distance makes the heart grow fonder."

"I'm not sure Robin feels that way."

"Finch will recover."

"I hope so. Hummingbirds are so fragile."

"Don't worry. *Pigeon*'s stronger than she looks."

Luke glanced down at his feet. And then without saying anything, he turned to go inside.

"Hey, one last thing!" I called.

He pivoted back around. "Yeah?"

I swallowed, then said it, "You're going to want the noise machine."

He barely reacted. He just gave me this look, eyebrow half-raised. "You think?"

"In my professional opinion, yes."

Luke smirked. "So I should have my mom send the noise machine?"

I felt myself nod.

"Okay, cool. Thanks for the tip."

"Anytime," I said, quieter than I meant to. I cleared my throat and started to blindly back down the terrace steps. I was definitely going to be late. "I'll see you later..."

Luke leaned against the side of the house, still smirking. "Give Hawk my best."

I shook my head. "She's playing Rapunzel."

"And that means…?"

I shrugged—to hide that I was shaking. "Do some research."

He laughed. "Am I going to be graded?"

"For skimming one Wikipedia page?"

"Wait, you consider Wikipedia a reliable source?"

I fake-gasped. "You mean it's not *the* pride and joy of the academic world?"

Luke rolled his eyes and fished his phone out of his pocket. I glanced over to see Sage talking to Cody Smith. She was using her arms to tell a story, and Cody was totally dialed in, nodding along. *Larchmont, New York*, I mused to myself. *What would Sage think of it?* Because I thought there was a good shot Cody would make it to hometowns week. He wouldn't receive the final rose, but cracking the top four? Yes, I could definitely picture it.

"Ah, I see," Luke said. "Rapunzel is indeed a princess, but"— he looked up from his phone and caught my eye—"she is *not* Prince Charming's love interest."

CHAPTER 3
SAGE

"SO WHAT'S EVERYONE DOING TOMORROW night?" Luke asked at dinner Friday evening, the first week almost over. Like most boarding schools, Bexley had Saturday-morning classes, so that night was when our "weekend" really began.

"Scandalous things," Charlie answered, taking a bite of his cheeseburger. Sitting next to him, I used one hand to zap his waist underneath the table and laughed when he jumped.

"It depends on who you ask," Reese said. "If you're like Charlie over there"—she nodded at him—"then you take a girl to a secluded spot on campus..."

"He gets it, Reese," Charlie cut in curtly.

"And if you're Nick Carmichael," Jennie added, unaware that Luke had yet to officially meet Nick, "you spend the entire night playing air hockey or video games in Mortimer's common room with your friends."

Charlie chuckled. "*So* accurate."

I giggled too, the image easily coming together in my head. Nicholas Carmichael, hair rumpled and sporting his usual sweatpants with the ugliest Patagonia pullover known to man (some tribal pattern in a bunch of clashing colors: teal, red, brown, and a mustard yellow), lounging on the Mortimer common room's giant sectional couch, an Xbox controller in hand. Nick liked to hunker down and relax on the weekends with his best friends, giving no shits about the Bexley social scene and disappointing his own fans. If a girl didn't have a crush on Charlie, chances were she liked his twin, despite his lack of public appearances on Saturday nights.

"And what about you guys?" Luke asked, twirling noodles around his fork. He'd gone to the make-your-own stir-fry station for dinner, and the result looked *delicious.* I'd been eyeing it for the last several minutes, debating whether or not to ask for a taste. "What do you do? I've heard some people talking about a dance?"

"You want to hang out tomorrow night?!" Nina gasped as if Luke were Harry Styles, saying he would much rather spend an evening with us instead of on some yacht crawling with supermodels.

"Well, to be honest," Luke said, "I've already gotten a bunch of invites for tomorrow. The football players on my floor are practically *begging* me to come to their poker game..." Charlie snorted next to me. "But maybe I'll consider gracing you with my presence if I like what I hear." He shrugged as we giggled around him.

"Okay, so this is what we do." Nina clapped her hands, smile a mile wide. "We—"

"Shh!" I interrupted. "Don't tell him a single thing, Nina Davies!"

Nina shot me a confused expression, but kept her mouth shut.

Reese caught my drift, saying to Luke: "As *thrilling* as that poker game sounds, I'm assuming you *will* be hanging out with us tomorrow, right?"

He sighed. "Yeah. I don't want to rob them completely this early in the year. So, yes, if you don't mind, I'll join you."

Reese and I exchanged evil grins. "Awesome," she said. "But you have to promise that you'll participate in *any* and *all* activities we do. Okay?"

"Reese..." Charlie warned, but she waved him off.

"Okay, Luke?" she repeated, her face the portrait of innocence.

"We're not pulling a bank job, are we?" he asked.

"No, that's not on the agenda as of now."

He nodded. "Then, sure, I'm in."

Charlie groaned as I picked up where Reese left off. "Meet us in your common room at 8:30 tomorrow night. *Sharp.* We have a tight schedule."

"Do I get any clues?"

The girls and I shook our heads.

"Carmichael?" he asked, turning toward Charlie.

"Just go with it, Morrissey," Charlie advised. "It's best to just go with it."

∞∞∞∞∞∞∞∞∞∞∞∞∞

As promised, Luke was waiting for us in Brooks House's gigantic common room the next evening. The hangout spot was pretty much empty, most guys having taken off for whatever was in their night's lineup.

Sprawled out on one of the room's couches, Luke had a phone

pressed to his ear. "No, Bec, it's nothing like TV," I heard him say in a hushed voice. "There's actually legit schoolwork and rules here."

"*Luke...*" Nina singsonged, and when he turned to look at us, his eyes grew large behind his glasses.

"Becca, I have to go," he told his sister, the youngest Morrissey. Luke also had two older sisters. "Tell Mom I said hi," he added before hanging up.

"I know, we look *amazing*," Reese remarked when it was clear we'd rendered him speechless.

"Do people really go all-out on the dance's theme?" he asked, rising from the couch and shoving his hands in his gray sweatshirt's center pocket.

"No," Nina replied. "But we do!"

"And so are you," Jennie said.

Luke opened his mouth to protest, but Reese reminded him: "Any and all activities."

He sighed. "Okay, fine. But I guarantee I have nothing that goes with..."

"Red Hot American Summer," Jennie supplied, and indeed, all four of us were representing the theme quite admirably. I wore white gym shorts with blue stars sprinkled all over them, along with a red tank top, knee-high blue socks, and my favorite white Nikes. Jennie and Nina had on similar getups, while Reese had been a little more daring with her outfit choice, sporting a red bikini top underneath a white mesh crop top, metallic blue spandex leggings, and white Converse. We were quite the crew.

"Well," I said to Luke, "it's fine if you don't have anything, because I happen to know someone who *does*."

Ten minutes later, Luke and I quietly slipped through Daggett's front door. The girls had volunteered to wait outside on the porch. "Are we allowed to be doing this?" Luke whispered as I led the way up the house's back stairs.

"Yes and no," I whispered back. "You are, because you're a guy, but girls have to get permission from the faculty duty-master to go upstairs in boys' houses. But I guess, technically, since we're not *with* anyone from Daggett, this little mission would be frowned upon."

We peeled off the staircase once we hit the second floor, and I took off for the end of the hallway, Luke right on my heels. I skidded to a stop in front of the door whose nameplate read:

CHARLES CARMICHAEL

SENIOR PREFECT

DARIEN, CONNECTICUT

Without giving it a second thought, I turned Charlie's doorknob and was greeted by his neat-as-a-pin, clearly empty room. It was nearing 9:00 p.m., so he was probably hanging out with Dove. I hadn't even texted to see if what we were doing was okay, but I didn't think he would mind, so long as we left his room in one piece.

I began to dig through his dresser and moved to grab a few things from his closet, all the while hearing Luke walk slowly around the room. Once I found the final thing on my list, I turned to see him surveying Charlie's wall decor, his gaze moving over the black-and-silver Daggett House flag tacked up next to a triangular red-white-and-blue flag for the Edgartown Yacht Club on Martha's Vineyard. Finally, he turned around. "So whatchya got?"

I smiled and held the clothes out to him. "I'll wait outside."

◇◇◇◇◇◇◇◇◇◇◇◇◇◇◇◇◇◇◇◇

The girls whistled when I reemerged from Daggett with a star-spangled Luke in tow. "God bless Charlie!" Reese declared.

"You look *fantastic*," Nina breathed.

"Totally Red Hot American Summer." Jennie nodded.

"I feel like I'm in a Halloween costume," Luke said.

"You pull it off, trust me." I gave his arm a reassuring squeeze. Even though Luke was skinny, Charlie's clothes fit him well enough. I'd decked Luke out in some of his most patriotic pieces, featuring a pair of screaming loud American flag-patterned shorts.

"So," Jennie prompted, "off to part one of the evening?" We stepped off Daggett's front porch and turned right in the direction of the field house, where the dance was being held.

"There's more than one part?" Luke asked.

"Oh, yes," I said. "Definitely more than one part."

"How many?"

"Three," Reese informed him. "Three parts."

"Okay." Luke straightened his shoulders. "Bring it."

◇◇◇◇◇◇◇◇◇◇◇◇◇◇◇◇◇◇◇◇

I knew as soon as we walked into the wrestling room that the five of us were the best dressed theme-wise. While the girls I spotted did honor the appropriate color scheme, anyone would think the guys just so happened to stumble upon the dance. They were all wearing variations of the same athletic clothing, black, blue, or gray.

So disappointing, gentlemen!

Reese, Jennie, and Nina immediately danced off into the crowd, but Luke stayed by my side, absorbing the entire scene. I touched his arm, and when he looked at me, I shouted that we had to dance. It was a rule between the four of us; every time we went to a dance, the girls and I had to dance like there was no tomorrow.

Luke raised an eyebrow and said something back, but the music was too loud to hear. Luckily, though, I could read his lips: *We do?*

I nodded enthusiastically.

His eyes darted around, and I took that to mean dancing wasn't his thing. I rose up onto my tiptoes and leaned in close, so close that my lips brushed against his ear. "Can you not dance or something?" I asked.

Luke pulled away so he could flash me an expression that said, *That's what you think?*

In response, I smirked at him, grabbed his arm, and tugged him into the mass of sweaty people with me.

And man, Luke *could* dance. His body moved effortlessly to the beat, lost in the music, and before long, I grabbed the collar of his shirt and pulled him to me. I was smiling and he was smiling, and when the song called for it, I spun around and shook my hips. Only when I heard Jack Healy's voice did I remember we were in a crush of people, that it wasn't just the two of us.

"Hot stuff, Sage!" Jack shouted, bopping by us. "You? Me? Turf? Ten minutes?"

Still dancing with Luke, I shook my head and flipped him the bird. I *did* plan on visiting the turf field tonight, but *not* with Jack.

◇◇◇◇◇◇◇◇◇◇◇◇◇◇◇◇◇

"Where are we going?" Luke whispered.

"The turf field," I whispered back, grinning into the darkness. "The primo hookup spot on campus."

Ahead of me, Reese snorted. "I would call the turf a lot of things before describing it as the primo spot," she said, Jennie and Nina laughing.

"Don't worry, we're not going to make you hook up with one of us," I said quickly, squeezing his hand.

About fifteen minutes after Jack's proposition, Luke and I were mocking the junior boys by doing their favorite fist-pump move when Nina had come twirling up to us. Chestnut hair flying everywhere, she announced that it was *time* before grabbing hold of Luke's sweaty T-shirt and dragging him out of the mob.

"Okay, here it is," Jennie whisper-yelled from a few yards away. The turf field was completely dark, so we blindly followed her voice to the locked metal contraption housing the controls that turned on the overhead lights.

"Fuck!" Reese muttered after I heard the clang of her foot banging into the metal post.

Meanwhile, Jennie illuminated her iPhone so she could type in the four-digit code on the keypad, and then pulled open the door. "One..." she counted. "Two..."

And on *three* she flipped a switch.

Turning on *all* the turf's high-powered lights.

I didn't need to ask Luke to know the sight he was treated to was like nothing he'd ever seen before. It was like the scene in the movie *Ratatouille* when the chefs come into the kitchen and the rats instantly scatter. There were couples *everywhere*, all in various states of undress. I spotted Lucy Rosales push a guy off her so she could grab her shirt and make a run for it, and by one of the field hockey goals, I saw more of Jack than I ever needed—or wanted—to see.

After about ten seconds of watching our classmates run for their lives, Jennie shut off the lights, and I grabbed Luke's hand again. "Run!" I whisper-yelled before taking off for the woods to hide. By the time we made it under the trees, everyone's breathing was heavy with excitement.

"What—the—fuck—was—*that*?" Luke asked.

The girls and I laughed. "That," Reese answered, "was Bexley's favorite use for the turf field."

"That's literally the grossest thing I've ever seen!" he exclaimed. "I feel sick! I can only imagine what my mother will say when I tell her I've been corrupted!" We kept laughing, and Luke soon joined in. "Where did you get the combination?"

Jennie collected herself first. "When I was president of Hardcastle last year, I organized a nighttime Ultimate Frisbee game, so obviously the lights needed to be on, and AD Calder gave me the code that unlocks the control box. It hasn't been changed since then."

"How many times have you done this?"

"This is only the third," Nina said. "We do it really infrequently to make sure people don't catch on."

"The next time will probably be in the winter," I added.

Luke was incredulous. "People come up here when it's cold?"

"If it means they're gonna get some," Reese said, "then yes, they'll brave the cold."

There were a few heartbeats of silence before Luke deadpanned: "Toto, I've a feeling we're *not* in Michigan anymore."

"Not even close," I replied, my grin invisible in the darkness, so happy that Luke was here with us. "Now it's time for the finale."

⟨⟨⟨⟨⟨⟨⟨⟨⟩⟩⟩⟩⟩⟩⟩⟩

Some would say that the finale was anticlimactic, but after expending most of our energy on the dance floor and bringing some unlucky Bexleyans' illicit activities to an abrupt end, we just wanted to catch our breath and chill.

Before our next destination, the five of us made a quick detour to Simmons, where Nina raced inside to grab the tote bag of essentials we needed. Then we set off for Thayer House, where all the freshmen boys lived. Predictably, their common room was a ghost town when we arrived, since they were still busy showing off their moves at the dance. "Okay, so *Mamma Mia* or *Mamma Mia 2*?" Nina posed, grabbing my laptop from the bag, along with some candy: M&M's, Sour Patch Kids, and my favorite, Junior Mints.

"Oh, please not the first one," Luke said. "I've seen it well over a *thousand* times."

We gave him quizzical looks.

"I have *three* sisters!"

"So number two it is!" I declared, taking the computer from

Nina and crouching down in front of the TV to plug it into the HDMI cord.

My friends and I capped off almost every Saturday night like this. We went to a boys' house and took over their common room by popping in a chick flick and lounging on their furniture, eating junk food. The dorm rotated every week, and no matter which one, it was always a mixed bag of reactions whenever the guys returned for the night; some told us to beat it, while others did their best high-pitched giggles and joined us on the couches. The freshmen boys, though, especially since it was the year's *first* Saturday night, would most likely walk into the common room, exchange a *what's going on?* look with one another, and then walk right back out again.

After hitting play, I saw that everyone had settled down in their movie-watching position of choice. Reese snagged the leather recliner, and Jennie was in the armchair to the right of the couch, hugging her legs to her chest. I moved a few paces to plop down on the couch with Luke...and Nina. She was lounging on the left end, using the couch's arm as a backrest, while her legs were stretched out across Luke's lap.

It's official, I thought. *Nina Davies likes Luke Morrissey.*

But Luke was keeping his hands to himself, ignoring Nina's silent invitation for him to rest them on her legs. Instead, his arms were folded across his chest. To me, the message was clear: He wasn't interested. And deep down, I had a feeling that even if they became super close and Nina's flirting continued, Luke *still* wouldn't be interested.

I felt my phone buzz toward the end of the movie, right when Donna's ghost sings the heartfelt "My Love, My Life" to her daughter Sophie. Before checking it, I flicked my gaze to Luke to see if he was crying. "I won't need tissues," he'd said when I jokingly offered them to him. "I've seen this movie too...but only a hundred times, not a thousand." Now, his face was noticeably tear-free, expression completely neutral. Nina's legs were still draped over him, and sure enough, Luke still hadn't taken the bait; his arms now rested on the back of the couch. I glanced down at my iPhone, then blinked to double-check the name on-screen. I swiped to see the message:

So word on campus is the turf saw more action than usual tonight...

I fought the urge to smile.

Retweet, I typed back. The most epic light show!

Epic? came his reply. Impossible!

Guess again, I was about to write, but before I could, he quickly buzzed in: Because you and I both know there's only ONE epic light show.

And then a third message: Up for an adventure?

Something rippled through me. *Up for an adventure?* Yes, I was always up for an adventure, and he knew it. So my thumbs dashed off a response, but hovered over the send button for a couple of seconds before sending back: I'm listening...

◇◇◇◇◇◇◇◇◇◇◇◇◇◇◇◇◇◇◇

A few minutes later, I jogged along Belmont Way toward The Meadow.

"Where are you going?" Jennie had asked when I'd stood to leave Thayer.

"Oh, Charlie needs me for something," I'd said, adjusting my obnoxious *MERICA* trucker hat. "I'll see you guys tomorrow? At brunch?"

I waited until Reese nodded in confirmation before making my exit. Although I managed to catch Nina telling Luke, "We all think she's in love with him. I mean, I know you've only been here a week, but you see it, right?"

It was close to 11:00 p.m., so unsurprisingly there were a ton of underclassmen loitering on the house porches, trying to make every last second count before their curfew.

Dusk-to-dawn lights dotted the Bexley golf course, lighting the way as I ran the final stretch to our meeting place: the sixth hole. I wished I had Stinger, but leaving tire tracks on the meticulously manicured grass wasn't the best idea. Breathing now shallow and a ringing noise in my ears, I let out a sigh when I heard Perry Lake's calming waves. The sixth hole was small and secluded, right on the lakeshore. I leaned against a streetlamp's post, figuring I'd beaten him here, since he was nowhere to be found, but when my breaths slowed and the ringing died away, I heard someone say, "What the hell are you wearing?"

Then, stepping out of the darkness and into the lamplight's glow, heinous fleece and all, was Nicholas Carmichael.

Once again, I felt that ripple. New, a little strange, but full of excitement.

"It was my outfit for the dance tonight," I explained, noticing the Hudson's Bay blanket he had thrown over his shoulder.

"Right, right." Nick nodded. "What was the theme again?"

"Red Hot American Summer," I answered, tilting my head. "Did you *really* not know that?"

One side of his mouth curled up in a smile. "Oh, come on, Sage. You know those aren't my thing."

I watched him shake out the blanket and spread it on the putting green. "Yes, how could I forget? The Carmichael twins are *far* too good for Bexley's dances."

"You mean *Charlie* is too good for dances," Nick corrected as he dropped to the ground. "I don't go because my couch is *so* comfortable."

I rolled my eyes. "You were totally a lapdog in another life."

He laughed and patted the spot next to him.

I hesitated for a second, then joined him. "You're right," I said after stretching out on my back. "Nothing is more epic than this."

The sky was breathtakingly bright tonight, the stars above dazzling—shimmering without the cover of clouds. "That's Polaris," Nick said after a moment, pointing to a single diamond-shaped star. "Also known as 'true north.' And if you look over there, you can see Andromeda."

His finger traced out the constellation.

I smiled in the darkness. Nick considered himself an astronomer of sorts, reading books and obsessed with some stargazing app on his phone. "And that's Perseus," I said, also reaching up to connect some stars. I'd downloaded the same app. "Right?"

Nick didn't answer. Instead, he just said, "I can't stop thinking about it."

My heart hitched.

"That night," he went on. "At the beach..."

"That night..." I echoed, grabbing for the hair tie on my wrist and stretching it out. "At the beach..." It sounded like I had no clue what he was talking about.

But I did, eyes fluttering shut for a second. To see it again, to be there again: Martha's Vineyard, back in July. The beach, the bonfire, the s'mores and "borrowed" beer. "Come on, let's play spin the bottle!" someone had shouted.

So I'd spun. I remembered spinning first, the empty Bud Light bottle slowing to a stop halfway between the twins. "Get ready, groom." I'd flashed Charlie a grin, at the same time one of his friends said, "No, no, Sage, it's totally leaning toward Nick..."

Totally leaning toward Nick.

I'd felt him smiling at me from across the fire, but even with its heat, I froze. Kiss Nick? Kiss *Nick* Carmichael? Half of me couldn't fathom it; we were friends. Just friends. *Always* just friends.

But then my ice broke, that first crack rippling through me.

Because somehow the other half *could* imagine it—kissing him.

Just once, I'd told myself. *Just once, to see what it's like.*

Now, I snapped my hair tie back against my wrist and sat up. Nick did too, and it was so quiet that I heard him swallow before he gave my ponytail a teasing tug. "What do you think?" he asked.

"Nick..." I began, but didn't get to finish, Nick suddenly taking my face in his hands and kissing me. And just like that, it felt like back at the bonfire. Nervous and clumsy at first, but then deep and drowning—all-consuming. Afterward, I felt so light-headed that I swore I would float up, up, and away, so I took one of his hands to anchor myself.

Nick grinned. "You taste like Junior Mints."

I grinned back. "And you taste like a Milky Way."

"Not a great combination," he replied, a dimple popping in his left cheek. I loved that dimple.

So I leaned in again.

"Wow," he sighed a few minutes later. "This time..."

"A bottle." I sucked in a breath, snapping back to reality. Here, now, Bexley. My spine straightened. "This time there isn't a bottle."

Nick chuckled. "Well, does there need to be?"

My heart twisted, knowing what he meant. *Everything will change*, I thought. *If we do this*, everything *will change...*

"I mean, would you want to?" he asked. "Because I think we could be really good." He squeezed my hand. "You know, good together. I've always thought so, but I've never had the nerve to say it..."

I stayed quiet, unsure how to respond. Nicholas Carmichael was a romantic and a traditionalist; he was imagining a girlfriend to love and adore, to hold hands with while walking to class, to take to prom. The idea made me think of my parents—that had been them, years and years ago. High school sweethearts, married straight out of college but divorced by the time I hit middle school. "Too young," my mom said now. "We loved each other, Sage, but we were too young to really know what we wanted. You shouldn't get serious with someone until you've lived your own life first."

Nick kissed my knuckles. "Sage?"

"We'd need to keep it a secret," I said before I could stop myself. I mean, what was the harm? We could keep it casual and under wraps.

Oh, and his lips were so warm and wonderful against my skin.

"A secret?" Nick gave me a look, eyebrows furrowed. "Why?"

"Because..." I tried to think of a good reason, unable to tell him the truth. He wouldn't get it. *Think! Think, think, think!* "Because people talk," I said, forcing out a laugh. "This place is a fishbowl." My heart pounded. "Like, remember when Charlie was with Schuyler Cole? They were *all* anyone could talk about, all anyone was interested in."

"Yeah, because that relationship was absurd," Nick responded. "You'd think he *wanted* people to talk about it..." He trailed off and shook his head, not convinced.

"Please?" I asked. "It should stay quiet. That way it'll be just us."

"Just us?"

"Yeah," I said, even though warning alarms sounded in my head. "Just us, just you and me."

"Well, okay, then." He untangled our fingers, and I let him pull me close. There was no campfire tonight, but somehow he still vaguely smelled like one. I smiled into his Patagonia. "So are you gonna kiss me again?" he whispered a beat later. "Or not?"

I did. I kissed Nick and Nick kissed me, kissed me so senseless that I had to cling to his arm when we headed back toward main campus. All around me there were stars, but I didn't think half of them could be seen by anyone else.

CHAPTER 4
CHARLIE

"WHAT DO YOU HAVE GOING ON LATER?" I ASKED Nick the first Saturday night, as we worked to straighten his red Arsenal flag. That was the overall theme of Nick's room: flags. There was a standard American flag, along with his crimson-and-gray Mortimer House flag, and a New York Rangers banner. He also had a black tapestry with a glow-in-the-dark map of the constellations (Sage had given it to him for our birthday last year, saying: "But don't tell him it's from the women's section of Urban Outfitters!"). So far, only about half the flags were tacked up, because Nick always had to wait until after the fire marshal's official visit to transform his room into the inside of a frat house/circus tent. It was *the* example of a fire hazard.

"Not much," my brother responded. "Probably will just hang here." He motioned for me to hand over another Command Strip. I watched him position it on the wall and put the flag in place. Then we stood back to admire it before tackling the constellation tapestry.

Nick was a prefect in Mortimer, an underclassmen dorm two houses down from Daggett. His house was like a secret society: the guys referred to one another as *brothers*—walking around in packs and eating every meal together—and outsiders only gained inside access if they knew the password. This week's was "Andromeda."

"Not the dance?" I joked. Dances were a Saturday-night staple at Bexley, and the student council was in charge of picking the theme, but when we were throwing around ideas during Thursday night's meeting, people just weren't on the same page. Nick sort of lost it after a while. "This is *ridiculous*," he'd said, falling into what Sage called his *exasperated mom* persona (executed by closing his eyes, biting his tongue, and releasing a deep, disappointed sigh). "Let's keep it simple. USA beach-themed or something."

And thus, the Red Hot American Summer dance had been born.

But as usual, Nick and I weren't going.

Nick, because he was a cringe-inducing dancer.

"How about you?" He grabbed the tapestry we would hang over his desk. "Plans?"

I shrugged. "Dove." Hence why I didn't go to dances. I mean, when you had a girlfriend, they were kind of a waste of time. You hung out until that magical hour struck (10:00 p.m.), then you went on a "walk" together. It was routine.

Nick nodded. "You like her?"

"Yeah," I said, both of us now standing on the desk. We were pretty tall, but Mortimer had outrageously high ceilings. "She's fun."

"Really? I heard she's kind of clingy."

I rolled my eyes. "Are you in cahoots with Sage?"

Nick laughed. "So what if I am?"

We continued hanging the flags, and later, when I grabbed my backpack to leave, I asked if we were on for brunch tomorrow. He and I always had Sunday brunch together. We called it *family meal*.

"Wouldn't miss it," he confirmed, and just as I was twisting his doorknob, I heard him clear his throat. "What's Sage doing tonight?"

"Oh, you know." I turned back around and shrugged. "What she always does. Sage is doing Sage."

◇◇◇◇◇◇◇◇◇◇◇◇◇◇◇

Dove and I decided to hang out on Hardcastle's porch, since I wasn't allowed inside the actual dorm. And no, it wasn't because I was a guy. Technically, girls and guys could hang out in one another's common rooms whenever, but Hardcastle's housemaster had banned me from entering period. "Front porch *only*, Mr. Carmichael," Mrs. Collings said last spring, after catching me with Catherine Howe on the common room couch, not at all paying attention to the movie we'd been watching.

We were sitting in rocking chairs while Blake Shelton crooned through Dove's speaker. Her chair was turned, facing mine, with her legs perched on my knees. I didn't particularly like country music, but I'd learned to tolerate it since Nick was obsessed. His go-to playlist was twenty-four hours of Nashville's best.

"Tell me a secret," Dove said after the song ended. We'd dropped into a lull after spending the last half hour talking about the musical and how Taylor Swift should really go back to country (which was 100 percent Dove's opinion; I just nodded along).

"Wait, what?" I glanced up from my phone.

Do you like country music? I'd texted a few minutes ago, fingers sort of shaking, but had yet to get a response. Not surprising. It was 9:45, so he was with Sage, and Sage's Saturday-night itinerary didn't factor in much time for texting.

"You sure you don't want to come?" she'd asked earlier, like she always did. And I loved her for it, never giving up hope that one night I might say yes.

"A secret," Dove repeated. "Let's trade secrets."

I locked my phone and flipped it over. "Okay, you're on." I summoned a smirk while trying to ignore the heat at the back of my neck. "Ladies first."

She smiled and shook her head. "No way. I asked *you* first."

I resisted rolling my eyes. I wasn't in the mood to play this game. "Fine. I have a bottle of Jack Daniel's hidden in my room."

Dove giggled. "Where?"

"In my closet." Lie. The whiskey was actually buried deep in the depths of my steamer trunk. Nick and I both had trunks, presents from Granddad and Nana Carmichael after we'd been accepted to Bexley. They were big and black, our initials embossed just underneath the locks, and heavy as hell. Nana had also been horrified to see that we'd both covered them in bumper stickers. I took Dove's hand. "Now take it away. I'm all ears."

She sucked in a breath. "I cheated on a Spanish test last year, by copying off Randall Washington."

I laughed. "I don't think you're alone there." Because with Bexley's Harkness tables, I'd felt the weight of people's gazes a hundred times as they carefully leaned closer to me. ("You know..." I once told Eva Alpert after a calculus test, my voice dripping with sarcasm, "if you need help, I'd be more than happy to tutor you.")

"It was me!" Dove blurted after I admitted Redbone's '70s hit "Come and Get Your Love" was my go-to shower song (and yes, also the opening to *Guardians of the Galaxy*). "It's my fault you're banned from coming inside. I'm the one who told Mrs. Collings about you and Catherine. I was jealous." She sighed. "I was always *so* jealous when you hung out with her. I thought you were so cute and funny and nice." She giggled. "I mean, I obviously still do, but..."

I squeezed her hand and smiled, letting her know I understood. I'd dated Catherine for two weeks, and it had felt like the *longest* two weeks of my life. I remembered telling Nick I was going to shave my head because Catherine never stopped raking her hands through my hair. "It's painful," I'd said. "Care to join me in getting a buzz cut?"

I was on the verge of zoning out when Dove spoke again. "I'm glad you're the one who asked for my number," she whispered. "Because I never know what to say when I want a guy's number."

"Really?" I asked, because clingy or not, Dove McKenzie was a cute girl. She could easily go up to any guy and request a phone number.

She let out a breathy laugh. "Yeah, I get nervous. My mind goes totally blank." She smiled at me. "I bet that never happens to you though, right?"

"Actually no." I shifted in my seat, itching to check my phone. "Once I was so nervous about asking for this one person's number that I just *didn't.*"

Dove's eyebrows knitted together. "So you never got it?"

My heart quickened. "No." I shook my head. "I did, but I didn't directly *ask* for it. Instead, I convinced our class that it would be smart to make a group chat"—I shrugged—"and there you go. Mission accomplished."

Dove giggled. "When? Your freshman year?"

I shrugged, leaving it up for interpretation. In reality, the Bexley Bunch chat had been created just over seventy-two hours ago, after I told everyone in Frontier Lit about the elusive Mr. Magnusson. "He's never around during consultation and doesn't respond to emails, so I think we should band together on this one, and form a gang of our own."

But of course, the second the chat blew up (as most did), I'd marked it as Do Not Disturb. Then I'd stared at my screen until Luke finally buzzed in, a text just to me: You're an IDIOT.

Mission accomplished.

I'd grinned while tapping a text back, but also felt a simultaneous lump forming in my throat. *Shit*, I thought, shivering when my phone vibrated again. *What did you just do?*

"Who was the girl?" Dove asked now, her face sort of crumpling when I let go of her hand.

I fiddled with the faded green-and-white rope bracelet on my wrist. "No one you'd know." I stood from my chair and held out my hand. "Should we go for a walk?"

Dove brightened, smiling and nodding, and when she ran inside to grab a sweater, I finally got to check my phone; six new messages, but only one I wanted to read.

Nope, it said. So you better give your extra Blake Shelton ticket to someone else.

There were so many places we could've gone, but I took Dove to the Zen rock garden, down one of the streetlamp-lit cross-country trails. *It's been a while*, I thought to myself as I spotted two pairs of initials carved into the massive sycamore tree nearby: *CCC + NMD*.

Dove clung to me on our way back, arms locked around my waist and face buried in my shoulder. "Why are you walking so fast?" she asked. We were all but jogging up Belmont Way, closer and closer to Hardcastle.

"Because it's almost eleven," I answered. Curfew for under-classmen was 11:00 p.m. on Saturdays, and midnight for seniors. So while Dove's evening was ending, I had a whole other set of plans.

She sighed and picked up her pace, not wanting to face the wrath of Mrs. Collings. And when we made it to The Meadow, I scooped her up fireman-style and did my best to hightail it across to ensure we'd beat the clock. Her laughter rang out into the night. "Don't you drop me, Charlie!"

The girls' porches were packed, and from the sea of stars and stripes, it looked like Nick's brainchild had been a raging success. Dove rose on her tiptoes and slung her arms around my neck, and I put a hand on her lower back. "Good night, Dove darling," I said after a quick kiss. "Feel free to dream about me."

Mrs. Collings was standing behind us. She looked the same as always: wearing a BEXLEY SWIMMING windbreaker, her salt-and-pepper hair pulled back, and smiling tightly. "While I am glad to see you haven't forgotten our arrangement," she said to me, "it's time for you to say goodbye to Miss McKenzie for tonight."

I nodded, not needing to be told twice—in my mind, I was already en route to my next stop. "Of course."

◇◇◇◇◇◇◇◇◇◇◇◇◇◇◇◇◇

Thayer, Sage had texted me earlier, before dinner. We're ending the night in Thayer. Feel free to crash! So I wasn't surprised when I walked into the common room and found my friends lounging on the furniture. Reese, Jennie, Luke with Nina's legs across his lap, and interestingly enough, Sage was missing. *Hmm*, I thought.

I groaned when I realized what they were watching: *Mamma Mia.* "Jesus, what are you doing to him?" I flipped on the lights and glanced at Luke. "Did you lose a bet or something?"

He opened his mouth, but the girls spoke first:

"He said it was okay!" Nina exclaimed.

"He has sisters," Jennie said.

"Did Sage find you?" Reese asked.

I nodded, never one to be slow on the uptake. "Yup." I watched one of her eyebrows un-arch itself. "All good." And before any of them could inquire about Sage's *current* whereabouts—I'd text her later to find out—I looked back at Luke and jerked my chin toward the door. "Let's go."

"What are you doing?" Jennie asked.

"Guy stuff," I answered as Nina slipped her legs off Luke's lap. "Something to get—"

He was wearing my clothes. I hadn't noticed it at first, with Nina draped all over him, but Luke was wearing my clothes. I'd recognize the T-shirt anywhere: blue with an American flag and reading BACK-TO-BACK WORLD WAR CHAMPS. My brother, a World War II aficionado, had given them out as Christmas presents last year. Red sweatbands were on his head and wrists, leftover from some half-assed Halloween costume a few years back. I suddenly wished I hadn't turned the lights on; it was a thousand degrees and I felt sort of dizzy. *Get it together*, I blinked. *Ignore it.*

"So what is this guy stuff, pray tell?" Luke asked once we were outside, cutting across the freshman grove toward Darby Road. I released a deep breath. Without the underclassmen around, Bexley was quieter, calmer, more relaxed. It was easier to breathe.

"I don't know." I shrugged. "I didn't have anything specific in mind. I just said that to get you out of there. You should *not* be spending your Saturday night watching *Mamma Mia*..."

"It was actually *Mamma Mia 2*."

"Is there a difference?"

Luke laughed, and our shoulders brushed—I hadn't realized how close we were walking. "You'd be surprised," he said as I put a couple of feet between us.

I nodded, but before I could say anything, my stomach rumbled. Dinner tonight felt like days ago.

"Time for a midnight snack?" Luke suggested.

"More like a midnight *dinner*." I motioned for us to turn left. "I've been craving a steak all day." At home, Dad always grilled steak on Saturday nights.

"How do you like it?"

"Rare, obviously."

"Good, because that's the only way I do it."

"You can grill?"

"In my sleep."

I laughed. "I never would've expected that."

"Why?" he asked, a slight edge to his voice. "Because I look fourteen?"

I was glad it was dark because I felt myself go red. It was true; Luke didn't look like a senior, but that wasn't it. "No." I shook my head. "It's because I don't know anyone our age who can actually cook." I cleared my throat. "I mean, I haven't even mastered pasta yet."

I saw Luke shrug as we passed under a streetlight. "I was very food-motivated when I was younger," he said, "while you probably wanted to be a NASCAR driver or something."

I sighed. "It was *one* Halloween."

He smirked. "Are there pictures?"

"Try a whole album." I rolled my eyes. Mom was obsessed with making photo albums; there had to be at least twenty in our basement.

Luke let out an impressed whistle, and we brushed shoulders again, having somehow moved back together. My legs went a little weak, so I couldn't step away this time.

"I wish we could build a fire," I randomly said, and straightened one of my rope bracelets. "It's a great night for s'mores." I thought of Nick, and the summer bonfires we loved to build. Always on the beach, with plenty of marshmallows and chocolate packed in the Yeti.

Luke laughed. "But that's a 'major school rule violation,' is it not?"

I elbowed him. "You didn't *actually* read the handbook..." *The*

Bexley School Student Handbook. We all owned a copy. Mine was currently a paperweight.

Luke was quiet, maybe a little embarrassed, and then, "Too bad I left my browning torch at home. It's for crème brûlée, but I use it to toast marshmallows in the kitchen sometimes."

My mouth watered. "Have your mom overnight it, then. Along with the cute little pots. I love crème brûlée."

"I'm assuming you mean the ramekins?"

I smirked at him, but sort of shuddered inside. "Sure."

Luke rolled his eyes. "We could rob a casino."

"I think that might involve too many moving parts for tonight," I said, still looking at him. He was wearing his contacts right now, instead of the glasses Sage referred to as his *hipster specs.*

I like the glasses better, I wanted to tell him.

"We went to the dance earlier," he said. "I thought my glasses would probably fog up, so I unearthed my contacts. I almost never wear them."

"Smart," I said, but my pulse pitched. *How did he literally just read my mind?*

Luke nodded.

"So, uh, how was it?" I kicked a stray rock. "The dance?"

He thought for a second. "Slippery."

"Sounds about right."

"But," he added, "Sage is an amazing dancer."

"Yeah, she is." I tried to sound casual. Because instead of picturing Sage shaking it, I found myself wondering what Luke looked like on the dance floor, if he was stiff and awkward, or loose and smooth. My chest tightened. *Dove,* I told myself, and inhaled a breath, trying to recall her sugar-cookie scent. No such luck—there was never any such luck.

We walked in silence for the final stretch, but Luke groaned when we arrived at the Miller Athletic Center. "No way." He shook his head. "I do not want to play you one-on-one in basketball. Let's get something to eat."

I laughed and reached into my pocket for my keys. The field house was locked up tight for the night, but I was lucky enough to have acquired a campus master key. A family friend had given it to me. "I'm not telling you where I got it," I remembered Leni saying, with her usual wink. "But it's yours now." I put the key in the lock and twisted it. "We aren't playing basketball," I told Luke. "I want to show you something."

<hr>

Next to the second-floor equipment room was a locked door, and inside was a staircase that led up to an attic of sorts. Said attic was used as a storage room for extra uniforms and equipment, old trophies, and an assortment of other random crap. And just above the attic was the roof, stars were visible through a couple of skylights. "I hope you're not afraid of heights," I said once we reached the top of the stairs. I switched on my iPhone flashlight, on the hunt for a ladder.

"No, I don't have *acrophobia*," Luke replied. "So I'm game."

I smiled. "Has anyone ever told you that you're kind of a smart-ass?"

"Not today."

I laughed and dragged the ladder over to where he was standing, right underneath a skylight. "After you." I gestured when it was in place. "It should be unlocked." I waited for him to disappear through the skylight before climbing up myself.

The MAC's roof was the best view on campus. The field house was set close to the woods, so all the illuminated buildings and streetlights were specks in the distance, letting the night sky shine for all it was worth. "Wow," Luke breathed. "This is incredible."

"Yeah, it's pretty cool," I agreed, pulling off my quarter-zip to use as a pillow before stretching out in a good stargazing position. Part of me wished Nick were here to point out Hercules and Cassiopeia and Orion. Maybe Luke would pay closer attention than I did. But then again, Nick had no idea about my rooftop visits, and neither did anyone else. And I liked it that way. This place was an escape—people could always find me in my room, but they could never find me here.

Luke dropped down next to me. "But not as cool as that giant orgy on the turf."

"So they *did* do it." I smirked. I wasn't the only one with secret keys and combinations. I'd never witnessed it, but from what Sage said, all hell broke loose. ("There's screaming, squealing, running, and *so* many bare-naked butts!" she'd told me.)

He laughed. "I'm guessing you and Flamingo weren't there?"

"Stop it." I knocked his foot with mine. "It's *Dove*."

"Like the chocolate? Or the soap?"

I snapped my fingers. "You know, I actually haven't asked."

Luke laughed again, and I did too. "How did you even find out how to get up here?" he asked a minute later, when we'd pulled ourselves together, our breathing in tune again.

"Family friend." I turned my head so I could look at him, and a chill ran up my spine when I did—he was already looking at me. I swallowed hard. "Leni Hardcastle."

"Same...?"

"Yes, same Hardcastle."

He nodded. "Okay, proceed."

"She graduated with Kitsey," I continued. "And apparently she used to *really* get around when she was here, which she loves to talk about after a couple vodka tonics."

"What's the story behind this place?" Luke asked. "Did she lose her virginity up here or something?"

I opened my mouth, then shut it.

He groaned. "My research did not prepare me for this!"

"So you *did* read the handbook!" I joked.

Luke shook his head. "How many girls have you brought here?"

In response, I literally froze, unable to say or do anything.

And he could tell. "Oh crap, I'm sorry. That was..."

"No, don't worry about it." I hoped my voice was calm. "It's fine. I've actually"—I bit the inside of my cheek—"never brought anyone up here before."

Then it was silent.

For what felt like three hours.

I couldn't handle it.

"So my ex-girlfriend really seems to like you," I said.

"Your ex-girlfriend?" Luke asked, confused. I could feel him looking at me again, but I refused to make eye contact, instead focusing on the collection of the stars above us. Was that Aquila or Cepheus?

I swallowed again. "Nina."

"Oh...you two dated?"

"Yeah." I nodded. "Freshman year." *CCC+NMD,* the initials on the sycamore tree read: Charles Christopher Carmichael and Nina Michelle Davies. And no lie, I sort of wanted to laugh. I remembered Nina and I had such trouble making our mark that I'd texted Nick to come and get the job done.

Luke shifted next to me. "Why'd it end?"

I sighed. "Because she didn't want to hurt Sage." Which brought up the fact that the entire school thought Sage and I were suffering from one of those *we're actually in love but haven't totally realized it yet* scenarios.

Nina and I were together for about a month before she latched on to that idea. "I just can't, Charlie," she'd said. "I really like you, but I *love* Sage. I can't do this to her."

Now I cleared my throat and said, "I love her madly, but not in that way."

"Well," Luke murmured, "you might want to tell people that."

And this time it was me who went silent. *I can't,* I wanted to say. *I know I should, but I can't, because I don't want anything to change. I like the way things are. I* need *them to be the way they are.*

But I didn't say any of that. Instead, I pointed up at the sky. "Do you see those stars up there? The ones that form sort of a house? That's Cepheus."

CHAPTER 5
SAGE

CHARLIE POUNCED ON ME AS SOON AS WE MET outside Daggett on Monday morning for our run. I'd stayed up late the night before finishing an essay—okay, *writing* an essay—so I was still half-asleep when he greeted me with: "So the other night, huh?"

But at that, I was suddenly *wide awake*, his words the equivalent of an ice-cold bucket of water being dumped over my head. "Wait, what?" was my eloquent response.

Charlie gulped some water from his Gatorade bottle and smiled at me after swallowing. "Saturday night." The smile twisted into a smirk. "What exactly did I need your *help* with?"

Shit, I inwardly groaned, remembering the lie: "Oh, Charlie needs me for something." Even though I'd invited him to Thayer, I didn't think he'd actually show up. He never did.

"Don't worry," Charlie said. "I covered for you."

"Thanks," I mumbled, trying to piece together why he *did* come. *What made this time different?*

Charlie stretched his arms above his head. "Tell me, who was it? Paddy? Cody? Jack?" His smirk shifted into his most mischie-vous grin. "Or might there be a dark horse out there?"

"Oh, please." I started stretching too, so my hands wouldn't shake at my side. *Dark horse.* "Charlie can't know," I'd told Nick before we parted on Saturday. "Don't tell him."

Nick had chuckled. "Why not? He was at that bonfire too. He saw."

"Yeah, I know," I said, but couldn't voice the next part—about how after the game, later when the fire was only crackling coals, Charlie had cornered me. "Hey," I'd said, noticing the handle of whiskey in his hand. "Where'd that come from?"

He'd shrugged and taken a long pull. "So you kissed him," he said. "You kissed Nicky."

"I did." I smiled, a flutter inside me. "You jealous?" I winked, knowing he wasn't. Charlie and I'd kissed before, and while it was *everything* for a first kiss, it was also somehow *nothing*. We'd been thirteen, at a bar mitzvah. "I love you," I would never forget him saying, with me saying back, "I love you too."

Then we silently agreed: *Just not in that way.*

"I mean, *man*..." Charlie went on, slugging more whiskey. "You've got him hooked now. I *know* when Knickknack's hooked." He waved a frenetic hand toward Nick, who was watching us from across the fire, and then Charlie stepped closer, so drunk his blue eyes were crossed. But his voice was so low and dark that it was like he was staring straight at me. "Don't hurt him, Sage. Don't hurt my brother. Don't touch his heart."

It'd been a balmy night, but a chill had slowly seeped into my veins. "Oh, relax," I told him. "It was a game. Just a silly kiss."

I mean, it hadn't *felt* like a silly kiss, but I couldn't admit that. Because that was the thing about Charlie and me; as best friends, we knew all each other's secrets. He knew that I didn't want a serious relationship because of what happened with my parents. "Yeah, I get that," he'd said after I'd first told him, and then smiled brightly. "We won't tie the knot until we're thirty..."

So, of course, he wouldn't want me to pursue anything with his brother. He didn't want Nick to just be some guy I hooked up with a few times. There hadn't been many—nothing compared to Charlie's line of ladies—but I saw how guys looked at me sometimes, and, hey, I was allowed to have some fun too.

He can't know, I thought again now, toeing the ground with my sneaker. I didn't like hiding things from Charlie, but he couldn't find out. No way.

"Are you ready to go?" Charlie asked.

I couldn't nod fast enough.

"Let's go left today," he suggested as we fell into step beside each other. "To pass Gatsby's."

"Why do we need to pass Brooks?"

Charlie's eyes met mine, but then quickly darted away. "So we can pick up Morrissey..."

"You invited Luke to come?" I asked. It was always just the two of us.

"Um, yes, I did," he said. "Is that okay?"

"Of course!" I playfully punched him in the arm. "The more, the merrier!"

Okay, Sage, why so enthusiastic? You guys are just running.

"All right, cool."

As we approached the senior guys' dorm, I spotted Luke sitting on the stone wall that surrounded the house's terrace, his legs dangling over the edge. *He really is cute*, I thought, just as Charlie whispered, "Paddy, Jack, or Cody?"

I tightened my ponytail. "Cut the crap."

"Ah, dark horse, then."

All of a sudden there was that coldness again, sinking into me. *Don't hurt my brother.* "Okay, listen..." I began.

"You guys are late!" Luke called out, tapping his wrist.

I laughed, relieved that Luke had rescued me, but then my ears pricked up, because something strange happened when Charlie's confident comeback came. "Oh, Morrissey!" he called back. "Counting the seconds until you see me, are you?"

He wavered.

Charlie *never* wavered.

∞∞∞∞∞∞∞∞∞∞∞

Wednesday afternoon, I was trying to multitask—walk and text at the same time—as I headed for my human anatomy class in the CSC, when I heard: "Need a lift?"

I looked up to see Nick cruising toward me on the most *ridiculous* bike I'd ever seen. Not Ace, his usual mountain bike, but a tandem bike, whose colors were far from subtle: stop-sign red and school-bus yellow. "Where the hell did you get that thing?" I asked once he'd braked beside me.

Nick grinned and rang the bike's bell, the dimple in his cheek cute as could be. My heart cartwheeled. "Meet Cherry Bomb," he said. "Nana and Granddad wanted to declutter their life, so I offered to take this winner off their hands."

I laughed and climbed onto the back seat. We started pedaling. "It's so obnoxious!"

"Yeah, I love it too..." he said dreamily as he stretched a hand back to take one of mine.

I tangled our fingers together for a few moments, which felt strangely automatic. I quickly kissed his knuckles before letting go. Nick needed to focus on the road, since our fellow Bexleyans were everywhere.

Riding Cherry Bomb together was different than riding side by side like we usually did. Nick and I loved racing our mountain bikes back home, deep in the woods behind our neighborhood. "Grinds," we called those rides. We'd laugh and trash-talk, always trying to one-up each other. The first time Nick tried to jump his bike over a boulder was classic. We were twelve. "Watch this!" he'd shouted, but instead of a clean landing, he'd wrecked the bike and dislocated his shoulder. My doctor dad had popped it back in for him in our driveway.

I liked this leisurely pace too, though. It was natural; it made me smile.

Soon, we slowed to stop in front of his grandfather's building. "Here we are, miss," Nick said in a deep voice. "The CSC, erected in 2014..."

"And named after the highly esteemed Carmichael family..." I joked, but trailed off when I noticed two guys several yards ahead of us, walking up Belmont Way toward the Buck Building. *Charlie and Luke*, I realized, and squinted to see Charlie saying something, with Luke nodding along, his hands in his pockets. But he must've made some sarcastic comment, because Charlie then reached out to shove him. And when Luke stumbled over the cobblestones, Charlie grabbed his sleeve to keep him from tripping over. I only looked away when Nick spoke.

"I guess Charlie hasn't memorized his schedule yet," he said.

My eyebrows knitted together. "What do you mean?"

Nick gestured at his twin. "I'm pretty sure he has French last period."

"Oh yeah." I felt a little jolt go through me, because Charlie *did* have French next, while Luke had history. And the two buildings, Knowles and Buck, were nowhere near each other. Charlie was going to be late to class, so he could walk Luke to his.

Huh, I thought.

Nick flicked Cherry Bomb's bell, getting ready to take off. "Do you want me to come pick you up?"

My heart flipped, but I shook my head. "No, that's okay. Mrs. Collings will probably let us out late."

"I'll still come."

"Only if you want." I smiled, now walking backward down the CSC's pathway. "Thanks for the ride, Nicholas."

He rang the bell again. "Anything for you, Morgan."

CHAPTER 6
CHARLIE

"WHEN'S A GOOD TIME TO WORK ON THIS?" LUKE asked as we trekked to our last stops of the day.

Mr. Magnusson had assigned us a project for English. "I want you to create a map of one of the texts we've read so far," he'd explained, "and then write a brief essay that discusses how your map enlightens that text." It was a cryptic assignment, but I knew Luke and I would think of something good.

"How about tonight?" I proposed.

"What time?"

"Anytime."

Out of the corner of my eye, I saw him tuck his hands into his pockets. "Would you want to do dinner?" His throat bobbed. "Pandora's or something?"

The word *dinner* rang a bell. "Oh, wait," I said. "Dinnertime's a no-go. Dove and I are getting dumplings with some people from the musical." Humpty Dumplings was the newest restaurant in town.

He nodded. "After, then? Eight?"

I hesitated.

"Okay, you're the one who suggested tonight..."

"No," I said quickly. "We can do eight. Sounds good."

"But you clearly have something going on at eight."

I sighed. "One of my favorite shows premieres tonight, that's all."

Luke glanced at me, an eyebrow raised. *What show?*

"*Survivor.*"

He shook his head. "Nope. No way. You do *not* watch *Survivor.*"

I laughed. "Yeah, I do. It's great!"

"I can't believe I'm hearing this."

"What's that supposed to mean?" I reached over to shove him. But when he lost his footing on Belmont Way's cobblestones, I grabbed his sleeve so he didn't totally eat it.

We looked at each other, neither of us blinking until Luke spoke. I was suddenly very aware that I hadn't let go of his arm yet. My chest ached. "I didn't know that show was still relevant," he said drily. "When did we time-travel back to 2005?"

I dropped his arm. "How dare you?!"

He shrugged.

"Have you ever even seen it?"

No response.

"Well, that settles it," I said, the two of us peeling off Belmont and onto the Buck Building's flagstone pathway. "Please be at Daggett by 7:45 tonight. We'll watch *Survivor*, and then chart out our map."

Luke sighed. "Will there be snacks?"

I smirked. "Do you *want* snacks?"

"If you're forcing me to watch reality TV, then yes."

"Listen, it's a reality TV *competition*," I told him. "Like *The Amazing Race*, or *Top Chef*."

"Which I'm guessing you also watch."

I smiled. "*Amazing Race* starts Friday."

Luke rolled his eyes, and I laughed as I pulled open the building's front door. We crossed the lobby's well-worn marble floor and then turned left down the hallway, Dr. Latham's classroom at the very end. Luke was in his Immigration Theories elective.

"What kind of snacks?" I asked once we were outside the door. "Sweet? Savory?"

"How about," Luke said, "a nice cheese plate, with some charcuterie"—he thought for a second—"and maybe an assortment of macarons for dessert."

I nodded. "And sparkling or still water?"

"Still."

"Okay."

"With a lemon wedge."

"Ice?"

"Yes, crushed."

"Of course."

"Thank you for being so accommodating."

"I try."

Luke smirked and turned to go. "See you later."

"7:45," I responded, and after waiting for him to disappear inside the classroom, I retraced my steps down the hall and broke into a sprint once I was back outside.

Because the Buck Building was for history, and I had French.

French was in Knowles Hall.

Eight minutes in the opposite direction.

And class started in three.

◇◇◇◇◇◇◇◇◇◇◇◇◇◇◇◇◇◇

I showered after dinner, since the rumor about Humpty Dumplings turned out to be true; you walked out smelling like you'd bathed in Chinese food.

Luke texted just as I was setting up our spread, saying he was outside. I pulled on a sweatshirt and went downstairs to get him. He sprang up from one of the porch's Adirondack chairs when I shouldered open the door. "Right on time, Morrissey."

"Actually, Carmichael," he said, "I'm early." He held up his phone. "It's only 7:39."

I smirked. "So eager."

He shrugged. "I was promised a cheese plate."

I laughed and waved him inside, leading the way back upstairs. Daggett was three floors, and my room was on the second. It wasn't completely unlike Nick's room in Mortimer. I had my own flags tacked up, and prefects also got first dibs on rooms, so mine was hands down one of the biggest. Dad and I had lofted my bed up high to make the most of the floor space and then lugged this brown leather chesterfield couch upstairs. Nick had its twin, another present from Nana, who always talked about the furniture she had in storage. So after Nick and I dropped some light hints, we managed to take them off her hands. Across from the chesterfield was my TV.

"Now"—I pushed open the door—"I didn't exactly have time to jet to France this afternoon, so I hope this will suffice." I gestured at the coffee table (steamer trunk), where I'd assembled tonight's snacks: Pandora's famous chips-salsa-and-guacamole combo, and something sweet from their treasure trove of desserts. Dove had gone with me to pick everything up after dumplings. "Friends are coming over to watch TV," I'd explained as I handed over my debit card, and then was treated to what I called an *I'm annoyed but I'm not going to tell you why* sigh. But I didn't take the bait; I just let Dove stew, acting like everything was fine.

Luke glanced at the plate of food, then back at me with this confused expression on his face—eyebrows furrowed and lips slightly parted as if he was about to say something. But nothing came out. My heart started to race.

"Oh, right." I moved across the room, sort of stumbling over my feet. "Drinks." I pulled open the door of my mini fridge and grabbed two seltzers, offering one to Luke. "It's not still, but it *is* lemon-infused."

He took it from me. "No, this is great," he said quietly, and then shook his head. "Sorry, I wasn't expecting all this."

"Well, microwaving popcorn isn't exactly one of my strengths," I told him. "I burn it every time."

Luke smiled. "The trick is—" but he got cut off, thanks to someone pounding on my door.

"Yeah?" I called.

The door opened and Kyle Thompson and Randall Washington, two juniors, entered. I saw them both notice the chips and salsa as they flopped down on the couch. *No*, I thought.

"Charlie, Thompson needs your help," Randall said.

"Your prefect wisdom," Kyle rephrased, dunking a chip in the guacamole.

I half-glanced at Luke. "Okay." I turned back to the guys. "You have five minutes." *Because I am* not *missing the opening of the show.*

Kyle laughed. "Oh, right... It's *Wednesday.*"

Randall caught on. "Outwit, outplay, outlast!"

I nodded. "Talk."

"Mikayla and Joseph broke up," Kyle said. "And I sort of want to get in there, but don't want to be too obvious..."

Randall snorted. "You mean aggressive."

Kyle flipped him off.

Good, I thought, *an easy one.* "Set up a mixer with Merriman," I responded, since Kyle was our house's social chair. "That way it'll seem casual, but you'll still get to lay some groundwork." I shrugged. "A game of Twister is always fun." I reached up and ran a hand through my hair. It felt weird talking about this stuff with Luke here.

They beat it after that, taking some food with them. Once the door clicked shut, I turned to see Luke looking at my bulletin board. So I took the opportunity to look at *him*. Cool and casual in his denim jacket and navy sweatpants with white stripes down the sides. Backward baseball hat too. I quickly blinked when he pivoted to face me.

"Who's this?" He pointed to a photo. "With you?"

I stiffened at the shot. It was an old one, taken on the Vineyard... of me and Cal. We were in Edgartown, Mad Martha's Ice Cream in the background. Cal licked his cone beside me, his wheat-colored hair shining in the sunlight. Meanwhile, I was smiling so hard my jaw ached, because Cal's arm...well, it was slung around me. Loosely, lazily, and to everyone but me, brotherly. I remembered not wanting to look at the camera, instead feeling the pull of Cal's dangling fingers, wishing I could...

"Carmichael?"

"Oh, that's Cal," I said, hoping my voice stayed level. "Kitsey's high school boyfriend."

"Gotcha." Luke reached to smooth one of the photo's curling edges. My eyes followed his fingers, long and tapered. I hooked two of mine onto my rope bracelets and squeezed as tightly as I could. "How old are you here?" he asked.

"Fourteen."

He nodded. "You look really happy."

"I was," I said before I could stop myself. *And I haven't been that happy in a long time.* I cleared my throat. "You can tell because my eyes are crinkling...or so my mom has told me."

Luke nodded again. "I know. I noticed that." He motioned to a few other pictures, most of them from summers past. "You're a cute kid."

I shifted from one foot to the other. *You're a cute kid.*

You're.

You are.

Present tense.

I released a deep breath. "So it's almost eight..."

We sat on the couch, a couple of feet between us. Luke dipped a chip in the salsa while I grabbed the remote and turned on CBS. Then I got up to nix the lights after asking him if it was okay.

Survivor was always better in the dark; it was easier to lose yourself in the show.

"Okay," I said when I was seated again, this time closer. My knee bumped his as I shifted to get comfortable. "This year, it's in Thailand, and the theme is..."

"Shh," Luke cut in, right as an island appeared on-screen, familiar music beginning to play. "Stop. This is your show; don't worry about me. Just watch like you always do, and I'll ask any necessary questions during a break."

And with that, he submerged another chip and leaned back, focusing on Jeff Probst hanging out of a helicopter.

I watched him for a moment, and then did the same.

◇◇◇◇◇◇◇◇◇◇◇◇◇◇◇◇◇◇

He spoke when a Geico commercial came on, during the first break. "Well, Alyssa's a complete moron."

I glanced at him. "Why do you say that?"

"Because," Luke said, "she found the hidden immunity idol, and literally told the first person she saw." He shook his head. "I guarantee it spreads around camp, and then all the votes will be put on her tonight so they can flush it out."

"Their tribe has to lose the immunity challenge, though," I reminded him.

"Oh, they will. The other one obviously has the physical edge."

I smirked. "Well, aren't you just a student of the game?"

"So you agree?"

I nodded.

Luke grinned and shifted so his body was angled toward mine. "And what do you think about—"

Someone was banging on the door again, and it swung open half a second later. "Thompson said you had guac," Carter Monaghan said as he flipped on the lights. Eddie Brown and Dhiraj were with him. They didn't waste any time making themselves at home on my floor, only an arm's reach away from the food. *Thank god for commercial breaks*, I thought to myself.

"Hey, Luke," Dhiraj said, giving him a nod. They knew each other from cross-country.

Luke nodded back and then reached up to adjust his glasses. It had only taken me a couple of meals with Luke to realize he was shy. He was always more of a listener, giving Sage or the girls his undivided attention, and every now and then, he'd unleash a sarcastic comment or two (which was always met with a laugh). But whenever other people stopped by the table to say hi, he took a vow of silence and started to fiddle with the salt and pepper shakers.

"All right, I hate to ask this," I said, barely moving to knock my knee against his, "but why aren't you three in your rooms?"

Eddie and Dhiraj stopped chewing and glanced at the door; Carter didn't. "Why would we be in our rooms?" he asked innocently.

"Oh, Monaghan." I shook my head. "I expected more from you. You of all people should know that study hall is from eight to ten." I looked at Eddie. "And what time is it?"

The sophomore swallowed. "8:24."

"We were just taking a five-minute break," Dhiraj added, the two of them jumping up and hurrying out of the room. "See you later!"

"Really, Charlie?" Carter snorted. "Enforcing study hall? You sound like Steve." He then grabbed the remainder of the chips and guac and left before I could do anything.

More food, I thought. *Next week, I'll get more food and leave half of it outside the door. With a sign that says*, PLEASE TAKE ONE.

"Steve?" Luke asked.

"Stephen Carver." I rose from the couch to retrieve dessert. "He's one of the other prefects. Lives on the third floor." I grabbed a white bag from on top of my fridge. "Wears noise-canceling headphones when he does homework." Seniors didn't have mandatory study hall, but I had no doubt Stephen was upstairs with his head buried in a book. "He had the second-highest GPA in Dag last year."

Luke raised an eyebrow. "Who had the highest?"

I dropped back down next to him and ignored the question. Instead, I handed over the bag. "There's a bunch of flavors," I told him, "but raspberry isn't my thing, so you have to eat those."

Luke reached inside and pulled out a chocolate macaron. And then, he gave me this look. "You do know I was kidding, right? You seriously could've gotten pretzels or goldfish and I would have eaten them. You didn't..." He took a bite and groaned. "Oh god, these are *so* good."

I laughed. "They aren't legit, but Pandora's does a hell of a knockoff."

He munched. "Thank you."

I let myself smile. "You're welcome."

◇◇◇◇◇◇◇◇◇◇◇◇◇◇◇◇

By midnight, the only homework I'd accomplished was an econ problem set, something that should've been done in forty minutes, but ended up taking an hour and some change.

Because I couldn't stop thinking about him.

After *Survivor* ended (Luke was right: Alyssa had no choice but to play her idol), we got to work on our map assignment, and it came together pretty quickly. The text we chose was an 1803 letter Thomas Jefferson wrote to Meriwether Lewis, appointing him to head up a cross-country journey to explore the Pacific Northwest. It was several pages' worth of material, and one second, Luke was laughing as I read the letter aloud in my President Jefferson voice (which sounded a lot like Mr. Magnusson), and the next, we were both hunched over Luke's laptop, surfing the internet for examples of FBI dossiers. "Because that's totally what this is!" he exclaimed. "I mean, come on, Lewis is the agent, and Jefferson's briefing him on the operation—telling him to cipher his notes, providing him with foreign passports, and to abort if something goes wrong..."

"An expedition?" I mused. "Or a covert mission?"

Luke looked up from the screen—our eyes met. "That'll be the title for the essay."

I laughed. "You really like this stuff, don't you?"

"What stuff?" he asked, now pounding his keys. UNITED STATES OF AMERICA appeared in the top left-hand corner of our blank Google doc, and underneath, CONFIDENTIAL!

"This stuff," I repeated, thinking of all the movies and TV shows we'd talked about: the Jason Bourne trilogy, *White Collar*, James Bond, *Bones*, etc.

He understood what I was getting at, nodding. "Yeah, I *really* like this stuff."

After we finished, I walked him downstairs, and Mrs. Shepherd intercepted us in the front hall. She was on duty tonight, and I'd forgotten she also was Luke's math teacher. "Are you ready for the test tomorrow?" she asked, total news to me. Had he even studied yet? Mrs. Shepherd wasn't exactly known for being the easiest teacher in the math department.

"One can only hope," Luke said smoothly, but his shyness was creeping up. I felt him take half a step closer to me, the backs of his fingers brushing against mine.

At 12:30 a.m., I gave up on French and texted Paddy: Milk and cookies?

Oreos okay? he responded.

Fine, I wrote, even though it didn't matter. I wasn't hungry. And I didn't even wait for his usual thumbs-up emoji before unlocking my trunk and digging through winter sweaters until I found what I was looking for. I'd already downed one splash of whiskey by the time he slipped into my room. He tossed the package of Oreos at me and went to grab a glass. I was stretched out on the chesterfield, so after helping himself to the bottle and taking a few cookies, Paddy settled down in my swivel chair. I poured myself another two fingers. We did this sometimes, just hung out and drank a little to take the edge off.

But never in the middle of the week.

And Paddy wasn't an idiot.

"So…" he said. "What's up?"

I didn't answer.

"Something wrong?"

I stared at the ceiling.

"Is Bowdoin pressuring you?"

I shook my head, not in the mood to talk hockey tonight.

Paddy didn't believe me. "If you don't want to commit, then don't commit. You also have Williams and Trinity, plus..."

"Hamilton," I shut my eyes. "Please don't tell anyone."

"I won't," he replied. "You know I won't."

"Thanks."

"But for what it's worth," he added, "you're going to light it up at whatever one you pick."

"Yeah, since I won't have to get past you on the blue line."

Paddy chuckled. "Nick better get ready."

"Trust me, he knows." I forced myself to laugh. "It's what keeps him up at night." With Nick at Yale next year, and Paddy at Princeton, I knew their first game against each other would be one for the books.

It was silent for the next few minutes, both of us sipping our drinks and listening to the creaking of the house. My eyes were still closed, allowing myself to picture Luke: his slim body with long limbs that I sort of wanted to hug as hard as humanly possible. But they snapped open when Paddy got up and switched on my fan. "It's a sauna in here."

At that, I drained my glass, and said it: "I'm going to end things with Dove."

Paddy sighed. "Seriously, Charlie? After only two weeks?"

I nodded.

"Is there someone else?"

"Yeah," I responded. "I think there is."

CHAPTER 7
SAGE

THURSDAY NIGHT, I WAITED FOR NICK ON Mortimer's back stoop, the dorm's outdoor lights having already flickered on for the evening. For the most part, campus was calm—dinner had come and gone, and so had underclassmen curfew. We seniors had an hour before check-in at 9:00 p.m.

"Hey," Nick said a minute later, pushing through the door. He gave me a hug, my whole body humming in his arms. "You ready?"

"Hell yeah." I nodded and followed him over to the bike rack.

How's your day going? he'd texted during lunch, when I was stirring my spoon aimlessly around in my soup.

Not great, I responded.

Why not? he asked.

Mrs. Collings, I wrote, which was all that needed to be said. Mrs. Collings was the evil queen of the science department, and I'd less than impressed her on our latest test. Basically the whole class had bombed it, but that was beside the point. I should've studied harder.

Nick sent back an angry-face emoji, along with, We'll do some cheering up later!

Now we gripped Cherry Bomb's handlebars and took off, bumping over Bexley's cobblestones. Him up front, me in back. We passed under a streetlamp, and the breeze rustled his thick hair. "Do you wanna talk about it?" he asked as we veered onto Darby Road. "The test?"

"Not really," I answered. "It was a total nightmare, and now Jack's suggesting we stage a coup."

Nick stretched his hand back. I latched on to his fingers and smiled against his knuckles before kissing them. "Makes sense," he said. "His mind was definitely elsewhere at soccer this afternoon. Passes were off, and he kept missing the net." He chuckled. "I bet he was in the middle of plotting."

I giggled.

"See, there we go!" Nick exclaimed. "There's a laugh!" He glanced over his shoulder and flashed me a grin before directing us through Bexley's wrought-iron gates, toward town.

"Where're we going?" I asked once we'd gone beyond Main Street. Instead of crossing back over to campus, Nick had turned onto a quiet lane. It was lined with shingled cottages, lights on in most of them. Through one window, I could see a football game playing out on TV.

"Oh, up through the back neighborhoods," he replied. "I think it really clears the head. Getting away for a little." A shrug. "At least it does for me."

I leaned forward to kiss the back of his neck. "Keep pedaling."

◇◇◇◇◇◇◇◇◇◇◇◇◇◇◇◇◇◇

"How about your day?" I asked later, as we circled a cul-de-sac. "Busy? I didn't see you at lunch."

"Yeah," Nick said. "Extremely busy. I had to hit the gym during lunch because my college counseling meeting ate up my entire free period." He sighed.

I sighed right along with him. College counseling and applications basically added another class to our schedule, piling onto an already huge workload. I had a session with my counselor tomorrow, to continue brainstorming my Common App essay. Two meetings already, and all I had was an outline. "Was it about your essay?" I asked Nick.

"Uh-huh," he answered. "One of Yale's supplementary questions." He laughed, but I could tell it was forced. "I have a draft, but it's rough, Morgan. I'm sending it to the magician so he can work his magic."

I didn't need to ask who "the magician" was, my eyes suddenly prickling. It wasn't his fault, but Charlie was so extraordinary academically that he made me feel overwhelmingly *ordinary* at times. I know he worked hard for it, staying up late and operating on very little sleep some days, but still. Did Nick feel the same way? Because obviously this college process was no big deal for his twin; he'd barely mentioned his applications. Half of me wondered if they'd already been submitted.

"You know he's gonna break up with Dove," I found myself saying, to change the subject. Enough college talk. "Tomorrow. He's taking her to Captain Smitty's."

Nick was quiet, then let out a slow whistle. "Well, that's a shame."

My eyebrows knitted together. "A shame?"

"Yeah, because from now on, she's going to associate Captain Smitty's with getting dumped. Ice cream will be ruined for her." He snorted. "Such a bummer."

I laughed.

"What's the deal breaker this time?" Nick asked.

"Not sure," I said, since I never asked why Charlie broke up with these girls so suddenly. Sometimes he told me, sometimes he didn't. It didn't matter, though. Because deep down, buried beneath all the *better as friends* and *it's not you, it's me* bullshit, I knew the truth...or at least *suspected*. This morning's run came to mind: the way Charlie and Luke spoke so quickly as they ran, so in sync that they'd picked up their pace and left me behind. "Hey!" I'd said after catching up. "I might be a third wheel, but I'm still here!"

While Luke laughed, Charlie's cheeks colored and he hadn't spoken to Luke for the rest of the run. Not one word.

Now, I swallowed hard. "Too clingy, probably," I told Nick. "They spend *way* too much time together."

"You've been clocking them?" he asked drily.

"Haha." I rolled my eyes. "I meant especially because of the musical. They've started extending rehearsals to three hours, I think."

"I wouldn't mind spending three hours with you," he said.

A ripple went through me.

"Would that make me clingy?"

I bit my lip. Was that rhetorical? Or did he really want me to respond?

Nick steered the bike off the street, braking beside a community park. There was a playground and maple trees with paper lanterns dangling from their branches. Nick hit the kickstand and wandered over to the nearby gazebo. I grinned once he sat down, catching his drift.

"Whoa there, tiger," he said a couple minutes later, kissing me as I ran my hands through his hair—or *raked*, possibly. "Take it easy."

"You take it easy." I kissed him back. He was just as bad, pulling me onto his lap and tugging my hair out of its ponytail. Warmth burst in my chest. It was like we'd both been waiting forever for a chance to do this. We didn't have hours and hours like Charlie and Dove; we had secret and stolen moments.

No, it wouldn't make you clingy, I caught myself thinking, heart racing. *Not at all, because I feel the same way. Hours and hours. We might've started with a stupid game of spin the bottle, but now we're* something, *something not stupid, something...*

Nick broke our kiss. "Your head all clear?" he whispered.

"Yes," I whispered back, even though it was a lie. So many thoughts were swirling around in my mind. "My head's all clear."

CHAPTER 8
CHARLIE

IT ALWAYS CRACKED ME UP WHEN PEOPLE ASKED if Nick and I were identical—we weren't. Sure, we had the same red hair and blue eyes, and yeah, our height difference wasn't too drastic, but if we stood right next to each other, it couldn't be more obvious who was who. Nick looked like a hockey player, built and broad-shouldered, while I was lean. I was the fastest on the hockey team, but Coach Meyer wanted me to bulk up; hence, a trip to the gym with a customized workout plan. "If you want to play college hockey," he kept reminding me, "you *need* to put on some muscle."

I was on the slide board when Val Palacios walked by, dark braid swinging. She pretended to do a double take. "No, wait, Charlie, is that *really* you?"

Everyone knew I hated the gym.

"Nope," I said, shaking my head. "Wrong, per usual. I'm *Nick*, not Charlie."

Val smirked as she unrolled her yoga mat. "Nice try, but your twin's over there." She gestured to the left. "Singing along to Miranda Lambert while he does medicine ball slams."

"And to think that I'm the one in the musical."

She laughed, and I smiled. Val was cool, easy to talk to. She was like Sage in that way. "How's that going?" she asked. "Clearly you haven't lost your voice."

"Nah, not yet." I continued to slide from side to side while she started doing sit-ups. Her belly-button ring glinted in the light. Val was wearing nothing but a purple sports bra and black spandex. "That'll be more like mid-October."

"Stocking up tea, then?"

"More like *stockpiling.*"

She smiled. "What kinds do you like?"

I shrugged. "Nothing too wild. Lemon with honey, usually. But Morrissey told me that ginger tea is also pretty soothing, so I think I'll try some of that this year too."

Val switched from sit-ups to side planks. "Is that Super Cute Luke? The cross-country PG from Michigan?"

I kept my cool, only raising an eyebrow. "Super Cute Luke?"

"I had dinner with Nina the other night."

"Ah." I nodded. Sometimes it slipped my mind that Val was casual friends with Nina and Sage. They'd all roomed together in Merriman last year.

"Yeah." Val laughed. "I think this is...what? Like her tenth Bexley crush or something?"

I stopped sliding and stepped off the board. "Wouldn't be surprised."

"Speaking of crushes..." She dropped out of her plank. "I heard about you and Dove."

"Damn." I snapped my fingers. "The press release wasn't supposed to go out until tomorrow."

Val rolled her eyes, but her lips twitched, fighting a smile. "You're such a jerk."

I shrugged again. Dove and I were done. After rehearsal yesterday, I offered to buy her ice cream at Captain Smitty's in town, then I just sort of did it. As she licked her one-scoop-of-strawberry-in-a-sugar-cone, I told her I thought we should press pause on our relationship.

"What do you mean?" she'd asked, and I watched as her eyes welled up, two heavy teardrops slipping down her face a beat later.

I reached out and took her hand. "I really like you," I said. "But I don't think we should be together right now. I mean, with the show and everything, it's probably better if we go back to being friends."

To be honest, it wasn't my best effort.

"So, I heard Dag's having a mixer with Merriman tonight?" Val asked.

I tried not to smirk—*this* was the real reason for today's visit to the gym. I had a feeling Val would be here. "Yeah, at ten." After successfully pitching the idea to our housemasters, Daggett's house council had been prepping all week for tonight's get-together.

"Is there a theme?"

"Nope. We're just gonna play board games and Xbox and stuff."

Val nodded and took a sip from her S'well water bottle. It was bright orange like Luke's, but not as big. "I like to stay hydrated," he explained when Reese first teased him about it. He also had a blue one, always filled with coffee. "And caffeinated."

"You should come," I said. "Sage has told me about your legendary *Fortnite* skills."

Val laughed. "But I'm not in Merriman anymore."

"Who cares? You were a year ago."

"Well, sure, I guess that's true," she said as I invited myself to join her on the yoga mat. Partner stretching was pretty effective.

"Nobody will care," I assured her. "Come. It'll be fun."

She didn't respond.

I leaned forward to touch my toes.

"Okay," she said. "I'll be there."

<hr/>

There was shouting coming from the common room when I came back to Daggett after dinner, Luke right behind me. We'd gone to Peace Love Pizza with everyone.

"Dude, I'm telling you," I heard Paddy saying, "I don't know where it is! It was right here last time I checked!"

"Where *what* is?" I asked.

Kyle sighed. "Twister."

I eyed the bookcase where we kept all our board games. Monopoly, Clue, Life, Scrabble, and a few random others. But sure enough, there was no Twister. "Here, let me text Sage," I said, unlocking my phone. "She has one." The two of us had once played for hours, determined to master the game.

I'll come by @ 8:30, she responded, and I sent a thumbs-up back.

"All good," I told the guys, and after Kyle sighed in relief, Luke and I left to go upstairs.

"So what's a mixer?" he asked once we'd reached the second floor. "Is it like a date party?"

"Sort of," I said. "I mean, yes, the activities are usually similar, but a mixer's when one house invites another over, and a date party is when you ask someone from whatever house you want. Date parties are typically more formal too."

"Which do you like better?"

I didn't hesitate. "Mixers, because they're more relaxed. Less pressure."

"Yeah, because you're *so* awkward."

I responded by hip-checking him into the wall, and he crashed into Dhiraj's closed door. "Come in!" we heard him call from inside.

Luke didn't say anything; the look he gave me was enough. But then he did speak, his voice low, "I am going to *kill* you."

A surge of something shot up my spine as I took off down the hall, racing toward my door. Unfortunately, though, Luke was pretty damn fast. I was closing in on the last few feet when he launched himself up onto my back. We promptly fell to the floor.

No wrestling followed. If Luke was Nick or Paddy or Jack or basically anyone else, I'd guarantee we'd be rolling around on the ground right now, trying to get the other to concede first. But he *was* Luke, so I scrambled up before anything could happen.

"Okay, truce." I turned to unlock my door. My heart was trying to make a break from my chest. *Relax*, I told myself.

Luke grabbed the remote and flopped down on the chesterfield once we were inside. "Yup, cool," I said, after chugging about half a bottle of water. "I wanted to sit on the floor anyway." Now flipping through the channels, he was sprawled across the entire couch. "Don't worry about me."

"Copy that," he said, settling on *Law & Order: SVU.* It was past 7:30 p.m., so the episode was probably a little over halfway through.

I rolled my eyes and retrieved my laptop from my desk. And then, without me needing to employ more sarcasm, Luke made space for me. I sat and propped my feet up on the trunk.

"You're welcome," Luke said.

"Oh, *sincerest* apologies..." I started, but dropped off when I shifted to look at him. His legs were in the way, and I bit the inside of my cheek. I really liked being able to see his face. So before my conscience gave me the go-ahead, I found myself saying, "You know, you can stretch out if you want. It's fine."

Two seconds later, his legs were draped across my lap. I situated my MacBook on his shins and then tried to seem *really* interested in my Twitter feed to disguise the fact that I was sneaking way too many peeks at him, to figure out if he was as on edge as I was. Because he didn't look it; he had his TV-watching face on: stone-cold serious, with his arms folded over his chest. But each and every time I glanced up, his eyes were a little droopier. "Hey, do you mind if I take a nap?" he asked when the credits got going.

I looked to see his eyes already shut; he was going to sleep with or without my permission. He hadn't even taken his glasses off. I smiled, and said, "*Mi casa es su casa.*"

"That accent was terrible."

I laughed. "I take French."

"*Je le sais.*" (I know that.)

"You speak French?" I asked, curious since Luke was in Señor Cortez's Spanish class.

"*Un peu.*" (A bit.)

"*Comment?*" (How?)

"*Mon père.*" (My dad.)

"Your dad sounds pretty cool," I said, then sort of winced, remembering Luke's dad died when Luke was only twelve. ("Colon cancer," he'd told us in this matter-of-fact, but still thoughtful voice. "It was extremely aggressive.")

But Luke nodded, eyes still closed. "He was. He was an expat growing up, lived all over the world for my grandfather's job. He met *ma mère* in Tokyo." He yawned. "But Paris was his favorite."

Another yawn, and then he nestled deeper into the couch.

I got the message. "*Fais de beaux rêves.*" (Sweet dreams.)

"*Merci,*" he whispered, and it didn't take long for his breathing to slow. I watched him for a few beats, and then went back to my computer—but not before putting my hand on his knee.

When he didn't wake up, I left it there.

<hr />

Luke slept like a rock. Totally and completely knocked out. There was no movement when a bunch of guys started playing broomball in the hall, and he didn't even hear Sage's arrival. I did, though, her voice loud and clear before she swept into the room: "No, Dhiraj, Sage isn't really here! I'm a ghost!" Girls weren't allowed upstairs, but Sage ignored that rule most of the time. I was sitting at my desk by the time the door opened. "Have you heard from Luke?" she asked, setting the Twister box on the trunk before noticing him. "Oh my gosh," she breathed. "How long has he been like this?"

"About a half hour," I said.

Sage knelt down and snapped a picture with her phone. "Nina's going to die."

I rolled my eyes. "Oh, come on, she has to know it's never going to happen."

"It isn't?" Sage looked at me. "Did he say something to you?"

"No."

She shrugged. "Then I wouldn't be so sure."

Bullshit, I thought. Because again, I'd known Sage for seventeen years. I *knew* her. So I wasn't buying the pleasant *anything is possible!* expression on her face. I think she had the same gut feeling I did, that Nina would be smart to find crush #11, because crush #10 wasn't ever going to pan out. Nothing was said, though; Sage had already moved on.

"Luke." She gently shook him. "Time to wake up."

"Mmm," I heard him mumble. "Pass."

Sage laughed. "Come on. It's almost time to rumble in the jungle!" That was the dance theme that had won out for tonight: "Rumble in the Jungle." It had been my suggestion, and President Jennie had kicked Nick out of the meeting because he'd been laughing so hard. I couldn't understand why—it was only a mere coincidence that "Rumble in the Jungle" had been the theme of our fifth birthday party.

Luke sat up and took off his glasses so he could rub his eyes. He looked disoriented, like he could've slept until morning. "What's tonight's getup?"

"Well, I'm going as a tiger." Sage gestured to her outfit: black Converse and shorts with a cropped orange shirt. She even had a pair of tiger ears on her head and a tail dangling from her back belt loop. I honestly had no idea where she found this stuff. Whatever the theme, she never had any trouble pulling an outfit together. We hadn't agreed on Danny and Sandy until the night before last year's "Dynamic Duos" spirit day, and I sure as hell hadn't expected her to say, "Oh, yes! I have this black cat suit that'll be perfect!"

I rose from my swivel chair. "Really?" I went to dig through one of the plastic storage bins in my closet. "Because I was getting more of a zebra vibe."

"Hysterical as always, Charlie," she said drily. "So funny."

I laughed and found what I was looking for. "Here you go," I said to Luke, and tossed him his headgear for the dance: an official *Survivor* Buff bandanna that Mom and Dad put in my stocking a few Christmases ago. A jungle always backed up to whatever beach the castaways made camp on. I watched as he tugged it on over his bedhead.

"How do I look?" he asked after.

"Legit," I said, a lesser-known synonym for *super cute*.

"Awesome," he said, and then gave me a nod when he and Sage split. I face-planted on the still-warm couch and just lay there until it was time to go downstairs.

◇◇◇◇◇◇◇◇◇◇◇◇◇◇◇◇

People broke off into certain clusters right away, some to play Xbox, some to check out the board games, and others disappearing into the hall to face off in cornhole. I challenged Val to Twister about fifteen minutes after everyone showed up, and was now looking down at her. She was on all fours, as if about to do a crab walk. I was above her, my feet planted so that the sides of my calves were pressed up against her thighs, and bent over so I could touch a hand down to the green dot over her shoulder. "Cinnamon Orbit?" she guessed after I let out a deep breath.

"Altoids." I winked.

"Okay," Dhiraj said. "Right hand yellow."

The eight or so people around us laughed as we shifted, because in three-two-one, we got even closer. My hand was now under Val's back. *You really can't script this stuff*, I thought.

Dhiraj spun the spinner again. "Yellow again. Left hand."

Val sighed. Both my hands were now underneath her back, arms pretty much wrapped around her. "Fancy meeting you here," I said.

She rolled her eyes, but there was that secret smile again. "How are you so good at this?"

"Raw talent."

She shook her head. "No way."

I laughed. "Lots of practice."

"Really?"

I nodded and told her to search "Ultimate Twister Fails" on YouTube. Nick had pulled one over on me and Sage, offering to be our cameraman for critique purposes. Half a million views and counting.

Val smirked as we moved again. "Oh, I absolutely will. Right when I get home."

I whistled. "Have you gotten sick of the walk yet?" Sage had her bike, but if you lived in Simmons House, you got your steps in during the day.

Val made a valiant attempt to shrug. "I like to walk."

"Must get lonely, though."

"That's why I wear headphones."

I nodded. "Smart."

Then there was a beat of silence except for our breathing and Dhiraj's latest call: "Right leg green!" but I knew I had her when she bit her lip and whispered, "Although I actually forgot them tonight..."

CHAPTER 9
SAGE

"WELL, YEAH, THE CAMPUS WAS NICE," REESE SAID after a spoonful of ice cream, "but I don't think I'll apply...I mean, I just didn't get that *vibe*, you know? The feeling of being at home?"

Everyone at our table nodded. "Plus," Nina said, "there's the whole *no guys* thing."

"Oh my god, Nina." Jennie laughed. "You are..."

"I believe the phrase you're looking for is *boy-obsessed*," Luke said drily when she trailed off. He popped a cherry into his mouth. No ice cream for him, only a bowl of maraschino cherries. His fingertips were stained with red juice. ("You're going to make yourself sick," Charlie warned earlier, with Luke smirking back: "Impossible. My stomach has built up a high level of tolerance over the years.")

The girls laughed, but Charlie sat up straighter in his chair as Val dropped into the empty seat next to him. She was wearing her soccer uniform. "Hey," he said, slinging an arm around her. "How'd the game go?"

"But you're right, Nina," Reese agreed. "Girls-only does kind of suck." She'd gotten back from her visit to Wellesley this afternoon.

It seemed like every day we seniors were MIA, getting excused from classes to go on college tours. Last week, Charlie had gone up to Maine to visit Bowdoin. The hockey coaches had shown him around.

Meanwhile, Luke's college conundrum had been solved surprisingly quickly; he was applying ED to the University of Virginia. "My dad went there," he'd told us. "He took me to his reunion when I was ten, and I remember telling him afterward that I was going go there too." He laughed. "My counselor joked that it's a sign, because UVA has all the programs I want, and she thinks I'd be a strong candidate for this one scholarship..."

Charlie teased him. "Following in your father's footsteps!"

Luke rolled his eyes. "Says the person whose list only consists of tiny New England schools. And your dad went to Bowdoin, right?"

"Hockey offers." Charlie shrugged. "You only play where they want you."

Luke shrugged back. "Who said you had to play?"

Instead of answering, Charlie seemed to consider.

"He really *is* your new best friend!" I'd joked earlier, although the words had sounded hollow. *Because*, my heart now sank, *you're the* worst *one, keeping secrets from him...*

"Hey!" Nina snapped me out of my thoughts. "Earth to Sage!" She gestured to Luke's cherries. "Take yours."

"Um, why?" I asked as someone called out a hello, and I turned to see Nick approaching our table. Strangely he was alone, no Mortimer guys flanking him. "What're you guys doing?"

"About to pop our cherries," Reese answered.

I almost choked on my saliva. "Relax, she's kidding," Nina said, holding up her cherry's stem. "We're gonna try to tie these in knots with our tongues. Rumor has it that whoever does it first is the best kisser." Then she did a terrible job of not smiling at Luke, and he did an exceptional one of not noticing. *He could be a world-class poker player*, I thought, because I knew Luke noticed everything.

"Wanna join, Nick?" Jennie asked.

"But the table's full!" I blurted before he could answer. My pulse raced. Biking together was one thing, but *this*? In front of everyone? In front of *Charlie*? "Sorry," I added. "There aren't any seats."

"Here," Val said. "He can have mine." She slid onto Charlie's lap.

"What innovative thinking," Luke muttered.

But then Charlie deposited Val back into her own chair. "Take mine instead," he said, voice hitching a little. "I forgot that there's a theater meeting tonight." He kissed Val's cheek but wasn't really looking at her. His eyes darted across the table, where Luke looked back at him.

"You can leave," he deadpanned. "Permission granted."

Charlie's lips curled, and he fell into his role, straightening to attention and saluting Luke. "Sir, yes sir!"

Nick eyed his brother's abandoned seat once Charlie had hurried out of the dining hall and the laughter died down. I quickly swiped into my phone and went to Messages.

"So are you game, Nick?" Reese asked as I fumbled to type and hit send.

"Nah." Nick looked up from his phone. He rubbed the back of his neck. "Not tonight." He smiled, but tightly…and not at me. "You guys have fun."

◇◇◇◇◇◇◇◇◇◇◇◇◇◇◇◇◇◇

I couldn't run fast enough to the golf course on Saturday, Nick spreading out his blanket when I got there. It went without saying that the sixth hole had become our spot. Late September still brought warm nights, and astronomy lessons if the sky was clear. "What was tonight's movie?" Nick asked, but I didn't answer; I just shucked off my backpack and threw myself at him. Nick held the bench-pressing record at the gym, but instead of catching me, he let us fall to the ground.

We didn't kiss, though.

"Hi," I whispered.

"Hi," he whispered back.

Then he *did* try to kiss me, but I dodged him. Not yet. "You're going to roll your eyes," I said, "but we watched an age-old classic. *Sweet Home Alabama.*"

"*Sweet Home Alabama*? I love that one!"

"What?!" I said, lightly slapping him on the chest. "You've seen it?"

"Of course! It's epic!" He shook his head and chuckled, then quoted: "'Why would you want to marry me for, anyhow?'"

"'So I can kiss you anytime I want,'" I quickly quoted back.

"Well." Nick grinned. "Now that we have that settled..." He leaned close again.

"Wait." I untangled myself from his arms. "Wait, I have something..." I unzipped my backpack. "I got these..."

Nick didn't say anything when I handed him the jar of maraschino cherries, so at first I thought he didn't get it. "Remember?" I nudged him. "The other day?"

He nodded, but still didn't speak—he just looked at the jar, stared at the label. "What was up with that?" he asked eventually. "Why didn't you want me to stay?"

My heart twisted.

No! I'd texted him, so he wouldn't take Charlie's chair. Say no! Just leave!

"I mean, yeah, we're in stealth mode," Nick went on. "But we're still friends."

"No, I know," I replied, swallowing hard. "I know we're friends."

But ever since Nick and I had started hooking up, being his friend on campus had become more complicated.

We were both silent for a minute.

"So who won?" he wondered. "Who's the best kisser?"

"Oh," I said. "Um, Val."

"Ah," he said, hand finding mine. "Well, good for Charlie, I guess."

I squeezed his fingers, not having the heart to tell him the truth—that Val hadn't won the contest, that we hadn't even attempted it. We'd talked about Nick instead. *Gossiped*, more like. "Okay, what's his deal?" Val had asked me. "Tell us, why isn't he with anyone?"

And for whatever reason, I'd tried to channel my nervousness into coyness: "Who says he's not?"

"Emma!" Nina exclaimed once the guessing had begun. "I bet it's Emma."

"Right?" Val grinned. "I think this is their year!"

I'd laughed and nodded along while strangling my hairband under the table. It was the worst-kept secret on campus that Emma Brisbane been doodling Nick's name in her notebook since freshman year. They always did partner projects together, and she'd even baked him cupcakes for his birthday last fall. She was exactly the type of girlfriend I knew Nick had always imagined. One who would hold his hand while walking to class, one who would fix his tie before the homecoming dance. The one I couldn't be right now.

Someday, but not now.

◇◇◇◇◇◇◇◇◇◇◇◇◇◇◇◇◇◇◇

My heart flipped when Nick finally twisted the lid off the jar. The moon had disappeared behind some clouds, so I switched on my iPhone flashlight for us to see. "Should we make a wager?" he asked once we'd chewed and swallowed our cherries, now left with stems.

"Yeah," I said, smiling. "Loser has to eat the whole jar."

"Deal." Nick tugged my ponytail. "Ready?"

Five seconds later, I knew I wasn't going to win. The stem kept sliding all over the place and nearly went down my throat. My hands were balled into fists, trying to concentrate. At the ten-second mark, I could tell Nick was frustrated too—openly whining. I almost choked with giggles, so I spit the stem out and flicked it at him. "Okay, stop. This is ridiculous."

Nick threw back his head and laughed. I glanced around, worried that someone would hear us, but then relaxed and felt myself melt into a grin. I loved Nick's laugh, so full yet boyish. "Maybe," he said. "But how will we ever know now?"

"Easy," I replied, already climbing onto his lap. "The *old-fashioned* way." I felt his fingers running along my waist as I dramatically cupped his face with my hands. His jaw was strong, his cheeks warm. "I'll kiss you, Nicholas."

"Yeah, okay," he whispered, so gently his voice rippled through me. "You can kiss me anytime you want, Morgan."

◇◇◇◇◇◇◇◇◇◇◇◇◇◇◇◇

"Is that new?" I asked later, as Nick tugged his crewneck back on. Nothing had happened beyond pulling off our shirts. "Oh, sorry, I'm sorry," Nick had stammered when I'd stopped him from unclasping my bra. "No, no, it's fine," I'd whispered, my lips on his neck. "It's just..."

Things were still so new. It had only been a month, and I was probably a little gun-shy from this last time I'd gone this far. Last year, Mrs. Collings had nearly caught Matt Gallant and me rolling around under The Meadow's willow tree together. If we hadn't heard her bloodhound's warning bark, detention could've come calling.

"Uh-huh," Nick said now. "Came in the mail yesterday." His sweatshirt was navy with YALE embroidered across the chest in white letters.

"I like it," I told him. "And I'm so happy for you."

Nick kissed my forehead. "Thank you, but I haven't really gotten in yet. Still a couple of months to wait."

"But you will," I said, leaning into his side. "You will."

"So will you," he replied. "Wherever you want to go." He paused. "Have you made headway?"

My stomach swirled. My college counseling meetings still didn't feel like successes because none of the schools on my list aligned with the twins'. My mom and I'd visited some cool places, but now I thought about Charlie and his Bowdoin visit, and Nick and Yale. "Reaches," my counselor called both of them. I remembered brushing away tears in her office that day, realizing I would be alone next year. For the first time ever, the Carmichaels would not be at my side. I would have to start from scratch, and it was daunting. Making friends had never been difficult for me, but without the twins to lean on? That scared me.

"Yeah, I have plans," I told Nick, then bit down hard on my lip to hold back the next part: *Although they don't yet involve you.*

Maybe it was better to spend the next four years on my own. I had to live my own life, to figure out who I really was and what I really wanted for the future. And that wouldn't happen if I was so deeply entwined with someone else. I knew that firsthand.

It couldn't last. No matter how much I liked being entwined with Nick. We were still buddies, but now I loved how his arms felt around me and how we talked about the most random stuff. "There are two types of s'more makers," he said later, giving me a piggy-back ride back to main campus. "JV and varsity."

"And how does one differentiate?" I asked.

"Simple," he answered, all confidence. "A varsity s'more maker possesses patience, while the JV team is overeager."

"Because you need to wait for the fire to burn down the coals." I smiled to myself, remembering a summer bonfire when we were younger. "The best way to get that golden-brown shell and gooey inside is when there's barely a flame."

"Exactly, or else you'll bungle the whole thing," he said, then somehow shifted us so that I was now a koala clinging to his side. He flashed me a dimpled grin. "You're varsity."

"Thanks." I grinned back. "You're varsity too."

Then we just smiled at each other before he leaned in to kiss me.

CHAPTER 10
CHARLIE

NICK AND I WENT HOME FOR OUR BIRTHDAY, October 2. It fell on a Saturday, so we caught a train after classes and would stay in Darien for the weekend. I packed for an overnight, but Nick packed like we were going home for winter break, showing up at the station with his rolling suitcase in tow. "I have a ton of laundry," he said. "So why not?"

Mom was waiting at the end of the platform, a loose grip on Cassidy and Sundance's leashes. Our black labs sat at her feet, but they started wagging their tails wildly when they spotted us. "Happy birthday!" Mom exclaimed, the signal for Nick and me to engage in one of our favorite bits: pushing and shoving each other in an attempt to be the first twin to hug Mom. This time, it was me. (Nick's luggage didn't do him any favors.)

"I think it might be time for a haircut, Nicky," Mom said as I chauffeured us home in the Jeep. "A little too long."

"Nah, not yet, Mom," Nick responded. "Girls love it like this."

There was a second of silence as I flipped on the blinker and made a left-hand turn, something knotting in me. *Sage.* I knew he was really talking about Sage. She was so confident with guys that they had hope they'd get their chance with her, that she was interested. My brother included. I gripped the steering wheel tighter, remembering Nick and Sage kissing this summer, during spin the bottle. "I'm sorry," Nick had said to me afterward, looking anything but—he was Hercules when they gave him back his godliness. "I know you two..." He shook his head, drunk and dazed. "I mean, you *know*, you know?"

No, I'd thought. *No, I don't know. I've never had a kiss like that. I never will.*

But I just clapped him on the shoulder. "Yeah, yeah, all good," I said. "It was a one-time thing. I get it."

Then I'd gone off to find the whiskey and Sage. I wasn't going to let her string along my twin.

◇◇◇◇◇◇◇◇◇◇◇◇◇◇◇◇◇

Two hours later, we were on another train. Tonight the Rangers were playing the Red Wings, and Mom and Dad had gotten center ice seats, with the Hardcastles joining us for dinner. Dad and Uncle Theo had been best friends since their own Bexley days.

"Happy birthday!" Aunt Whitney called out when we got to the restaurant, and I tried not to let my shoulders slump. Because I could never catch a break with Aunt Whit. Everything I did elicited some sort of comment from her.

"You certainly have a lot of *tea*, Charlie," she'd told me at one of my parents' dinner parties, when Nick and I were working on the dishes and she'd come in asking for a cup of Earl Grey.

"Well, yes," I responded as I dug through our tea cabinet, pulse pounding. "Otherwise I'd probably have no voice, and what kind of world would that be?"

She was a master at subtext.

Tonight's Q-and-A session began as soon as the drinks were served. "So, Nick," Uncle Theo said, "how's soccer shaping up?"

"Good," Nick answered. "It's definitely going to be a winning season; the only problem is that I'm pretty bored most of the time. We control most of the play, so I don't get a lot of shots. Randall Washington knows what he's doing up front."

"See?" I said. "You didn't even need me."

Nick laughed. "Every year I try to get Charlie to join the team, and he always says no."

"I would've loved to see that," Dad agreed. "It's a shame the play is in the fall."

"I believe it's a *musical*, not a play," Aunt Whit said, sipping her wine. "There's a difference. Musicals are song and dance." She looked at me. "Right, Charlie? You're singing and dancing?"

My chest tightened as I nodded.

"But Charlie has some monologues too," Nick added. He would know, after all—I had two *Into the Woods* scripts so I could run lines with him before anyone else. He took it seriously, always giving insightful feedback. "It's not all singing."

Aunt Whit considered. "Yes, that's true, Nicky," she said. "Charlie, you've always been great at pretending, ever since you were little." She turned to me and smiled like the Big Bad Wolf. "So now you're pretending on a bigger stage, playing a part."

Everything in me clenched.

Pretending, playing a part.

I glanced around the table to see if anyone noticed.

But thankfully they just laughed, and then Dad and Uncle Theo launched in on the latest quandary: where I should commit for hockey. The offers had come in over the past couple of months, and they'd been obsessed ever since. It was the same when Nick's future was still up in the air. "I mean, why not Trinity?" Uncle Theo said now. "They're at the top of the NESCAC, and..."

Nick kicked me under the table, getting me to make eye contact. *You haven't told them?*

I shook my head. *No.*

He glared at me. *Tell them, Charlie. Now.*

"Yes, all true," Dad agreed. "But there's talk going around that their coach is in the running for the Colgate job. I don't think—"

"Dad," I interrupted. "Trinity's out."

He looked at me. "What?"

"Trinity's *out*." I fumbled for a bracelet under the table. "I called them last week, and said no."

"Without talking to us first?"

"Jay..." Mom started.

I shrugged. "I talked to Coach Meyer." (Who'd caught on: "Just let your dad down gently," he advised the last time we spoke.)

"And me," Nick said. "We made a pro/con list and everything."

Dad's expression stayed serious. "Have you turned down anyone else?"

I swallowed and nodded. "Bowdoin."

"Well, okay." He nodded back. "Then I guess it's Hamilton or Williams."

◇◇◇◇◇◇◇◇◇◇◇◇◇◇◇◇

We had cake when we got home, a little before midnight. The game had gone into overtime, and then a shoot-out, so we'd left after the Rangers nabbed the 4–3 win in the final round. Nick and I had the same cake every year: vanilla with chocolate icing. Mom always ordered two of them, so we could blow out our own candles (and have more leftovers).

"Make a wish!" Dad said once they were gleaming in front of us, just as Mom blinded us with her camera flash. I watched Nick squeeze his eyes shut and extinguish his cake in one go. I quickly did the same, wondering what his wish was.

Our numbers started dwindling around 12:15 a.m. Mom gave us all good-night hugs before going upstairs. Dad soon followed, and afterward Nick and I sprang into action. I went to the garage to get the beers, and he retrieved one of the cakes from the kitchen. We reconvened in the family room.

"So." He handed me a fork. "Did we think it was a good birthday?"

I nodded and hacked off a hunk. "Yeah, great birthday."

Nick popped open his Budweiser. "That didn't sound very convincing."

I rolled my eyes. "Well, sorry. It's just that 'Rumble in the Jungle' was one *hell* of a party..."

Nick laughed mid-sip of beer, spraying it all over the half-eaten cake. I cracked up and then started coughing when my cake-beer combination went down the wrong pipe. "I'm glad we came home," Nick said once I was stable. "I love being home."

"Me too," I responded. Because Aunt Whit aside, I did. It was looser here, the clench I always felt inside me. Only on the Vineyard did it ever really disappear, and it was the worst at Bexley. This was somewhere in the middle.

Nick switched on the TV and asked, "You also said no to Bowdoin?"

"Uh-huh," I said. *Before saying no to Trinity.* I felt him looking at me, but I kept my eyes glued to the *SVU* rerun on-screen.

Nick released a deep breath. "You don't want to play, do you?"

I shook my head.

He was quiet for a second, and then I glanced over to see him nod. "I wouldn't keep dragging this out then," he said. "It's not fair to the coaches. They need to know you aren't interested, so they can move on and make offers to other players."

"I know," I told him. "You think I don't know that?"

Nick backed off, but tried again a couple of minutes later. "So, uh, where are you applying?"

I cleared my throat. "Nowhere near here."

Nick laughed. "Very funny."

I didn't say anything. Instead, I picked at what was left of the birthday cake. When he stopped laughing, I wondered if he'd gotten the message. I didn't want to go to college in New England. I didn't want to graduate from Bexley just to move to another small campus a state or few away.

"I want something different," I'd told Luke. "I'm tired. I'm tired of being in a fishbowl." My voice sort of cracked. "I *need* something different."

I'd thought he'd laugh at me, the person whose name everyone knew, but he didn't. He nodded thoughtfully. "You want a big pond," he said. "You want to be swallowed up."

I nodded back. "Exactly."

Now, I rubbed my forehead. "I'm sorry."

"What?" Nick gave me a look. "Are you kidding? Don't be. Yeah, it'll be weird if you're far away, but we knew we weren't gonna end up at the same place..." He paused. "You should tell Mom and Dad, though."

I sighed. "I think that's Future Charlie's problem."

"How about *Tomorrow* Charlie's problem?"

"Okay, fine. But only if Tomorrow Nick is there for moral support."

"Sure, I've got you."

"Really?"

"Of course," he said, mid-yawn. "You're my twin. I've always got you."

◇◇◇◇◇◇◇◇◇◇◇◇◇◇◇◇

Nick fell asleep on the couch, hugging Sundance close. Cass followed me upstairs after I cleaned up any incriminating evidence and shut off the downstairs lights. He made himself at home on the foot of my bed while I brushed my teeth, and then I stripped down to my boxers and pulled back the covers. It was only October, but Mom had already put on my flannel sheets. She knew I liked them best.

My room at home was silent, so silent that you could hear my watch ticking from over on my dresser. Sage's nickname for it was *the tomb*. She sometimes slept over when we were home on break, usually when one of us was upset about something. I remembered in sixth grade, when her parents said they were getting a divorce. She was really torn up about it, so I'd snuck into her house after they went to sleep and hugged her while she cried.

Cass instantly passed out, and I listened to his heavy breathing for a couple of minutes before I reached for my phone. I swiped and tapped and then waited.

He picked up after two rings. "Hello?"

"Hi," I said.

"Oh, hey..."

"Did I wake you up?" I asked—his voice sounded off. I wouldn't have called him if I thought he'd be asleep. It was just past 1:00 a.m., and Luke told me that his bedtime was around 2:00 on Saturday nights.

"I just fuck around on my computer," he'd explained. "One minute, I'll be on YouTube watching a Jimmy Kimmel interview with Matt Damon, and then a half hour later, I'll be on Wikipedia reading about the history of vampires." I'd since dubbed his nocturnal activities "Saturday-Night Spirals," and now woke up to random facts on Sunday mornings.

Abraham Lincoln was a fan of imported oysters, he'd messaged me last week.

"No." He released a deep breath. "I wasn't asleep."

"You okay, though?"

There was a second or two of silence, but then I heard him clear his throat. "Yeah, I'm fine," he said, voice low. "I'm just not great at talking on the phone. My sisters never even let me order the pizza."

I grinned. "But you're not ordering pizza. You're talking to me."

Another moment of quiet, before: "I guess that's true."

"How was your day?" I asked, rolling onto my back. Cass didn't react when I accidentally kicked his side. He slept like the dead.

"It was obviously a Saturday," Luke replied. "I went to class, and then took a nap…"

I smiled. Luke never went to lunch on Wednesdays or Saturdays, both half days. Instead, he went back to his room to get some shut-eye before cross-country in the afternoon.

"…and I had this nightmare where a ham was chasing me."

I raised an eyebrow. "Wait, come again? A *ham* was chasing you?"

"Yeah, it's this recurring thing from when I was a kid."

"Are we talking a honey-glazed ham? Or…"

"A slice of deli meat, with Mickey Mouse hands and feet."

I shook my head. "You are so *weird*."

"What do you think it means?"

I laughed. "I don't think I'm qualified to answer that."

"You aren't the leading expert in dream interpretation?"

"If only."

He didn't respond, probably smirking.

"Okay, moving on." I grabbed one of my pillows and hugged it. "What happened post-siesta?"

"I had a very nutritional lunch from Tuck: a chocolate muffin. And then I stopped by the mail room—"

"For your Halloween care package?" I interrupted. So far this year, Luke's mom had sent him two care packages, and apparently she hinted that the next several were going to be *festive*.

"No, not the care package," he said. "We're *two* days into October. Calm down."

"Three," I corrected. "It's past midnight. Three days into October."

"And you are now eighteen," Luke said.

I nodded, even though he couldn't see. "As of 9:26 p.m."

"That's a good time."

"Thanks. When were you born?" I knew Luke's birthday was back in August. He looked younger, but was definitely older than most of our grade. A lot of PGs were.

"8:15 a.m."

"Wait, you were born at 8:15 *on* 8/15?"

"Yup."

"Creepy."

"Or a moment of perfect symmetry?"

I opened my mouth, but didn't respond, hearing something out in the hall. *Nick zombie-walking off to bed*, I determined. I didn't speak until I heard his door shut. "So," I whispered, "what did you pick up from the mail room?"

Luke's voice dropped to a whisper too. "I can't tell you."

"Why not?"

"Because it would ruin the surprise."

It took a second, but then it clicked. "Did you get me a birthday present?"

"It's nothing big."

"Well, return it then." I swallowed the lump in my throat. "I only accept big presents."

Luke laughed, and I hugged my pillow tighter. He had the best laugh, one that could always make you smile. One you wanted to record so you could use it as your ringtone. "What did your parents give you?" he asked.

I sighed. "Nick and I always ask for Rangers tickets. We're not very creative."

"For Christmas too?"

"No, that's when we put the thinking caps on."

"Good. You can't make it too easy on them."

"We don't," I joked. "That's why they sent us to boarding school."

More laughter.

"How about you?" I asked. "What did your mom get you for the big one-eight?"

He cleared his throat. "An American Express card."

"Wow," I said. "She must really trust you."

"More like she wants to *track* me. I think she has the account set up so that she gets notified every time I use it."

"So a weekend jaunt to Paris isn't in the cards?"

"Sadly, no."

I laughed, and then asked how the dance was. This week's was called the "Eurotrash Bash." The other day, Nina had talked about bleaching her hair, and Sage had mentioned something about a pair of leopard-print boots.

"Oh," Luke said. "I didn't go."

"You didn't? No leather pants for you?"

"Nope. I just kind of stayed in... It's tiring, you know? Being around people all the time?"

"That's Bexley for you," I said. "You're never not around people."

He sighed. "Yeah, I'm figuring that out. I'm jealous that you're at home right now."

"Eh, it's not that great."

"Bullshit."

I smiled. "Okay, it's pretty nice."

Luke groaned. "And I bet your mom's gonna make you French toast tomorrow."

My smile grew. "It's her specialty."

"You're the worst," he mumbled, and I half-laughed, half-yawned in response. "Well, it might be time for me to hang up," he said after. "Sounds like the birthday boy's all tuckered out."

"No." I shifted so I was back on my side, sleep mode. "Keep talking." I yawned again. "I like hearing you talk."

"Really?" He sounded amused.

I nodded against my pillow. "Yeah."

"I'm not completely hopeless on the phone?"

I let my eyes drift shut and nodded again, too tired to realize that Luke couldn't see me.

"You still there?" I heard him ask a few beats later. Distantly, like in a dream.

So I answered like maybe it really *was* all a dream. "I wish you were here," I said. "It would've been better with you here."

And by then, I was too out of it to fully grasp his reply, but it sounded a lot like, "I miss you too."

CHAPTER 11
SAGE

PARENTS' WEEKEND WAS SUPPOSED TO BE A picturesque late October weekend on campus, with blue skies and leaves the color of the twins' hair fluttering to the ground. But this year, it was no such thing. Instead, it was raining. Umbrellas bounced up and down Belmont Way as our parents attended teacher conferences, with the students getting Saturday off from classes. Most people were hanging out in Knowles Basement, but Luke and I decided to hunker down in my room.

"What are you thinking about?" I asked him at one point, noticing he was biting his lip.

"How much I want to clean this place," he said, gesturing around. My room was a mess. "It looks like a war zone."

I laughed as my phone chimed. Nicholas! was displayed on the screen.

"If it's Nina," Luke said, "I'm *not* here."

"It's not her." I giggled. Nick's message said: Rain, rain, go away...

"Ah, so it's the other Carmichael, your secret boyfriend."

My head jerked up. "What are you talking about?"

Luke gave me a look. "Nick Carmichael is who you run off to meet on Saturday nights." He shook his head. "It's not that hard to put together. Whenever he walks into Addison, you automatically fix your hair and try your best not to stare at him every ten seconds, and when you're not looking at him, he's looking at you." He laughed. "And whenever you guys *do* make eye contact, you smile and look at the floor."

Damn you, Luke Morrissey! I thought. *Why do you have to be so observant?*

I nodded, but reluctantly. "Yeah, but he's not my boyfriend. Someday, maybe. But not today."

Luke's eyebrows furrowed, but my phone pinged again before he could say anything else. This time, it really *was* Nina. I swiped to read: Do you think Luke would go to homecoming with me?

Yikes, I thought, and must've blanched because Luke sighed.

"That's Nina getting your opinion on asking me to homecoming, right?"

The look on his face made it impossible for me to hold back: "Can I ask you something personal?"

"Sure."

I hesitated, unsure what to say. I'd never asked anyone what I was about to ask before. Was there a right or wrong way to say it? "Um..." I grasped at the extra hairband on my wrist. "Are you gay?"

I glanced up to find a bemused smile on Luke's face. Suddenly, my cheeks were a thousand degrees and probably as red as Taylor Swift's lipstick.

"Oh my god!" I exclaimed, completely frazzled, and desperately wanting a do-over. "You're not, are you? I'm such an idiot. You really just don't like Nina. Luke, I'm so—"

"Hey, hey," he interrupted, laughing. "Calm down."

"I'm so *embarrassed*," I groaned.

"You don't need to be embarrassed!"

"So if you don't like her, what type of girls do you like?"

The laughter stopped. "I don't like girls."

I opened my mouth, but nothing came out.

"You were right," Luke said. "I think boys are just as cute as you do."

"Then why are you laughing?"

"Because you're the first person to ever outright ask me that question."

I grabbed one of my pillows and hugged it close. "You mean nobody else knows?"

"No, no." He shook his head. "My mom and my sisters know and some friends...and Charlie's aunt and uncle do too. I told my mom before she ever asked, but, you know, didn't get the chance to tell my dad..." He shrugged, a slight sadness in it. "So, yeah."

"When did you tell your mom?" I leaned forward, fascinated. My uncle Eric was gay, but I didn't know how or when he came out.

"Three years ago, when I was fifteen," he said.

"How'd you do it?" I asked, then, "Sorry if I'm prying!"

"No, it's fine. I actually wrote her a letter...I've written her letters ever since I was a little kid. Some were about stupid stuff like asking if we could get ice cream that day, some were to complain about Bec using my bike without asking, but most of them were just to tell her how awesome she is and how much I love her." He went silent for a moment. "I left it on her desk, and later that night, I found a letter from her in my room."

I smiled at him. "She sounds like the best."

He nodded, grinning. "Keiko Morrissey is the cat's pajamas." He trailed off. "But, Sage?"

"Yeah?"

"It's fine that you know. Actually, I'm happy you do…but can you not tell anyone else yet? I just…don't want them to treat me differently. I'm not ashamed of who I am, but I don't want it to be this big deal or anything. I'd rather be known as the 'cross-country PG' or the 'PG from Michigan' than the 'gay PG.'"

"Of course," I agreed, incredibly touched that he'd shared all this with me. "And for the record, Luke Morrissey, I happen to think *you're* the cat's pajamas."

He blushed.

"So tell me." I grinned. "Do you like anyone?"

Luke adjusted his glasses. "Sorry, Sage, but you gotta give me a whole lot of maraschino cherries to get me to answer that one."

◇◇◇◇◇◇◇◇◇◇◇◇◇◇◇◇◇◇

Since Nick's afternoon soccer game had been canceled along with all the others, *Into The Woods* had become the main event.

"Okay, what's this about?" my dad had asked once we'd snagged seats.

My mom was cradling a bouquet of roses for Charlie. "A cross-over event with all the classic fairy-tale figures?"

Now after a spectacular musical, it was still downpouring, so everyone had retreated inside for the night. The girls and I were listening to Nina pluck out "Sparks Fly" on her guitar while rummaging through Reese's nail polish basket. C'mon, Nick texted after I Snapchatted him some possible color choices. Come hang?

I sent him another color instead of a text. He wanted me to brave the rain to chill in Mortimer's common room, but I couldn't. No other girls would be there tonight. Even though I wanted to go, I knew it would just be me, and how obvious would that be?

Nick didn't respond right away, so I locked my phone and applauded Nina before deciding on a blue Essie shade: "After School Boy Blazer." I smiled—it was such a familiar color, so easy to picture Bexley boys in their coats and ties on special occasions. My phone didn't buzz again until my second coat of polish was dry. Nick, again: Password?

With a winky-face emoji.

And there he was once I'd raced downstairs, standing outside the back door. Only Mortimer had a password, but our student IDs beeped us into just our own dorms.

"What're you doing here?" I pushed open the door, shouting over the storm. Soaking wet, he was shivering on the stoop. "No umbrella?"

Nick didn't say anything, pulling me in close. Raindrops dripped from his hair onto my cheeks. "I wanted to see you," he said. "And you weren't gonna come to me, so..."

I couldn't help but grin. "You're like the guy in that Taylor Swift song. The one who kisses her in the rain."

Nick chuckled. "Which song?" He kissed my forehead. "She sings a lot about the rain."

"Very true," I agreed. Nick wasn't shy about his devotion to Country Taylor. I took his arm to tug him upstairs. I'd text the girls that Charlie had come over or something. They left us alone whenever he did.

But Nick hesitated. It was too late in the night to get parietal permission from my housemaster, so we'd get in trouble if he was caught in my room. Detention, for sure. Maybe even a Major (shorthand for *major school rule violation*). "I don't know, Morgan..."

"Oh, come on," I said. "Charlie does it all the time, and nobody ever finds out." I laughed. "Only one close call—Mrs. Butler knocked on my door, so he hid under my covers and I piled pillows on top of him."

In the stairwell's dim light, Nick's jaw tightened.

I tugged him again. "We can watch a movie, and I have *chocolate*..."

"You do?" Nick had a huge sweet tooth.

"We made these ridiculously yummy pretzel-M&M things last night."

"Mmm," Nick said, groaning. "Those things are epic."

"Yeah." I kissed his neck. "Too bad they're upstairs..."

<hr/>

We settled on my bed, backs against the wall with my laptop balanced on Nick's knees and the Tupperware of goodies between us. His drenched Barbour was draped over my desk chair, and he'd shaken his hair like a golden retriever. I kept combing my fingers through his curls. Nick's hair always got super curly when it rained.

"I can't believe you've never seen this," he said through a mouthful of pretzels and chocolate. "It's a classic."

Ever since Nick had revealed his love for *Sweet Home Alabama*, we'd talked about our favorite rom-coms, and he'd been shocked to learn that I had no idea who Nancy Meyers was. "Are you serious?" he'd asked, eyes wide. "Nancy Meyers? She directed *The Parent Trap*?"

"Well, yeah," I said. "Of course I've seen that. The girls who feud at summer camp before discovering they're twins, and then switch places to meet their other parent?" I smirked. "They also happen to be redheads..."

He chuckled. "Right, exactly." He nodded, then cleared his throat. "Now how about *The Holiday*?"

I'd given him a blank look.

So now the opening credits were rolling on this 2006 movie where two women, Amanda and Iris, swap houses for Christmas to escape their guy problems.

"Oh, wow," I said when Amanda's sweeping California property came on-screen. A gorgeous white mansion that sparkled in the sunlight. The complete opposite of gloomy Bexley. "I'd give anything to be there right now."

"Me too." Nick wrapped his arm around me. I leaned into him, feeling his lungs expand and contract. "I first watched this movie with my mom," he said a while later. "It was on when I had the flu once, and then rom-coms became our thing whenever I was home sick from school. She's the one who introduced me to *Sweet Home Alabama* too."

It took me a second to respond. I didn't know what to say. Nick and his mom watching rom-coms on the couch together?

Cutest thing ever.

But Nick misinterpreted my silence. "Yeah, yeah." He rolled his eyes. "I know it sounds gay. Like, *really* gay."

"No," I said quickly, trying not to wince at his words. "No, it doesn't, Nick. It's sweet..."

My eyes drifted away from the screen and over to my chaise. Or, as Luke called it, the *therapy couch*. Where he'd been sitting several hours ago, where he'd told me something so special...

Before I knew it, the fictional Iris and Amanda had swapped back houses after finding both self-love and true love. "Good, right?" Nick asked once the credits rolled.

"Absolutely." I nodded and kissed him. "I loved it." The fact that Amanda had ended up with Iris's brother was not lost on me. "An oldie but a goodie."

Nick grinned. "Told you."

"You did," I said softly, eyes going back to the therapy couch, but no longer thinking of Luke.

"Hey." Nick shut my laptop. "Where are you? It's like you're interstellar."

Interstellar was Nick-speak for spacing out.

"Oh, um, sorry," I said, and blinked a few times. "I was thinking about Charlie."

"Charlie?"

I plastered on a smile. "Yeah, tonight. It's just hitting me, how incredible he was." Charlie's Prince Charming had been larger than life onstage, so great that Reese remarked: "I will deny this later, but I seriously want to push him up against a wall and kiss his face off."

He'd cast a spell on everyone.

Nick nodded slowly, and only once. Now he'd gone interstellar.

"Everything good?" I asked.

"Don't let him under your covers again," he murmured.

I cocked my head. "Huh?"

Nick shut his eyes. "Please don't let Charlie in your bed again. Like you told me earlier." His throat bobbed. "If it's just going to be us..."

"Don't worry." I laughed and waved him off. It was all I could think to do. "You seriously have *nothing* to worry about. He needed a hiding spot, that's it."

I caught Nick throw a glance toward my overflowing closet, as if say, *Well, isn't that a perfectly good spot?*

No, I thought, heart beginning to race. *Nobody should have to hide in there.*

Nick missed my drift, saying, "Actually, I take that back. I bet that'd be pretty difficult." He chuckled. "You have so much stuff in there!"

I tried to laugh along. "Yeah, yeah, I'm a total hoarder."

He wrapped me in his arms. "I better go."

"No, don't." I buried my face in his chest and hugged him tight.

Nick squeezed me tighter, lifting me off the floor. Tears

suddenly welled up—it had become so hard recently, saying good night to him. *Always*, I thought. *I want to be with him always.*

But a minute later, he was zipping up his raincoat. "So I have a question," he said as I straightened his collar. "Do you want to go to homecoming together?"

My hand immediately dropped down to my side, and I sucked in a breath, hoping to god he didn't hear it.

He did. "I know we're not—"

"No, it's not that," I said quickly. "It's just, Charlie's always my date to homecoming."

"But he's still with Val."

"Well, yeah," I said. "But he'll break up with her before then." Granted, Charlie hadn't *told me* told me, but I knew he would. We'd gone to homecoming together every year.

"Oh...okay." Nick glanced toward my bed, pillows and blankets everywhere. *Please don't let Charlie in your bed again.* My heart plummeted. He still didn't believe me, and I wasn't sure what else I could say to *make* him believe me. I was worried only Charlie could do that.

Someday, I hoped. *Someday.*

"Feel free to take someone else," I added. "You know, if you want to."

"Do you actually mean that?" he asked.

"Yes!" I tried to sound upbeat. "I totally don't mind if you take a date."

"Do I need your, uh, approval for whoever I ask?"

I shook my head, even though my mind went to Emma Brisbane,

and the idea of Nick with his arm around her... "No, Nick," I said. "Of course you don't!"

Then after successfully sneaking him back downstairs, I let him pull me outside and kiss me in the rain.

Sparks fly, I thought, while at the same time a creepy feeling formed in the pit of my stomach. *Sage, what's happening? You're going to end up doing exactly as Charlie predicted back on the beach.*

CHAPTER 12
CHARLIE

THE MUSICAL'S AFTER-PARTY WAS SENIORS ONLY. Despite the serious rain, Greer and the guys and I met up at the baseball field around 11:00 p.m., armed with Gatorade and Grey Goose. "Mikey never disappoints!" Josh Dennings said, pulling down two handles of vodka from the dugout's rafters.

Mikey was this guy who worked for Bexley's Building and Grounds crew, and it was no secret that if students wanted something—alcohol, pot, etc.—he would get it for us. So far, I'd only visited him once this year, my inner pirate requesting some Bacardi. "Charlie," he'd said, giving me a fist bump. "I was wondering when I was gonna see you, man. How you been?"

I mixed the drinks, spilling Josh's Grey Goose into everyone's orange-flavored Gatorade and then advising people to shake well before sipping. Or in Greer's case, *chugging*.

"Oh, man," Josh said. "Cinderella's come to play!"

Then we all followed her, to prove that we too were capable of greatness. I killed my bottle first and chucked it at the dugout's concrete floor. *Victory is mine!*

"Okay, okay, Charlie," Greer said later, when she was halfway through another screwdriver. "I want to know the truth." She sighed. "Why did it never happen between us? You can't deny it, we're so *good* together."

I shrugged as I topped off my drink again. And then while Samir Khan and Josh argued over whether or not the rafters were strong enough to be used as a jungle gym, I began humming "Come and Get Your Love." A sign that I needed to slow down, because whenever I got really drunk, I acted like it was my own personal karaoke night. The last time Sage's ringtone went off, it was a voice memo of my latest performance. I'd groaned, but Sage cracked up. "I'll have to get Reese to send me the video," she said. "None of us knew you were so good at flipping your hair!"

"*Please* tell me, Charlie," Greer whined again.

"You know I'm with Val," I said.

"But—"

Josh cut her off. "Greer, why do you even want to be with Charlie? I don't understand the hype." He looked at me. "No offense, dude."

I rolled my eyes. "For the record, Dennings, a lot of people swoon over my dashing good looks and think I'm wickedly funny."

Greer giggled. "Exactly."

Josh sighed. "Yeah, fine, but you're forgetting about..."

"The Sage factor," Samir supplied.

"Right," Josh said. "Right!"

Greer looked confused. "Huh?"

I kept drinking while they explained. "If you were to date Charlie," Samir said, "you would *always* be second place to Sage. Just like every single girl he's been with has. They've known each other their whole lives, and yeah, they might *say* they're"—he made air quotes—"'just friends,' but we all know it's going to be more than that someday. It's, like, inevitable."

"Uh-huh." Josh nodded. "That's why things pretty much end after a month. Because *nobody* can compare to Sage Morgan."

"Wow," I said, in this bored voice. "That's quite the theory."

"It's true, isn't it?" Samir asked.

I shrugged, hoping they didn't notice me strangling my almost-empty plastic bottle. "Wouldn't you like to know?"

The guys laughed, and I drained my drink. Greer spoke then, with that melodramatic sigh: "I think you should go for it, Charlie. Go tell Sage how you *feel*. Live happily ever after!"

I rose from the bench and made sure I had my balance before trying to walk. Luckily the world wasn't totally spinning yet. "Thanks, Greer," I said, locating my backpack. "It means a lot." I turned to Samir and Josh. "Make sure she gets back to Simmons okay."

Josh took a step toward me. "Hey, we didn't mean anything by it, Charlie."

"Yeah," Samir added. "We just think you'd be good together, that's all."

I nodded. "I gotta go."

◇◇◇◇◇◇◇◇◇◇◇◇◇◇◇◇

It didn't occur to me until I was pounding up the stairs that I had no idea where Luke's room was...because I had never been there before. *Second floor or third?* I debated, stopping halfway up to the second for a breather. I'd somehow run most of the way back to main campus and now was feeling sort of dizzy. Not to mention, sopping wet from the rain. My stomach was also churning, but I didn't want to think about that.

Third floor, I decided. PGs usually lived on the top floor, in the unclaimed rooms from the room lottery the spring before. I remembered Jack being completely stoked about how he'd gotten first pick; he ended up choosing some room on the second floor with a private bathroom. "I'm living large now, Chuck!" he'd declared. "It's *triple* the size of our freshman room!"

It also didn't occur to me that Luke's door might be locked. I found his room about three-quarters of the way down the third-floor hallway, once my eyes focused in on his nameplate:

LUKE MORRISSEY

POSTGRADUATE

GROSSE POINTE, MICHIGAN

Although, the postgraduate part had been crossed out; instead, there was *SUPER SENIOR* written in chicken scratch off to the side. I shook my head, knowing it wasn't Luke's handwriting. Luke had nice handwriting, interesting handwriting. Half cursive, half print. I suddenly wondered what my name would look like in his handwriting. *Charles Christopher Carmichael*, I thought to myself, and then promptly grappled for his doorknob and heaved my shoulder into the door. But I went nowhere; it was locked. "No..." I whispered.

"Hello?" Luke called from inside.

"It's me!" I responded.

A beat later, I heard the click of the door unlocking, and then Luke was in front of me.

"I have something for you!" I blurted before he could say anything.

He let me inside. "What is it?"

"A souvenir," I answered, now unzipping my backpack. I pulled out my quarter-zip and unwrapped it, revealing my Prince Charming crown. It was gold and silver, and I was a thief because it was against the rules to take anything from the costume shop. *But whatever*, I thought. *What's done is done.* When I moved to give it to Luke, I laughed. He was wearing my blue *Survivor* bandanna, which I'd given him over a month ago for that dance.

Face on fire, he quickly ripped the thing off, messing up his hair. I quickly smoothed it back down, realizing he must've taken a shower recently. It was soft and damp, and the air smelled like peppermint. "Did you steal this?" he whispered as I crowned him.

I smirked. "Did you think I was good?"

"Yes." He didn't blink. "Magnetic."

I laughed again and put my hands on his shoulders. *Thin*, I thought, feeling his bones through his T-shirt. *But perfect.* Then I started to run my hands down his arms, touching his warm skin. The vodka made this so easy, no longer a dream. "I almost forgot them," I murmured.

Luke shivered. "What? Your lines?"

I closed my eyes and nodded. "Right when I came onstage. I saw you, wearing the sweatshirt..."

I trailed off; he was now combing his fingers through my slick hair—gently, slowly, agonizingly.

"The sweatshirt...?" he asked.

"Right." I felt goose bumps on the back of my neck. I licked my lips and kept my eyes shut. "The gray sweatshirt, with the black Adidas logo on the front." I paused. "The one you left in my room the first weekend."

"Yeah, that sounds vaguely familiar." Luke laughed, and I opened my eyes to see him smiling at me. My heart squirmed.

You could do it, I realized, body quaking. *You could just lean forward and kiss him.*

So I sort of did—or *started* to, at least. Luke took a few steps backward, putting several feet between us. I released a deep breath and watched as he reached up and adjusted the crown. "Do you want a glass of water?" he asked, and then gestured to the Keurig on top of his mini fridge. "Or maybe some coffee?"

I coughed. "No, why?"

Luke looked at the floor. "You're drunk."

"No, I'm not," I lied.

"Yeah, you are," he said, kneeling to open the fridge. I noticed his pants right then: red-and-black plaid pajama bottoms. *Shit*, I thought, connecting the sight of Luke in pajamas to bedtime, and then bedtime to curfew. What time was it?

I fumbled around in my pocket for my phone and jolted: 11:56 p.m. I had four minutes. "I have to go," I told Luke when he handed me a water bottle.

He nodded. "Okay."

I didn't move.

Luke cut his eyes toward the closed door. The hallway was far from silent: footsteps, laughter, shouting. Everyone coming back for the night. He cleared his throat. "You're going to be late."

"I know," I said, voice sounding distorted. I could hear the blood pumping through my ears. "I just…"

One of Luke's eyebrows quirked up. *I'm listening.*

I swallowed. "You aren't interested in Nina, right?"

He shook his head.

"Or anyone else?"

"I don't know, maybe." He crossed his arms over his chest. "Why do you care?"

Everything in me lurched, and I opened my mouth to respond, but someone banging on the door stopped me. "Poker in Brewster's room, Morrissey!" a guy shouted. "Two minutes!"

I glanced at my phone again: 11:58 p.m.

CHAPTER 13
SAGE

IT RAINED SUNDAY TOO, AND THE SKY WAS STILL ominously cloudy when Charlie and I ran on Monday morning. "Slow down!" I shouted once he pulled ahead of me. I could see our puffs of breath in the air.

"'Winter is coming,'" Nick would've quoted.

"Sorry, sorry." He held back so I could catch up. Our paces were far from in sync, and I knew what that meant—he had something to say, or I had something to say, or both.

Both, I thought, since my secret was swirling inside me, and Charlie was running like something was chasing him.

So I tested the waters. "Is anything wrong?"

He thought for a moment, then shook his head.

"You preoccupied with something?" I rephrased.

"Should I break up with Val?" he asked.

"Oh," I said, and did the mental math. *Four weeks*, I surmised. That sounded about right.

"There's nothing there," he said flatly.

"Then break up with her."

He nodded, speeding up again. I pumped my arms harder to stay with him.

"You know, *I* know someone who's interested..." I teased, mind half elsewhere. Because someone definitely was. He'd told me, right after the musical.

Charlie gave me a look. "And who would that be?"

I bit down hard on my lip. *Shit.* My hands were tied, remembering that Luke trusted me not to say anything. I couldn't, *wouldn't* out him. No freaking way.

My genius comeback was: "Guess!"

Charlie chuckled. "Erica Lee?"

"No."

"Hannah Rogers?"

"Um, not sure..."

How do I get out of this? I worried while Charlie rattled off a few more names. *Lie?*

But then suddenly, the truth arrived. *Literally.* "Sorry I'm late," Luke said, catching up to us. He yawned. "Alarm didn't go off..."

"Or could you have slept through it?" Charlie joked.

Luke grumbled as we veered onto Darby Road. "Nina and I were up late FaceTiming," he said. "She needed help on her Spanish homework." Another yawn. "And then..."

"She asked you to homecoming?" I said, even though Nina had already broken the news to me. I'd woken up to a text: It's a date!!!

Luke nodded. "Affirmative."

Charlie glanced at him. "Did you say yes?"

"Of course," he said. "It'll be fun." He stretched his arms over his head. "I mean, it'd be much *more* fun if Nina were Shawn

Mendes, but..." He smoothly trailed off, and my heart began running faster than we were.

Much more fun if Nina were Shawn Mendes.

Holy crap, I thought. *He did it, just like that.*

And by way of a response, Charlie slowed a little. "Uh, Shawn Mendes?"

"Yeah, Shawn Mendes," Luke said drily. "Ever heard of him?"

Charlie bristled.

We ran in silence for a stretch.

"Well, sorry, Luke," I said. "But if anyone snags Shawn, it's *me*. Three concerts and counting, and my posters are *amazing*." I shrugged. "It's only a matter of time."

Luke rolled his eyes and laughed. "Okay, then who's that guy from—"

"Look, I should go," Charlie interrupted, stopping in the middle of the road. His jaw was clenched. "It's getting pretty late. Do you mind if we split here?"

"Yeah, sure," Luke said casually and turned to resume running, but I grabbed Charlie's sleeve to keep him from leaving. My secret swirled again.

"Wait," I breathed. "There's something..." I swallowed hard. "Do you want to go to homecoming together?"

Charlie gave me a funny look. "Well, yeah..." he said. "I thought that was a given." Something like panic flashed in his eyes. "Or did someone ask you?"

"No," I lied, cold sweat dripping down my back. I couldn't tell him about Nick. Maybe part of me wanted to, but no, Charlie couldn't know. "No one asked me. Everyone knows we go together."

CHAPTER 14
CHARLIE

SAGE AND THE GIRLS WERE MAKING AN EVENT out of homecoming. Not that it wasn't one already, but this year, they were going above and beyond. "What tie are you wearing tonight?" Sage asked me while we set up our beach chairs at the soccer field (that was our thing, pretending the bleachers didn't exist). "Because remember, my dress is blue."

"How convenient," I said. "I'm wearing the Chick Magnet tie."

She groaned. "Really?"

"It's tradition," I reminded her. Every year for the homecoming dance, Nick and I broke out our goofiest ties. Last year's were both food-related: I'd worn this green tie with tacos all over it, while Nick had gone with a red one covered in cheeseburgers and foaming pints of beer (which unfortunately underwhelmed the dance chaperones). My aforementioned Vineyard Vines Chick Magnet tie was light blue and sported hatching baby chicks and horseshoe-shaped magnets. It was a years-ago present from the Hardcastles.

"Your dad mentioned you have a bit of a reputation on campus?" Uncle Theo had joked after I'd unwrapped it, as my family cracked up.

"Thank you," I'd said and stared at the tie for a second. I couldn't take it out of the box, knowing my hands would shake. So I just summoned a smile. "I'll wear it all the time."

"Wonderful to hear." Aunt Whit smiled back. "Because unlike Theo, I worried that it wasn't really *you*..."

At first, I'd sworn to never touch the tie, but one day, I found myself knotting it around my neck. From then on it became some sort of talisman, a sign of self-assurance. If I wore the tie, if I tried my best, I could be that guy. The chick magnet.

<hr />

Everyone else showed up once Nick's soccer game was underway. "Nina, over here!" Sage waved her arms back and forth, the crowd all of a sudden cheering. Bexley had scored the first goal.

"Luke knows to meet us here after he's done," Nina announced, helping herself to a root beer from the Yeti cooler we'd brought.

"When was his race again?" Sage asked.

"An hour ago. I went to see the start."

"Ugh, you're the best." Sage smiled and handed Jennie a cream soda. We'd gone old school for the drinks. I looked over to see a handful of people in the stands staring at us. It was November, and we were acting like we were on a beach in July. *I know*, I wanted to tell them. *We're something else, all right.*

For the rest of the first half, everything the girls said went in one ear and out the other. I sat there drinking my orange soda and watching Nick play goalie. It was pretty entertaining, since Ames, our rival school, was actually good. *That's my brother*, I thought after he dove to redirect a shot. "Yeah, Nick!" Jack and Cody roared from the bench.

It wasn't until halftime that I looked away from the field, someone tapping my shoulder. "First place?" I asked, expecting Luke—fuck, *hoping* for Luke—but instead, turned to see Val smiling. My stomach started churning.

I had tried—tried breaking up with her the other day, but it hadn't happened. "I'm going to homecoming with Sage," had been my grand opening line, and it so did not get the point across.

Val hadn't even blinked. "Okay, that's cool," she said. "It's your tradition, right? Going to the dance together?"

"Yeah, every year." I avoided eye contact.

"Which is actually perfect," she added. "Because the soccer girls are all going together..." She laughed. "I was worried about telling you. I didn't want it to seem like I was completely ditching my boyfriend!"

Then she kissed my cheek, and my mouth went slack while the rest of me went numb. I couldn't clarify, couldn't do it. I couldn't break up with her right then.

I was a horrible person, but I wasn't *that* horrible.

Was I?

※※※※※※※※※※※

There were eight of us at homecoming dinner in town. Jennie's date was the crew team captain, while Nina had Luke, and after weeks of shutting him down, Reese was going with Jack. "But this means nothing," she'd said after telling him yes. "You should have *zero* expectations."

Jack had nodded solemnly. "We'll see."

"It must be love," Luke had whispered in my ear as we watched him walk away.

Of course my ball and chain for the night was *the* Sage Morgan—long blond hair rippling down her back, blue dress, and wearing the silver earrings I'd given her for her birthday last March.

"Will you marry me?" I asked after we hugged on Simmons' patio, making her giggle. I forced myself to smile. *I'm not entirely joking.* Sometimes I thought stuff like this, what it would be like if Sage and I were together. If we could actually be the way people thought we should be. If *I* could actually be the way people thought I was.

Then my chest would clench, knowing it was impossible.

∞∞∞∞∞∞∞∞∞∞∞∞∞

Bistro was sandwiched between the dry cleaners and Captain Smitty's, and ranked somewhere in the upper-middle of town's restaurants (the bottom was Peace Love Pizza, and the top was the Bluebird Inn). And dinner started off with a bang: Sage and I disagreed where to sit. While Nina and Luke moved to sit at one end of the table, Jack and Reese chose the other, and I wanted to sit with them. I just wanted to get lost in a conversation about hockey with Jack (he couldn't skate to save his life, but the guy knew the NHL backward and forward). Sage had other ideas, though, yanking my arm toward Nina and Luke.

"What?" I asked. "Jack and I need to touch base on our fantasy teams." We were in a pool with a bunch of Daggett guys, and as of now, Paddy was on top.

Sage laughed. "But I want to sit near Luke and Nina."

I didn't respond; instead, giving her a look that said, *We're actually going to fight about this?*

She flashed me her brightest without-teeth smile. *Yup!*

"You guys gonna join us anytime soon?" I heard Jennie say, and when I turned to look at her, I saw that she and her date had taken the seats closest to Reese and Jack.

I sighed. *Awesome.*

"Yes, let's sit." Sage moved to sit next to Luke, leaving me to sit across from him.

It was the lesser of two evils, I guess—sitting across from him. That way we wouldn't break off into a whispered side conversation, and I wouldn't be tempted to knock my knee against his under the table. But still, I stood next to the chair for a beat, sort of hoping that someone would offer to trade seats.

Then out of nowhere, Luke appeared at my side and pulled out my chair for me. His arm brushed mine, and I steeled myself from the shudder that felt so good. "Happy now?" he asked.

Immediately my eyes went to the other end of the table, where the other four hadn't seen anything, too busy listening to Jack talk about the Bruins. Then I sat down. "Thanks, Morrissey."

"What was that?" Nina giggled.

He shrugged. "The musical just ended. He's used to being treated like royalty." He looked at me, and our eyes locked. "You seem to be missing your crown, though. Did you lose it or something?"

I nearly jumped, but hid it by leaning back in my chair and folding my arms across my chest. Neither of us had brought up my pop-in to his room that night until now. "I'm not sure," I replied evenly. "Maybe I lost it..." I raised an eyebrow. "Or maybe someone *stole* it. Who knows?"

"Oh, well, that's too bad." Luke took a sip from his water glass. "It was a cool crown."

"You think so?" I cocked my head.

"For sure," he answered. "I think it—"

"Hello, my name is Isaac, and I'll be your server this evening," a new voice said. I blinked and looked away from Luke to see a bald guy standing at the ready to take our order.

"Hi," Sage said pleasantly. "Could we possibly get a few more minutes?"

◇◇◇◇◇◇◇◇◇◇◇◇◇◇◇◇◇◇◇◇◇

Just as we were finishing our appetizers, I glanced up to see Sage staring at something over my shoulder. Everyone else was oblivious, but I turned to see Nick. The first thing I spotted was his tie—it wasn't the skull-and-crossbones with dancing parrots one he'd mentioned earlier; it was a plain old crimson-and-gray checked tie. His Mortimer tie. *WTF?* I thought.

Then I noticed who was with him: Cody, Lucy Rosales, and Emma Brisbane. They sat down at a table by the front window, with Nick pulling out Emma's chair. She was smiling at him like he'd named a constellation after her. *Bravo, Nick*, I thought, since I'd suggested he invite her to homecoming. These Sage fantasies needed to end. Nick kept showing up at our dinner table, and while Sage was always friendly, nothing stopped her from texting as he talked. She wasn't interested. *C'mon*, I planned to say if he hesitated. *Emma's cute, and really likes you, Nick. She doesn't make cupcakes for just anyone. Ask her!*

Although surprisingly, he didn't hesitate. "I will." He'd nodded. "Good idea."

Sage was still eyeing their table a couple of minutes later. Her face looked a little pale. Luke noticed too. "You all right, Sage?" he asked before I could. "Shrimp not sitting well?"

"Oh, I'm fine," she answered brightly, but then mumbled, "Her? Really?"

Because for whatever reason, Sage wasn't a huge fan of Emma. "I just can't explain it," was how she phrased it. "But she *irks* me."

But she's nice, I wanted to say. *She's nice and won't break his heart.*

◇◇◇◇◇◇◇◇◇◇◇◇◇◇◇◇◇◇

The homecoming dance went down in the PAC's lobby, and it was my first dance of the year. There were two dance floors: one on the first floor, and then another on the second, which had its own lobby of sorts for the auditorium's balcony. It was designed as an overlook for the downstairs lobby, so you could see the DJ and everyone else down below. Almost like a cruise ship.

Our group mostly stuck to the first floor, dancing together amid the sea of people at first, but then we swam off in different directions. Sage and I ended up next to a group of freshmen girls, and we swayed together for a while, even during the fast songs. She seemed a million miles away. *Could she be jealous?* I wondered. Because when we'd gone and said hello to Nick's table on our way out of Bistro, I felt frustration radiating off Sage's body. "You guys look great!" Emma had told us, and I knew it had taken everything in Sage to say, "You too! I *love* your dress."

Meanwhile, I'd asked Nick why he bailed on the tie, and he kind of glared at me. "I guess I wasn't feeling it."

Now, though, Sage was checking out the second floor with Nina, and I was leaning against the wall near the DJ booth with Luke. We both had plastic cups of water (I wished it was something stronger) and he was holding his phone up, taking a video of Jack and Reese making out by the speakers. "For when she denies it," he'd reasoned.

He cut it off about a minute in, after Mrs. Collings broke things up. My phone buzzed and I fished it out of my pocket to see a message from Luke. The music was way too loud to talk.

The question is, it said, do I put it in the group chat now? Or later?

I glanced over to see him smirking, and when we made eye contact, he raised an eyebrow. *Which is it?*

I went back to my phone. I say bombs away...

So eager, he replied.

I looked at him again and rolled my eyes. He laughed, and my breath caught—even though the music pretty much drowned it out, his laugh made my heart jump. It was the best sound. My fingers flew across my touch screen and then hit the send button before I really thought about it. I love your laugh, appeared in a blue bubble.

I watched Luke read the message, smile slipping off his face. Then his phone shook in his hands as he tapped a text back. My stomach dropped when mine pinged: Is there somewhere we can talk?

We made eye contact again, and Luke looked like I felt: scared as shit. I could see the nervousness in his eyes as I bit the inside of my cheek and nodded.

◇◇◇◇◇◇◇◇◇◇◇◇◇◇◇◇◇◇◇◇

Down the hall, the Edelson Meeting Room was used as a green-room for guest speakers, and I couldn't decide whether I hoped it was already occupied or not when I opened the door and turned on the lights.

It was empty, and I swore loudly from the extreme brightness, squeezing my eyes shut. I hadn't been in a decently lit room since before dinner. The room was dark again when I reopened them, and Luke had his iPhone illuminated. "We're probably not supposed to be in here," he said quietly.

"No." I shook my head. "Probably not." I fumbled to switch on my flashlight as well—I wasn't sure it was a good idea for it to be so dark. I shined my way over to the couch, and my heart pressed down on the gas when Luke joined me. We sat in silence for what seemed like hours, and then Luke started to speak.

"Okay, I don't want to be this type of person," he said, not looking at me. "I never *thought* I'd be this type of person, someone who overanalyzes every interaction we have, right down to how many times we make eye contact." He paused, took a deep breath.

"So I'm just going to ask: Do you like me? As more than a friend? Because that's what I've been getting from you, but maybe I'm completely delusional."

I didn't say anything.

"Because I like you, Charlie," he added. "I like you so much..." He hesitated. "And I really hope you feel the same way."

Charlie, I thought. He'd called me Charlie. I hadn't heard him say my name since the first day of school, before we'd officially met. I remembered listening to his voice, wondering who he was—

But you can't do this, I reminded myself. *This* cannot *happen.*

I shoved my sweaty palms under my legs and took a deep breath. "Morrissey..."

"Like that!" His excitement made me flinch. "You don't call anyone else by their last name. Just me. And I think it's a shield. I think calling me 'Morrissey' forces you to keep some type of distance between us. Never once have I heard you say 'Luke.'"

I tried to swallow the lump in my throat. "But up until now," I whispered, "you've called me 'Carmichael.'"

"Yeah, well, I was trying to flirt with you," he admitted. "And you *know* that."

I said nothing. I did know that.

"And you walk me to class..."

I shook my head.

Luke called me on it. "Yes, you do, Charlie. I've seen your schedule. You have French when I have history, and we both know Knowles is nowhere near Buck."

God, he is so with it, I thought, because he'd never let on that he noticed.

"And what about after the musical?" he continued. "I know you were drunk, but what *was* that?"

"It was nothing," I responded, my vocal chords aching. "You're my friend. You're such a good…"

"I know you're scared," Luke whispered. "It's scary. I've never felt this way about anyone before. Ever since I met you, I've had butterflies in my stomach."

I felt the corners of my eyes start to sting.

Luke tried again. "Please tell me you like me, Charlie."

"You're my friend," I repeated, nodding like I actually believed it. I blinked, not wanting him to see I was now crying. "You're such a good friend. I, um, haven't clicked with anyone the way I click with you."

He put a hand on my knee, sending a series of tremors up my leg. "Then why can't we be something more? What's stopping you?"

I stood; I needed to leave. "Sage will be looking for me. Or Val—Val will be looking for me. She wanted at least one dance."

Luke stood too. "Charlie, wait…"

But I didn't wait. I shook him off, and then left him there in the dark.

CHAPTER 15
SAGE

I'D ALWAYS THOUGHT THE LIBRARY'S GLASS-walled study rooms were great for people-watching. You could be busy doing calculus homework, and then glance up to see anything happen. A librarian reshelving books, boys playing leapfrog down the long hallway, maybe even a couple sneaking downstairs to "explore" the stacks together.

It didn't occur to me that the windows worked both ways until Nick and I agreed to study together one night. *It's fine*, I told myself when the door clicked shut behind me. *It's totally fine. Keep it professional, like you're project partners or something.* Nick was already sitting at the cozy pine table, his hair disheveled.

"Hey," I said as I took the chair across from him. "How was practice?" Homecoming two weeks ago had brought the end of fall sports. Hockey season was now upon us. I felt a sudden burst of pride, thrilled that Nick had been named captain this year.

"Ugh," Nick said, groaning. "Good, but also *brutal*. It's No Puck Luck Week."

I sucked in a breath to commiserate with him. No Puck Luck

Week happened right after varsity tryouts, when the hockey coaches skated the team into the ground. The guys didn't touch the pucks at practice; it was all power skating and conditioning drills. "Yeah, I heard," I said. "Charlie was whining about it in architecture today."

Nick half-chuckled, half-rolled his eyes. "Yet he smokes us in sprints *every* time." He shook his head. "I still don't fully get it. He's so good, but he's not gonna play. All the top D3 programs, and he passed."

"Wait, what?" I stopped unloading my backpack. "He said *no?* He's not playing?"

Nick nodded.

"He didn't tell me," I whispered. Charlie hadn't mentioned college in a while, and I hadn't asked. I knew he'd turned down Bowdoin after his less-than-enthusiastic visit, but then he'd stopped talking about the process altogether. My stomach swirled. There was only a month left until early decisions were released. Only Nick knew where I'd decided to apply, his response shooting some confidence up my spine. "I like that." He'd nodded, smiling. "I can see you there."

"Yeah," he said now. "Back in October, he said he wanted to go..." He paused. "Nowhere near here."

My heart twisted. *Nowhere near here?*

"What does that mean?"

"Not New England. That's what he told Mom and Dad. He said he wants a lot of options, and that hockey limited them. Dad was bummed at first—he was really pulling for a NESCAC—but he's coming around. Mom too."

"Oh, that's good..." I heard myself say, but trailed off. Why hadn't Charlie told me? I suddenly felt sick from all these secrets piling up. *How did we get here?* I wondered. *And how can we get back to truly being us?*

"So I guess we'll see," Nick said.

"Yeah," I echoed. "We'll see."

We worked on homework quietly for the next hour, only pausing to nudge each other under the table. I giggled when Nick propped his heels up on my knees and leaned back in his chair. "Stop it," I said, covering my mouth. "People could see."

He smiled and shrugged, dimple deepening. I wanted to kiss it, but instead, buried my face in my history book. Not here, not now.

But Nick's dimple wasn't the only distraction; his phone kept vibrating. "Okay, who is it?" I asked once he'd unlocked it and was typing a text back.

"Emma," he said. "With a question about hockey stuff. She's our manager this season."

I nodded, but also gritted my teeth. Emma was perfectly *nice*, and I had no reason to dislike her, but here's the thing: In life, I think everyone has a person they can't explain why they don't like; they just don't like them. Emma was that person for me. Something about her bothered me, and it wasn't because she liked Nick.

Well, part of it was.

You have fun? I'd texted Nick after the dance, and he'd replied: Yeah, lots!

Lots? I mean, clearly they'd had fun. Nick and Emma were friends. I'd seen them on the dance floor together, laughing as he tripped over his own two feet. But *lots* of fun? He'd had *lots* of fun with Emma freaking Brisbane?

So when Nick asked how *my* night went, I sent back: No complaints!

Even though Charlie had basically dragged me out of the PAC. "Keep moving," he muttered as Nina asked where Luke was. "We need to leave…"

I risked stretching a hand across the study table for a quick second. Nick put down his pencil to lace our fingers and lift them to his lips. I expected a kiss, but a ripple reverberated when he playfully bit one of my knuckles.

My voice was breathy: "Nicholas Carmichael!"

The dimple appeared again. "What?" he asked, right as I heard footsteps outside in the hall. Someone was coming.

I unlaced my hand from his, and a beat later, Charlie strolled past our room with his arm casually slung over Val's shoulders, busy whispering something in her ear. Nick cleared his throat once they'd disappeared. "So that's something," he commented. "Those two?"

"Uh-huh," I agreed. Charlie and Val were still going strong, much to Bexley's surprise. Over a month now. I suspected Charlie was procrastinating dumping her, since his first attempt had failed miserably. "But it'll end soon," I added, unable to stop some truth slip out: "I *want* it to end soon."

Nick's eyebrows furrowed. "You do?"

"Yeah." I nodded. "I hope he realizes it soon, that she isn't right for him." I thought again of Charlie and me fleeing the dance, and Nina unable to find Luke. Something *had* to have happened, since Charlie started avoiding Luke since then. He ate every meal with the hockey guys now.

Nick didn't respond. I wanted to ask what he thought, if he had the same inkling I did, but I didn't. His eyes had already dropped down to his math notes.

So I reached to take his hand and playfully bit one of his knuckles, like he'd done earlier. When he didn't react, I did it again. He still didn't laugh or look at me, but I caught his lips curl into a small smile.

"People could see," he murmured.

Maybe I want them to, I murmured back.

Just not aloud, because I reminded myself I wasn't allowed.

It was dark when we slipped out the library's side door, and I let Nick walk me home. The back way on Darby Road, free of streetlamps. But somehow Nick had night vision. "Watch out!" he'd say every couple of minutes. "Massive pothole!"

Then I laughed as he curved his arm around my waist so he could pick me up and smoothly swing me forward. "Thanks for the warning."

Nick kissed my forehead. "I do what I can."

◇◇◇◇◇◇◇◇◇◇◇◇◇◇◇◇◇◇

Luke dumped the remainder of our popcorn in the trash as we left the movie theater Saturday. It was only the two of us, the girls hanging out with the guys tonight. *The flock*, we'd started calling our group. "So what did you think?"

"To be honest," I said, "I kinda fell asleep. Wes Anderson's dialogue is too talky for me sometimes."

"Oh, trust me, I *know* you fell asleep." Luke laughed. "Because when I said, 'Look behind us,' I got no response."

"What was behind us?"

Luke adjusted his backward hat. "This girl and her boyfriend were taking advantage of being in the back row."

"Gross." I rolled my eyes, but was really thinking, *Maybe Nick and I should do that.*

"It was," he confirmed. "Especially because we know them."

I stopped walking. "We do?"

"We do."

"Who was it?"

"I'll give you an excerpt from their conversation, okay?"

I nodded.

Luke cleared his throat and then said in a *no time for this shit* voice, "'God, this is so boring. All they're doing is standing there rambling in goofy outfits, while the narrator rambles over them...'" He switched into an impression of someone else. "'Yeah, Val, that's Wes Anderson's style.'" The annoyance returned, but then softened after a sigh. "'Well sorry, but I'm *way more* interested in *you* than Wes Anderson...'"

I cringed.

"And *then*," Luke added, "they started packing it on."

He seemed completely unaffected by the whole thing, but I still took his hand and squeezed it. "Do you think they saw us?" I asked.

Luke shook his head and twined our fingers together before we resumed walking. "I doubt it. They snuck out with ten minutes left."

Well, if he's not going to dwell on it, neither will I, I decided as I started swinging our arms back and forth. Luke laughed and raised his high so I could twirl underneath it.

"Am I as good as Tate?" I joked, since apparently Charlie's

cousin loved dancing with Luke when he babysat. ("Always to Disney," he'd told us.)

"It's a tight race." Luke smiled, just as someone called out: "Hey, Sage! Is that you?"

Uh-oh.

Luke and I both turned to see Val and Charlie. She now seemed anything but bored, clinging to his arm with it being impossible to miss her puffy lips. Meanwhile, Charlie was self-consciously trying to smooth down his standing-on-end hair. I glanced at Luke; his poker face was alive and well.

I plastered on a pleasant smile. "Hi, Val."

"What did you guys see?" Charlie asked, without bothering to say hello.

"The new Wes Anderson," Luke said nonchalantly.

Charlie's face drained of color, and he shifted from one foot to the other, but Luke stared him down and Val didn't bat an eye. Instead, she smiled at Luke and said, "Have you met Tristan Andrews, Luke?"

My heart skipped a beat the same way it had last week, when it had spread around campus that Luke was gay. Like wildfire. "I promise I didn't say anything," I'd whispered when he sat down for lunch that day at our usual table, everyone pretending not to stare at him.

"Oh, I know," he'd said calmly. "Because it was me. Relax. I'm the source."

"When?" I asked, shifting in my seat. "Where?"

He sighed. "It was in Spanish, and the topic of our discussion was…" He made air quotes. "'Your ideal significant other,' and I used *el,* the male pronoun, when describing mine." He shrugged. "I guess people really *do* pay attention in that class. Because up until today, it certainly didn't seem like it."

Now, instead of pining for him, Nina was begging to know his first crush and who he thought was cute on campus. Reese too. "Tristan Andrews?" they asked hopefully, since he was really Bexley's only other openly gay guy.

"Yes," Luke told Val. "I know Tristan. He was in the musical with Carmichael." He nodded at Charlie, whose face had gone from pale to translucent.

"Oh, right!" Val exclaimed, then winked. "Well, I'm really glad you've met."

"Thanks," he said drily. "Keep an eye out for our 'Save the Date.'"

Nobody said anything. Val was once again wrapped up her boyfriend, not caring to comprehend the joke. I squeezed Luke's hand, and it stayed silent until Charlie blurted: "Can I talk to you for a second?"

I nodded, but then noticed he was looking at Luke, not me.

Luke disentangled our fingers. "Sure."

They walked across the lobby and stopped beside a giant cardboard cutout of Chris Hemsworth. Val asked if I was auditioning for Bexley's Winter Dance Expo, but I wasn't really paying attention, trying to send Charlie a mental hug from afar. He was doing the talking, but while staring at the floor. Luke was no wealth of information either, since his own expression was completely neutral as he looked at Charlie. *Homecoming*, I guessed again. *Something happened at homecoming.*

"It'll be great," Val said. "Emma's got some cool choreography ideas, and I'm trying to talk Charlie into auditioning, but might need your help..."

"Oh, yeah, sure," I replied as I saw Luke nod, and then he and Charlie were heading back over to us.

"Ready to go?" Luke asked me.

I nodded.

"What do you guys have planned for the rest of the night?" Val wondered. It was only 10:00 p.m., so we had plenty of time before our midnight curfew.

"We're seeing another movie in ten minutes," I lied.

"Yup," Luke said. "And we should probably go if we want *back-row* seats."

Val didn't catch the jab. "Have fun!" she chirped, tugging Charlie's arm. "Come on, Charlie..."

He gave us only the briefest of glances before following his girlfriend toward the exit.

◇◇◇◇◇◇◇◇◇◇◇◇◇◇◇◇◇

"What did he say to you?" I asked Luke as we waited for Main Street's traffic light to change so we could cross the street.

We'd hung out at the movies for a while after Charlie and Val left to avoid walking back to campus with them. I wanted to ask as soon as they were gone, but some hockey guys had spotted us. Paddy asked Luke how he'd done on their last AP Chem test. "Eh, okay." He shrugged, and Paddy nodded understandingly.

"Yeah, I shit the bed too," he said. "And apparently some asshole in our class aced it, so the curve's all fucked up."

Luke's gaze dropped to the floor. "Yeah, that sucks..."

"Nothing very interesting," he responded now. "He just wanted to brag about banging Val in the bathroom."

"Be serious."

"I am," he said, smirk visible in the streetlight's glow.

I rolled my eyes. "No, you're not."

"Okay, maybe he didn't say that," he caved. "But you *know* that's what happened."

The light finally changed and we crossed the street. "Well, what did he *actually* say?"

"Honestly, nothing. He mumbled an apology for this text he accidentally sent me the other day. That's all."

My spine straightened. "What'd it say?"

"I miss you," Luke cleared his throat. "He said it was meant for Val."

I let out a deep breath. "Do you believe that?"

"Yeah, totally," he answered, nodding emphatically. "The spellings of 'Morrissey' and 'Val' are so similar. It's an easy mistake to make."

I sighed.

"Look, it doesn't really matter. So what if he misses me? It's his fault. I put myself out there, and since then, he's removed himself from the picture. That text was the first I'd heard from him since homecoming."

So I'd been right—something *did* happen.

But it wasn't my place to ask.

"He really *does* miss you, though," I murmured. Because I knew he did. Charlie was different now...uneasy, tired all the time, and the light in his eyes dimmer than usual. I wondered if I was the only one who noticed it.

We walked in silence until reaching Brooks, where we would say goodbye for the night, since I was due to meet up with Nick on the golf course soon.

I gave Luke a hug. "Tonight was fun."

"You fell asleep."

I grinned. "Okay, so the movie wasn't my favorite, but being with you is always fun."

He grinned back. "You too, Sage. You make everything fun."

∞∞∞∞∞∞∞∞∞∞∞∞∞∞∞

It was like one of those staged, eye-roll-inducing scenes from *The Bachelor*: the girl squealing with excitement before flying into the guy's welcoming arms and kissing him as passionately as possible. But I didn't squeal, and any embarrassment vanished the second my legs locked around Nick's waist and he stumbled before laughing into my hair. "Be gentle," he said. "I'm barely hobbling around." He kissed my neck. "Still sore from practices."

"Oh, my poor captain," I said back, and pulled back to cup his cold cheeks with my hands. We looked at each other, breath warm between us. And all of a sudden, I was blinking back tears. Maybe because the temperature had dropped, so tonight's sixth-hole visit was probably our last, and definitely because I had *this* while Charlie... I remembered earlier, how pale his face had grown and how he couldn't even look Luke in the eye. A lump formed in my throat. "I'm so happy to see you," I whispered to Nick.

He grinned. "I'm so happy to see you too."

Then we kissed.

We kissed slowly for a while until Nick laid me down on our blanket and I grabbed his Patagonia to pull him on top of me. "Lose it," I breathed a few heartbeats later. "Lose the fleece."

Soon my hands were running through Nick's hair and his were under my shirt, fingers sparking on my skin. My heart—my *heart*. "You okay?" he murmured as we kissed, his lips leaving bursts of fire against mine. "You good?"

"Mmm-hmm," I murmured back. "So, so good."

Even though a part of me wasn't. *You shouldn't be doing this,* a voice said in the back of my mind. *You really shouldn't be doing this...*

But I want to, I thought. *I really*, really *want to.*

Nick's voice grew husky later, when jeans had been unbuttoned and unzipped and sweatpants slid off. "Have you ever done this before?" he asked as I pressed the sealed wrapper into his hand.

I shook my head. "No, never."

"Me either," he whispered, then coughed. "But I want to."

Everything in me rippled. Because this was Nick—this was *Nick Carmichael*, the boy I grew up riding bikes with, the boy who gave me piggybacks, the boy I'd kissed by the bonfire.

The boy I suddenly imagined marrying someday.

"Me too." I kissed him, as deeply as I could. "So let's do it."

◇◇◇◇◇◇◇◇◇◇◇◇◇◇◇

The phone didn't ring until afterward. Nick and I were fully entwined, with me wearing his Patagonia and him just in his old sweats and long-sleeved T-shirt. Every few seconds he'd fake-shiver so I'd snuggle closer. "Nothing could be better," he was saying softly. "This is the most epic night, with the most epic girl. I can't wait for more nights like this..."

I smiled as my eyes drifted shut, but they snapped open at the sound. It was a recording of Charlie slur-singing "Dancing Queen" from last June. Reese had thrown a party at her family's apartment in the city. "This one goes out to my favorite girl," Charlie had said, so trashed but grinning so wide. "This one's for you, Sagey Baby!"

I'd laughed then, but stayed quiet now. Nick held me close, and we let whoever it was go to voicemail.

But then Charlie began singing again, and a chill went through me. "I should get that," I whispered. "Twice in a row..."

Nick groaned and released me after one more kiss. I crawled over to my discarded jacket and pulled my iPhone from its pocket. Charlie, the screen read.

"Hey, everything all right?" I answered.

The line was quiet, before: "I need you."

I tried to laugh. "Sorry, but I'm busy right now."

Charlie didn't. "No, Sage. I *need* you."

His voice was dark. Low and *dark*. "Where are you?" I asked slowly.

"English class," Charlie said, right as his twin came up behind me and asked who was on the other end of the line. I stepped away from him.

"Are you alone? Is Val with you?"

"No, it's done, we're done," he said, then added, "Sage, my legs don't work."

"I'm sorry," I told Nick once I'd assured Charlie I was on my way. "But I have to go. Charlie needs help."

"Does he now?"

My spine straightened. If Charlie was dark and stormy right now, Nick sounded light and airy. I had a sinking feeling that too meant bad news. Nick was never sarcastic. "I'm going to go," I said again. "He's messed up."

A beat of silence passed.

"Seriously?" Nick said. "You're actually going to leave? After we just—" He cut himself off. "Charlie might've messed up, but he's fine." He sighed the exasperated mom sigh. "He's *always* fine."

Oh, Nick, I thought, tears welling up. *Have you talked to him lately?* Charlie was most definitely not fine. He called when he couldn't sleep, kept running after I stopped, and when we hung out, he wasn't really there. He'd lost so much weight and looked so sad all the time.

And I know why, I wanted to say. *I know what I've been suspecting is true. He's buried it for so long, but it's becoming harder and harder, because someone unexpected has come into play...and he's scared.*

But before I could really respond, Nick muttered something... something that sounded a lot like: "I can't do this anymore."

Suddenly my heart was in my throat. "Wait, what?"

Nick exhaled a deep breath. "I can't do this anymore," he repeated. "I'm sorry, Sage, but I can't. I can't do this anymore. I want you, but not if you don't want me."

"What?" I shoved my phone into my pocket. Charlie would have to hang tight for a second. "What are you talking about? Of course I want you!" I laughed. "I mean, we..." I gestured to the blanket.

Nick's voice got quiet. "Yeah, we did," he said. "We slept together."

And it was epic, I waited for him to add like earlier. *It was everything.*

He didn't. Instead, he said, "But it's time to cut the crap, Sage. I'm your second choice."

All I could do was shake my head.

Nick nodded his. "*Yes*, I am. We both know it. Stop pretending otherwise. I will *always* be second place to Charlie." He paused. "And I'm such an idiot. Because I hoped things would change. That if I did things your way—kept us a secret—you'd feel the same way I do, the way I've felt for *years*..." He stopped speaking and rubbed his forehead. "I can't do this anymore."

"No, it's not like that," I tried, stomach squirming. "Charlie and I, we're not—"

"But you *want* to be," he cut me off. "You two are all over each other whenever he's not with someone, you rejected me for homecoming to go with him, and whenever we *are* together, he's *all* you want to talk about." His voice dropped. "Now you're about to ditch me to rescue him. He's why you won't be my girlfriend. You're in love with him, and you want to be free when he finally realizes he's in love with you."

Tears streamed down my face. "Nick, please, you have to understand, that's not why I..." I trailed off, unsure what to say. I couldn't tell him about Charlie, and I still wasn't sure he'd understand the truth. I couldn't do this. I couldn't be all-in right now. I didn't even know where I wanted to go to school if it wasn't with Charlie and Nick! I wasn't sure I knew how to be my own person without them and that scared me. I couldn't be what Nick needed, I couldn't give that to him right now.

Nick took my silence to mean he was right. "If you really can't stay here, with me, and talk this out, then I can't do this. We'll go back to being friends, classmates, or neighbors," he said. "Whatever you want to call it. But I can't be with someone who doesn't *really* want to be with me...who wishes she were with my brother instead."

"That's not true," I blurted. "It's absolutely not true. You have no idea..."

"You should go, Sage," Nick murmured, turning away to start folding up our blanket. "Charlie needs you."

CHAPTER 16
CHARLIE

AFTER RUNNING INTO LUKE AND SAGE AT THE movies, the night sped up and soon broke into fragments. I first remembered getting really drunk and breaking up with Val. "So admit it, asshole," she'd said. "I want you to *admit* it. That you run away from anything remotely serious because you're incapable of feeling anything for anyone who isn't Sage. You love her, but you're too scared to do anything about it!"

Everything was swaying by the time Sage showed up later, old floorboards creaking beneath her feet. Her voice sounded warped, like we were underwater. "Charlie."

I'm sorry, I was about to say, because she was already crying. Her eyes were red-rimmed with tears trailing down her cheeks.

She stole the Bacardi from me. "What is this?"

"Rum!" I crowed, but my voice more so warbled. "It could do with some Coke, but—"

"No," she spat out. "What is this doing *here*? Where did you *get* it?"

I groaned.

"Answer me, Charlie."

"I'm so tired." I shook my head. "So, so tired."

"Well, yeah," she said, her voice still harshly distorted. "It looks you just drank a whole handle of *pure alcohol.*"

"No," I groaned again, letting my shoulders slump. "So tired of being *this guy*, Sage. So tired of practicing that smile, practicing those lines. So tired of not having—"

"A person?" she whispered a second after I'd dropped off. "So tired of not having a...true person?"

A true person. I pressed the heels of my palms hard against my eyes. Deep down, I knew Sage *knew.* About me. Somewhere along the way, she'd figured it out. It wasn't a shocker, and it wasn't the problem. My chest clenched. The problem was now I'd brought the whole thing up, up to the door; my closet had always been straight out of *The Lion, the Witch and the Wardrobe*, leading all the way back to Narnia. And I wanted it to stay that way.

Even if I was tired. Even if I was exhausted. Even if I wanted *him*.

When I looked at Sage again, her phone was pressed against her ear. "Are you still awake?" she was saying, and then I heard her mumble something about not needing help *burying* the body, but needing help *carrying* it.

My legs wobbled, and I squinted as Sage slung my lifeless arm over her shoulder. "Is that Nicky's Patagonia?" I asked, suddenly noticing her fleece's horrific tribal print.

She didn't answer.

I woke up on the chesterfield with a dry throat and a throbbing headache. I was underneath the plaid comforter he must've dragged down from my sky-high bed, with my trash can on standby. One of my towels was spread out on the floor in case my aim was off, and there was also a tall glass of water on the trunk. I reached for it and then noticed a bottle of Advil and a Post-it Note.

You are a moron, it said in half print, half cursive.

CHAPTER 17
SAGE

MY EYES WERE SWOLLEN ON SUNDAY MORNING. I'd slept restlessly, but couldn't drag myself out of bed or check my phone until the afternoon. 1:22 p.m., the screen read. There were also some missed texts; I ignored them, instead burrowing under my covers again. I didn't want to be alone, but couldn't reach out to the girls, no matter how much I loved them. Since they didn't know anything, they would want to know *everything*, and I didn't want to explain. So I called the one person who *did* know everything. "Please come," I croaked over the phone, like Charlie had last night. Not dark and demanding, but still cloudy and desperate. "I need you."

Twenty minutes later, Luke let me snuggle into his shoulder. He smelled like peppermint and released this deep sigh of something. Not relief, but *something*—like he hadn't gotten much sleep either. *Frustration*, I determined when I noticed how tense he was. *He's frustrated.*

"I'm sorry," I whispered, realizing this was the second time I'd summoned him in...what? Fifteen hours?

I shut my eyes and remembered Mr. Magnusson's classroom, creaky floor announcing Luke's arrival. He had his sweatshirt hood pulled up over his baseball hat, with his mouth in a straight line and an eyebrow barely raised. *What's the plan?* the expression said, but he hadn't uttered one word the entire time.

Now, he relaxed and wrapped his arms around me. "You don't need to be sorry, Sage," he said, then whispered: "And you don't have to tell me, but Charlie wasn't the only Carmichael-related problem last night, was he?"

"No." I shook my head. "He wasn't."

Then it all came spilling out, along with the tears I didn't know I had left. About how Nick thought he was a consolation prize, that I was just passing time until Charlie was slapped in the face with his love for me. "None of it's true," I said. "None of it. Yes, I love Charlie, but not in that way. Never in that way, you know that. The truth is..."

He was quiet after I finished telling him the history between my parents, with my mom later warning me that long-term relationships had no place in high school. *Well, what are you waiting for?* I almost said. *Say something!*

But then I realized he didn't know if I just wanted him to comfort me, or if I wanted him to offer his opinion.

"What do you think?" I eventually asked.

"I think you should try explaining yourself," Luke answered. "It sounds like he did most of the talking, and you the listening." He paused, then laughed a little. "I'm sorry, that might be terrible advice. This isn't exactly my area of expertise. I've dated, but have never had what you and Nick have."

What you and Nick have.

What did we have?

Love, I realized. Love, but a love I wasn't sure I was ready for. A love that scared me right now.

I sobbed.

Luke hugged me closer. "*Itai desu*," he whispered.

Japanese, I guessed.

"What does that mean?"

"It hurts," he translated, and hugged me again before adding, "But things will get better. Things will be good again."

I bit my lip hard so I didn't let out another wail. Nick said that all the time, ever since we were kids. "Things will be good again, Morgan," he'd say after talking through a bad test grade or a dumb argument with my mom. "Don't worry. Things will be good again."

<hr />

I planned to lay low on Monday, riding Stinger everywhere so I didn't have to talk to anyone—and by anyone, I meant Charlie. Part of me wanted to scream at him for his Saturday-night stupidity, while another part wanted to hug him and whisper that I was there for him no matter what. And a third part was nervous...really nervous that he'd put the puzzle pieces together about me and his twin. "Is that Nicky's Patagonia?" he'd said just before we'd left Mr. Magnusson's classroom. His eyebrows had furrowed as he touched the fuzzy sleeve. I'd swallowed hard and didn't answer, my heart never beating so fast.

But Charlie had different ideas. He found me in town during

consultation, since Pandora's had better coffee than the Tuck Shop. "Hi." I tried to play things cool. "How are you? I didn't see you yesterday."

"Because I was sleeping," he replied. "I slept almost the whole day."

And just like that, the worried best friend in me seized her chance, touching his arm. "Please don't do it again," I said. "You scared the *shit* out of me."

Charlie was silent.

"I know you're unhappy," I whispered. "The things you said..."

"I was drunk. Obviously I wasn't thinking."

"Charlie, please. You can tell me. I don't want this to get swept under the rug. I'm *really* worried about you."

"Well, you don't need to be," he muttered, glancing around the café. "I'm okay."

"No, you're not. You—"

Charlie cut me off with the look on his face. It sent the shivers down my spine, his head cocked and blue eyes wide, as if genuinely intrigued. "You want to talk about not okay?" he asked. "Fine. Let's talk about *not okay.*" His voice pitched, sounding scarily like Nick's on the sixth hole. Light and airy, sarcastic. I braced myself. "You and Nick, Sage," he said. "That's not okay."

Eyes prickling, I pulled him into Pandora's back hallway, toward the restrooms. "I'm sorry," I told him quickly. "I'm sorry I didn't tell you."

"Didn't tell me?" Charlie shook his head. "Yeah, well, that doesn't matter now, does it? What matters is that you've wrecked him. He's a *mess.* I went by his room last night, and he told me about you two, but wouldn't even let me inside. Locked the door and everything."

Because he's mad at you, I thought, heart twisting. *He thinks I want you and not him.*

"I knew this would happen," he went on. "If you ever got together." He raked a hand through his hair. "He'd fall fast and hard, and shatter the second you decided things had run their course." He gave me a look. "I thought I told you on the Vineyard not to hurt him."

My cheeks caught fire. "You are such a hypocrite, Charlie," I hissed. "You shatter girls all the time. Like Val, the other night. You give them this fairy tale and then with snap of a finger, it's *over*." I crossed my arms over my chest. "It's over so quickly that it almost makes you *wonder*..."

The second the words were out of my mouth, I wished I could take them back. All of a sudden, the bags under Charlie's eyes were more prominent and his shoulders slumped. He gritted his teeth. "This is different."

"Oh yeah?" My voice caught. Yes, they were different. Of course they were different, but I wanted him to tell me, to finally admit why. "How?"

"Because it's my brother," he said, giving me a hard stare. "And he's in love with you."

CHAPTER 18
CHARLIE

DURING HOCKEY SEASON, WE ATE AS A TEAM every night, commandeering three of Leighton's center tables so all eighteen of us could sit together. Captains sat at the head of the table, but Nick barely spoke tonight, instead shoveling Bexley's infamous taco lasagna into his mouth like he hadn't eaten in a month. I caught some sour cream dripping down onto his Patagonia.

The Patagonia. Last Saturday had gotten way out of hand, but not *blackout* out of hand. Because the next morning, I'd remembered Sage wearing Nick's fleece...and that was the tip-off, the tip-off that had highlighted all the little tip-offs I'd missed over the term: Sage missing from movie night, Nick stopping by our Addison table all the time and then abruptly leaving. *That's who Sage was always texting*, I realized. *Texting Nick, so he'd split. Probably worried he was too obvious with his smiles.*

Then homecoming, how strange Sage had acted that whole night. "Her? Really?" she'd grumbled upon seeing Emma Brisbane with Nick. It wasn't just that she didn't like Emma; it was because she was jealous of her.

Nice work, rook, I imagined Agent Luke Morrissey saying. *Now the motive for the secrecy?*

Easy, I would've said. *You're looking at him.*

It hurt that neither of them had told me, but as soon as I felt that clenching in my chest, I knew why. *The Sage factor*, someone once called it.

Sage was my best friend, but I also used her to an extent. I wasn't proud of it, but I did. She was my get-out-of-jail-free card— no one could suspect the truth if they believed I was in love with her. And how could they fault me for that? She was sunshine in human form, the most loyal and loving person I knew. She was, in so many ways, my soul mate. So I let people assume what they wanted to assume.

But what did she say to Nick? I wondered, as my brother rose from the table to get seconds. *To swear him to secrecy?* Perhaps protecting me wasn't her only motive. "Just leave, Charlie," Nick said through his door Sunday night, after I found his Patagonia abandoned on Mortimer's porch. Sage had returned it. "It got too complicated." He choked, like his heart was caught in his throat. "And was never that serious, anyway."

Then I heard him move away from the door. I pressed my forehead against the other side and squeezed my eyes shut. *Tell him*, I thought. *Tell him everything.*

◇◇◇◇◇◇◇◇◇◇◇◇◇◇◇

A few days later, Bexley battened down the hatches for final exams. I knew Sage and the flock had camped out in the library, in Jennie's personal study room. It was gigantic, complete with a Harkness table for our student council meetings. There was even a gold-embossed nameplate on the door: J. H. CHU, PRESIDENT.

I stayed in my room. Sage and I hadn't spoken since our fight, and it was easier that way—I didn't have to see Luke. Because for the most part, I'd been able to avoid him. I ate with the hockey guys, and obviously he didn't come over for *Survivor* anymore. The two tribes had merged, and I'd really wanted to ask him what he thought of Emily willing the legacy advantage to Hardy, but I didn't.

The only place I couldn't duck him was Frontier Lit, so I was relieved when classes ended. It meant I didn't have to sit across the table from him anymore, and hear the collective breath the class took every time someone finished speaking, waiting for Luke to launch into his counterargument. Because he didn't think twice about getting into it with people; he checked his shyness at the classroom door. He didn't pick apart everyone's opinion, but I always knew when he was about to—drumming his fingers lightly on the table, rolling his eyes at least twice, and taking a huge gulp from his water bottle to be plenty hydrated. He was the very defini-tion of a Harkness Warrior, someone who slayed class debates. And Mr. Magnusson loved it. If discussion was ever lacking, he would make some statement like, "*O Pioneers!* does not value Emil and Marie's love," and then look at Luke and go, "Mr. Morrissey, your thoughts?"

Our final for Frontier Lit was just a paper, so I finished that before monitoring the study group that had gathered in my room. Carter Monaghan was attempting to relearn the last three months of precalc, Eddie Brown conjugated French verbs, and Kyle

Thompson flipped through his bio flashcards. Dhiraj was waiting for me to edit his Euro paper.

But then I started thinking about Luke. "You're the one with the highest GPA, aren't you?" he'd asked while reading over our joint essay for that map assignment. He glanced up from his laptop and gave me a look, one of his eyebrows raised. *Yes? No?*

I'd shrugged. "It's probably by only a tenth of a point."

"Nope." Luke shook his head. "I bet it's a flat-out landslide."

I pretended to be downright fascinated by his backpack.

"Yet," he continued, "you don't like talking about it, when—from what I've gathered so far—you *do* enjoy talking about yourself quite a bit."

I glared at him. "Fuck off."

Luke laughed. "No, I didn't mean it like that. I just meant it's interesting." He paused. *"You're* interesting..."

God, I now shut my eyes, gut twisting. *I just—*

"Hey, Charlie!" Dhiraj called from across my room. "Is my paper hopeless?"

∞∞∞∞∞∞∞∞∞∞∞∞∞∞∞

Now, I lay in my bed and listened to the dial tone, hoping he would answer. Because if I were him, I probably wouldn't.

He picked up on the fourth ring. "Hi."

I exhaled—not realizing I hadn't been breathing. "Hi."

"What's up?"

"Not much."

"All right, good talk."

"No, wait." I gripped the phone tighter. "How'd your test go today?"

A beat of silence, and then, "An hour flat."

I grinned. Exam blocks were *three*. "Luke is so freaking humble," I'd heard Sage say on more than one occasion, but I'd always thought it was mostly bullshit. Luke had a low-key cocky side to him, and I *liked* that. I liked that he *knew* he was smart, and sharp, and quick as hell...

"Man, I love your brain," I whispered.

"What am I supposed to do with that?" Luke whispered back after a couple of seconds. "Because I seriously don't know."

I was quiet.

"I want to figure this out," he went on, now an edge to his voice. "Since it's getting a little confusing. You tell me that I'm your *friend* at homecoming, but after that, proceed to ghost me...and then you said you missed me a few weeks ago."

Again, I didn't say anything, and he didn't either for a while.

"And let's not forget," he picked up, "your nighttime English class. I somehow got you back to your room, which, I'm going to be candid with you, was pretty much Mission Impossible, and then you asked me to *stay*."

My stomach dropped. *Fuck.*

He kept going. "You told me to stay, saying that you didn't want to be alone, that you couldn't be alone, and that you feel like you're *always* alone..." He paused. "Unless I'm with you."

A lump formed in my throat, and I heard Luke sigh.

"Why did you call me?" he asked.

I closed my stinging eyes. "Because I think about you all the time."

"Likewise," he said.

So I dared myself to do it, swallowing hard and murmuring, "And I wish I was holding your hand."

Luke let out a deep breath. "I wish I was holding yours too, C."

My heart flickered. "What does it stand for?" I asked. "First or last?"

But he didn't tell me, instead saying, "I should probably go. It's late."

Which was probably code for *Think about it.*

"Okay," I told him. "Call me over break?"

"Yes," Luke said. "So please pick up."

CHAPTER 19
SAGE

THIS YEAR'S THANKSGIVING FESTIVITIES WERE IN full swing by the time the Carmichaels arrived, for the first time ever.

"It was supposed to be all set," Nick had said during another movie in my room, a few weeks before that horrible night on the golf course. "But Grammy and Poppy just epically pulled the plug. They want to visit friends in Florida, so everyone else is scattering. No road trip to Pennsylvania for us."

"Well..." I'd sighed an overdramatic sigh, "I guess you'll *just* have to come to the Morgans' Friendsgiving!" Without much extended family, my mom and I always hosted a big Thanksgiving party for whoever wanted to come in the neighborhood. Everyone brought food, and the day before was spent moving around furniture to set up as many dinner tables as possible. It was my favorite holiday.

"Yeah, I guess," Nick grumbled, but with a gleam in his eye. "It won't be the same as Grammy and Poppy's, though..."

"Oh, shut up, Nicholas!" I'd laughed, and then kissed him.

He grinned and pinched my side, making me giggle more. "I love that." He was flushed once we broke apart. "I love your laughter."

The memory made my heart ache now, as I refilled a six-year-old's plastic cup of apple cider. Nick had just walked into the kitchen and was heading straight for the impressive spread of hors d'oeuvres, everything from a baked Brie with raspberry jam to balsamic bacon-wrapped Brussels sprouts and butternut squash soup.

Try it, I remembered Luke telling me. *Try explaining yourself.*

"Here you go, Jenna," I said, handing the little girl her cup. "I'll see you a little later, okay?" I pointed to where Nick was now piling food onto a plate. "I have to go talk to Nick."

Jenna's eyes grew wide. "Is Nick your *boyfriend*?"

I ignored the grimy feeling in the pit of my stomach. "Nope. He's just a friend."

But someday, I prayed, hoping he would understand, hoping we could fix things.

"Well, *I* have a boyfriend," she informed me. "His name is Ryan, and he's in my class."

"Oh, that's great," I replied, glancing over to see Nick sitting at one of the island's barstools, only an arm's reach away from the appetizers for when it came time for seconds.

"But Tori doesn't believe he's my boyfriend," Jenna continued. "Because—"

"Have you checked out the dessert table yet?" I interrupted.

"No!" she exclaimed. "Where is it?"

"Oh my gosh! In the dining room!"

Five seconds later, she was gone, and I was moving toward Nick. "Hey," I said, my hand quivering as I lightly touched his shoulder. "How are you?"

Nick turned to look at me, and I half-expected his eyes to widen since this was our first time speaking post–golf course, but they didn't. They were as calm as could be. "Hey," he said after swallowing his mouthful of food. "I'm good. How're you?"

I nearly fell to the floor. *In pieces*, I thought. *I am in pieces.*

"Congrats on the big win!" I said instead, stalling. "First place. That's awesome!" Bexley had beaten Kent in overtime at their Thanksgiving tournament.

"Thanks," he replied, smiling without showing his teeth. Not even close to his real smile. "It bodes well for the rest of the season."

"Oh, definitely! I bet you guys have a ton of momentum now."

"Yeah, we're really pumped."

Then it got awkward, with neither of us saying anything. Even though my house was bursting at the seams with noise and an oven timer was going off, I could still hear crickets. *Okay*, I thought. *Here you go. Ask if he wants to talk somewhere—*

"I'm gonna go check out what's happening in the basement," Nick said. "I'll see you later?"

He didn't even wait for me to respond, nodding in confirmation and then hopping off the barstool to leave the room. Shoulders sinking, I barely had time to blink back tears before someone called my name. I turned to see Mrs. Carmichael. "Sage!" she said. "Happy Thanksgiving!"

"Happy Thanksgiving!" I replied. The twins' mom wrapped

me in a hug, Charlie behind her. We hadn't talked much about our fight, but we *were* talking again. He'd found me after exams, with Pandora's as a peace offering. "A CTL," was all he said. "Your favorite."

"I'm sorry we're late," Mrs. Carmichael apologized after giving me a quick kiss on the cheek. "There was"—she gestured to her son—"a wardrobe issue."

"Yeah, what are you wearing?" I asked Charlie, because I'd seen pictures of the Carmichael twins on Thanksgiving, and they always looked ready for an autumn family photo shoot. Nick looked so dashing in a pair of black watch plaid pants, but Charlie just had on a navy sweater and brown cords, with one of his usual striped ribbon belts cinched tight.

"None of it fits!" Mrs. Carmichael exclaimed, as if reading my mind. "He came downstairs and I thought he was wearing Nicky's clothes." She shook her head. "Sage, I don't care how you do it, but make sure my son eats tonight. I don't care if you have to hold his hand or force food down his throat. He *needs* to eat."

I nodded.

⬦⬦⬦⬦⬦⬦⬦⬦⬦⬦⬦⬦⬦⬦⬦

"It's hard to believe," my mom said as she handed the twins and me tumblers of her famous Thanksgiving cocktail, a sweet auburn-colored concoction. We were allowed one drink since it was a holiday. "It's hard to believe that in a few weeks, you'll hopefully know what's next." She and I exchanged a smile. "This is the place for you, Sage," she'd remarked after a college tour last month, crisp Vermont wind whipping through the air. "I can feel it."

I'd given her a big hug and told her I could feel it too. My heart was aflutter, excitement mixed with that familiar feeling of home. *This is it*, I thought. *This is where I want to go to college.*

Now I just had to get in.

"Oh, I know." Nick grinned. "I'm amped."

"Says the person who already knows what's next," Charlie said, elbowing him in the ribs.

Nick responded by trapping his twin in a one-armed headlock. I still wanted to retreat under my covers and cry, but also felt a flood of relief, seeing the twins joke together. Just like between me and Charlie, tension among the Carmichaels didn't last long. There was stuff swept under the rug, but they were too close for any ongoing tension.

My mom laughed. "And what about you, Charlie? Your parents said you're keeping your options open...?"

Charlie nodded and sipped his cocktail. "Yes, but that's all I'll say on the subject." He smiled slyly. "The rest is between me and the college counseling office."

"Okay, come on." I punched his arm. "Where do you want to go?"

"I don't know," Charlie said, and cocked his head. "Where do *you* want to go?"

I rolled my eyes. It had become a game now, trying to get the other to admit where they'd applied. "Definitely colleges," we usually joked. "Oh, and some universities."

It was fun, but in the back of my mind, I kept hearing Nick

say that Charlie wanted to go far away for school. *Nowhere near here.* Part of me worried he'd be living in a broom-closet-sized room at Oxford come next fall. All the way across the ocean. Who knew?

I took a sip of my drink and glanced over at Nick, only to catch him watching Charlie as he spoke. Quietly, thoughtfully, and maybe even a little sadly.

I'm not the only one, I knew. *He's going to miss him too. We're going to miss him so much.*

<hr/>

We went hard on dessert, so hard that I needed to take a moment and breathe after my first plate, but I watched Charlie dig right into his second one (an assortment including slices of pumpkin, pecan, and apple pie, plus a generous scoop of mint chip ice cream). We'd eaten dinner in the front hall with the DePietros from up the street, but now we sat in the kitchen's breakfast nook. "Does your mom think you have anorexia?" I asked, again noticing how thin he was.

Charlie shook his head. "I don't think so. I just told her the truth—that besides hockey, I run a lot, and Bexley's food options are at an all-time low—and she seemed to believe that."

"You look like the difficult child," I said. Just like Nick, Kitsey Carmichael looked ready for her Thanksgiving close-up. Her gold pleated skirt was stunning.

Charlie chuckled softly. "I *am* the difficult child. That's nothing new."

"No, you aren't," I protested. "You were just..."

"A challenge," he filled in the blank, lips curling up in a smile. "I was a challenge."

I laughed, remembering our younger days. Charlie had been a precocious child and constantly kept his parents on their toes. When we were in kindergarten, our parents started calling him *the mayor*, since Charlie knew everyone in the neighborhood and everyone knew him. And I had to smile now, since it was the same way at Bexley. You could drop him in the middle of any situation, and he'd come out with a handful of friends. I loved that about him.

But I also loved how low-key his twin was, how calm and collected. The way he could always put you at ease, the way he anchored you on both smooth and stormy days. The way he was just *Nick*. Suddenly I was choked up, remembering our hors d'oeuvres encounter, and how my plan to talk to him crashed and burned. *Try again*, my stomach stirred as something buzzed under my fingers. *The night's still young.*

"Hey," I heard Charlie say, and I snapped out of my Nick reverie to see him holding his phone against his ear. "Happy Turkey Day..." He trailed off, a smile breaking over his face. "Oh, really?" He pushed back his chair. "Well, tell them I say hi..."

As soon as Charlie was gone, I too was up and on my feet, dessert plates forgotten. Maybe Charlie could eat seconds, but I only knew one person whose sweet tooth was big enough for *thirds*. So, heart hammering, I weaved through guests until I found Nick eyeing the pumpkin pie in the dining room. Or, more accurately, mourning what *remained* of the pumpkin pie. Barely a slice, crust already crumbled. "You know..." I said hesitantly. "We have another one."

Nick sighed. "This is the other one," he said. "Your mom pulled it from the pantry after everyone ravaged the first few."

"No, Nick." I shook my head, even though he hadn't taken his eyes off the prize. "Trust me, there's *another* one."

◇◇◇◇◇◇◇◇◇◇◇◇◇◇◇◇◇◇

"Ah, the good old garage fridge," he said as I slid the pie off its shelf and into his awaiting arms. We hadn't brought plates, only forks. "Why didn't I think of that?"

I shrugged and moved next to him, leaning against the hood of my mom's SUV. Nick was already powering through the pan, but I squeezed the utensil in my hand, too anxious to eat. "Are you having fun?" I eventually asked, to break the silence.

Nick nodded. "Yeah," he said after swallowing a bite. "You and your mom really do Thanksgiving right." He pointed his fork at the mudroom door. "This party puts Grammy and Poppy to shame."

When he laughed, I tried to too, but it was pretty much impossible with tears also pooling in my eyes. "I'm sorry," I whispered. "Nick, I'm really, *really* sorry."

"It's all good," he replied, voice level. "You put me out of my misery..."

Misery.

The word felt like a knife through the heart.

"...by showing me where this baby was." He took a huge bite

of pie, and then smiled his without-teeth smile. Sarcastic Nick. I hated Sarcastic Nick. "So all's well that ends well—"

I grabbed the pan from him. "Nick, no," I said, pulse pounding. "I'm not talking about dessert."

"Why not? I could seriously *live* off dessert."

"I know," I said, a few tears falling. I hugged the pie pan close. "I know you can, and that's..." My voice turned thick. "One of my favorite things about you. I have so many..."

Nick straightened up from the car, face now solemn. "I do too," he said. "I have so many favorites." He fiddled with his fork. "Favorite things about you."

My heart fluttered. *Here we go*, I thought. *We're doing it, we're fixing it—*

"That's what makes us good friends," he continued, plastering on that stupid no-teeth smile again. "We're such good friends."

Such good friends.

My heartbeat slowed down so fast that the world went a little fuzzy. "Yeah." I barely felt myself nodding. "We're such good friends."

◇◇◇◇◇◇◇◇◇◇◇◇◇◇◇◇◇◇◇◇

Charlie never returned to the party. He didn't come back for the board games, or to claim leftovers, and not even for the serving of the farewell hot chocolate (with candy canes, to welcome the Christmas season). *Good*, I thought as my mom and I loaded the dishwasher later. *I don't want to see him anyway.*

Because part of me regretted it, regretted answering his call and leaving Nick on the golf course so I could rescue his twin from Mr. Magnusson's classroom. I hated myself for it, and right now, it was easy to hate him too.

Such good friends.

But I kept checking my phone, a complete hypocrite. I kept waiting for him to call, or for a text to pop up—to hear something about his conversation with Luke. Because seeing his smile earlier...

Midnight: nothing.

12:30 a.m.: nothing.

1:00 a.m.: nothing.

Which left me to my own thoughts. *Why didn't you fight?* I chastised myself. *Why did you agree with Nick, instead of shaking your head and telling him the truth?*

I sighed and rolled onto my back, to stare up at the ceiling, glimmering with a galaxy of glow-in-the-dark stars. My dad and I'd spent a whole afternoon sticking them up when I was little, and before freshman year at Bexley, I made my interior-designer mother promise not to take them down while I was away at school. I still loved them, always reminding me of when I visited the Carmichaels on the Vineyard. One of Nick's and my favorite things to do was go night kayaking, disappearing out on the Oyster Pond. Everything was pitch-black, except for the stars above us. Pure magic, in my eyes.

But tonight, my stars kind of haunted me, brought me back to the sixth hole. "You have no idea how much you mean to me, Nick Carmichael," I whispered to myself—what I'd wanted to say tonight. *You're the love of my life...*

I've known it for a while now. More than anything, I want to marry you someday. I want us to play street hockey with our kids in the driveway and teach them to bike mountain trails. I want to be that old couple who wins every bocce ball match at our Florida condo complex. And that's why I can't be your girlfriend right now. We're too young for it all to begin.

◇◇◇◇◇◇◇◇◇◇◇◇◇◇◇◇◇

At 1:30, after I'd finally fallen asleep, I woke up to my phone vibrating on my pillow. "Hello?"

"Are you awake?" Charlie asked.

"I am now."

"Oh, sorry..."

"No, don't apologize. What's up?"

I heard him sigh. "Is there any way you can come over? I know you're probably still in a food coma..." His voice trembled. "But I'd like to talk."

"Don't worry." I was already out of bed and pulling on my fuzzy boots. "I'm coming."

◇◇◇◇◇◇◇◇◇◇◇◇◇◇◇◇◇

"Is this about Luke?" I wondered once I'd crawled underneath Charlie's covers and, like he did whenever I was upset, wrapped my arms and legs around him. "What did you guys talk about?"

"Stuff," he said as I rested my cheek against his back. "A lot of stuff..."

Like being such good friends? I wondered bitterly, as we were quiet, so quiet that I could hear Charlie's watch ticking from over on his dresser. His room left you to face your own thoughts.

I started rubbing his back, something his mom used to do whenever he had a meltdown as a kid. He wanted to tell me, I could feel it.

After a few minutes, I heard him ask if I remembered our Pandora's fight.

"Yeah, I remember," I said, and hugged him tighter. I needed to push Nick aside for now. "And I'm so sorry. It was such a bitchy thing to say."

"But you were right," he whispered. "About all of it."

Then his body curled into a ball.

◇◇◇◇◇◇◇◇◇◇◇◇◇◇◇◇◇◇◇

"You're perfect, Charlie," I said after letting him cry for a while. "You're absolutely perfect, and I love you so much. I love you more than anyone else in the entire world. No matter what, I will always love you, and I want you to be happy."

"I don't know what to do." He wavered, fear in his voice. "I have no idea what to do."

I kissed his shoulder.

Silence.

"He said he loves me," Charlie whispered. "Before we hung up, he told me."

I gasped. "And what did you say?"

"Nothing. Just 'Happy Thanksgiving.'"

"But *do* you love him?"

My question hung in the air for a moment, and then I heard: "Promise you won't laugh?"

"Promise."

Charlie took a deep breath. "Yeah, I love him," he said. "I've been a goner for him since the day we met."

And I'm a goner for your brother, I thought, hugging and now crying with him. *I am an absolute goner for your brother.*

CHAPTER 20
CHARLIE

THE FLOCK WENT TO PEACE LOVE PIZZA TOGETHER on Saturday to celebrate the start of winter term, but as Nick would've said, I was interstellar the entire time. I didn't notice the gallon of grease that dripped off my barbeque chicken slice, and I didn't notice Val and her friends stabbing me with mental daggers from three tables away. All I noticed was that Luke wasn't there. Not feeling great, he'd texted our group chat. Out for tonight.

I fiddled with one of my bracelets under the table, the twisted leather cord with a brass anchor catch. Luke had been so stoic as I'd unwrapped the box in October, but then smirked with satisfaction once I told him I loved it, as if to say, *Yes, I'm a gift-giving genius.*

We'd seen each other around campus this week, but hadn't really spoken since Thanksgiving. There had been a blizzard in Grosse Pointe, so Luke had spent the holiday at my cousins' house. "So where are you now?" he'd asked after almost two hours of talking that night. "Still walking?"

I smiled. "No, sitting on some neighbor's porch." The DePietros were at Sage's, and I'd circled the neighborhood a hundred times already. "Where're you?"

"The upstairs den."

"Do they still have that red couch?" I couldn't remember the last time I'd been to Grosse Pointe, but I did remember my cousins' upstairs TV room: wood-paneled walls with built-in bookshelves and the deepest couch known to man. You literally *sank* into it.

"The one and only," Luke said. "Your aunt keeps saying they're going to get rid of it, though. The cushions are starting to tear."

"Shame."

"Yeah..."

"Okay, what are you thinking about?" I asked when he trailed off, shifting on the porch steps to get more comfortable.

A pause. "How do you know I'm thinking about something?"

"I can hear it in your voice," I said. "When you're lost in your head, it sort of drifts away..." I shut my eyes, so I could picture it. "And I know you're lying there, all stretched out, drumming your fingers on your leg. You're also staring at something across the room, but not *really* looking at it, and you're biting your tongue." Because Luke hadn't always been paying attention in class or at dinner. Even he could be a space cadet.

"It's a watercolor Banks did at school," Luke murmured after a second. "Of a pirate ship, armed with a shit-ton of cannons."

I laughed. "So what are you thinking about?"

No response.

"What was that?" I joked. "You're gonna need to speak up."

And again, silence, but then, "I'm thinking about how I'm in love with you."

⬩⬩⬩⬩⬩⬩⬩⬩⬩⬩⬩⬩⬩⬩⬩⬩⬩

I tripped going up the stairs, totally eating it halfway to Brooks' third floor. "You okay, Charlie?" Samir Khan asked from the landing. His voice made me flinch. I didn't know why I thought the house would be deserted, but I did. I hadn't expected to run into anyone.

"Yes, fine." I picked myself up off the ground. I hoped it wasn't obvious my whole body was shaking. *Now get out of my way.*

The third floor was quiet, and part of me considered making a pit stop in the bathroom so I could throw up. Because I had no idea what to do. *Do I just kiss him? Or do I tell him first? And what happens if he's changed his mind? Will it be different kissing a guy than kissing a girl? Will this change everything?*

I stood in front of his door for a long time, probably five minutes. And then I dared myself to knock. "My butler's out sick!" Luke called from inside. "Open it yourself!"

So I did, and there he was. I felt light-headed. Luke was alone, sitting on his bed with his computer, in a white T-shirt and the pajama pants I'd ordered off Vineyard Vines' website the day after Thanksgiving. Green with Santa hats. I paid for express shipping so he would get them before coming back to school. Christmas was his favorite holiday.

He looked up from his laptop screen, and we made eye contact. "Hey there." He shut his computer. "How's it going?"

"I'm sorry for taking so long!" I blurted.

Luke laughed and got up from his bed. "Yeah, I timed you. Five minutes outside my door. Now listen, the 'Super Senior' thing wasn't my—"

I didn't let him finish. Instead, I crossed the room and hugged him. Really, really hugged him. Both arms around him and burying my face in his neck. And Luke was very still for a beat before he started hugging me back. I sort of slumped against him. "I'm sorry for taking so long," I repeated. "But I'm all set now."

At least I hoped I was.

Luke pulled away to look at me. He cocked his head, pretending to be confused. Because I knew he knew what I meant. His gleaming eyes gave him away. But even so, he said, "Please elaborate."

"Be with me." I broke out of our hug so I could take his hand. Mine was shaking so hard, but our fingers somehow threaded together without a second thought, like we'd held hands a hundred times already. It was effortless. "Please. Let's be together. I'm in love with you. I've known we were going to be something since before we even met, when I heard you talking on the phone..." I squeezed his hand. "I've been all over the place, but this time, I'm ready." I paused. "That is, if you still want."

Luke was quiet for a second—the longest, quietest second ever—but then he smirked. "You're in love with me, huh?"

I exhaled. "That's the diagnosis, yes."

His whole face lit up. "I'm sorry to hear that."

"Yeah, I can tell." I smiled.

"Well, I'm in," he said with a nod. "As long as it's just me. Because according to my sisters, I've never been a good sharer..."

"You won't need to be," I told him. "It'll be you and me and no one else."

Then neither of us said anything. We just sort of looked at each other.

Luke spoke first. "I'm sick," he said, suddenly sounding all congested. "So I get it if you—"

"Doesn't matter." I shook my head, blood pulsing through my ears. "I have a good immune system."

"Proceed at your own risk."

I swallowed hard. "Have you ever...?" I started to ask, unable to say the whole thing. *Have you ever kissed a guy before?*

He knew what I meant. "Yes."

I glanced at the floor. *Well, I haven't*, I thought, but didn't say anything. Nothing had ever been more obvious.

"But I have never wanted to kiss anyone," Luke continued, voice quieter this time, "as much as I want to kiss *you*."

I lifted my head, and our eyes met. "Really?"

"Charlie." He gave me a long look. "You're a moron."

My heart throbbed.

"You're contagious," I said.

"You said you didn't care," he said back.

I took a deep breath. He was right; I didn't care. Not even a little bit. "Okay."

Luke nodded. "Okay."

"So how should we...?"

Luke smiled and shook his head, then slid an arm around my

side to pull me close, close enough to feel his heartbeat. His chest against mine. "You do way too much thinking," he murmured after holding me for a moment. He was so warm and steady that my eyes started to drift shut. "Relax, and let this happen." He knocked his forehead against mine. "All right?"

Eyes closed, I nodded.

"Good," he said, and then I opened my eyes in time to catch his grin before his lips landed on mine.

And just like him, they were warm and steady and somehow already so familiar. But my legs collapsed out of nowhere, and I fell back against his closed door, banging my head and dragging Luke down with me. A flailing mess of arms and legs, we kept kissing. Luke mumbled something unintelligible, and I mumbled something unintelligible back.

Whatever it was, I knew we were in agreement.

◇◇◇◇◇◇◇◇◇◇◇◇◇◇◇◇◇◇

I went into town early the next morning. Brunch in Addison didn't start until 11:00 a.m., but Pandora's opened at 7:00. Predictably, Luke was passed out when I got to his room, armed with coffee and breakfast sandwiches. "Sausage-egg-and-cheese on a cinnamon-sugar bagel," I'd ordered, remembering it was his favorite. "And make that two, please."

I knew his door was unlocked, because he'd asked me to turn out the lights on my way out last night. I put our bag of riches on his desk and took all of three steps over to his bed. I crouched down and touched his arm. "Hey," I whispered.

Luke's brown eyes snapped open so fast, and I saw his body tense up. "Holy shit," he mumbled when he realized it was me. "You are a psychopath."

I cocked my head. "Did I forget to mention that last night?"

"I don't remember it coming up, no." He rolled his eyes. "Otherwise, I'd like to think I would've at least locked the door."

"Oh, that wouldn't have done anything." I unbuttoned my coat and pulled off my boots. "I know how to pick locks."

"As every psychopath should."

"If they want to be able to hack it." I nodded, and then stood there for a second before Luke pushed back his covers and moved over to make room for me. He grinned.

"Get in here."

I grinned back and climbed in with him. He pulled the comforter back up as I rolled onto my side so we could share his pillow. Then he quickly kissed my cheek, not even my cheek— more like the corner of my mouth. I felt a deep tug. Still freaking out somewhat, but also excited. Here I was, in bed with a guy. I was kissing a guy—*Luke*. Finally.

I was me.

"Good morning," Luke whispered.

"Good morning," I whispered back.

He laughed softly, and I buried my head in his chest to feel the vibrations. Everything ached when I did. He really did have the best laugh. "What time is it?" he asked. "Seven?"

I smiled. "Almost nine."

He groaned. "Same thing."

"How so?"

"Addison isn't open yet."

I laughed. "Which is why I went off-site to bring you breakfast."

His eyes widened. "Pandora's?"

"What else?"

Luke sighed happily. "You're such a prince."

"Not a psychopath?"

"I might've been a little quick to judge."

I laughed again, and just like that, it clicked. *C.* I knew what it stood for, and it wasn't any part of my name. I raised an eyebrow and zapped Luke's side. "Charming?"

"Charming." He smirked and leaned in to kiss me again—right after whispering, "Your crown's in the closet."

CHAPTER 21
SAGE

THERE WERE TWO BIG PIECES OF NEWS BY breakfast on Monday. The first was that Charlie Carmichael apparently had a concussion. "You do *not* have a concussion," Luke said, looking up from scanning the news on his phone. "Calm down."

Charlie grinned, the corners of his eyes crinkling. "You know, I just might." He turned to the rest of us. "It was really hard to focus on my homework yesterday, and I woke up with this killer headache—"

"Try taking some Tylenol," Luke deadpanned. "Or Advil."

"Here," Jack said before Charlie could answer. "Follow my finger." He held up his index finger and slowly moved it back and forth, for Charlie's eyes to track. "Does this make you dizzy?"

Reese snorted. "And where did you get your medical degree, Dr. Healy?"

Jack shrugged. "Certified online." Then he smiled at her, and she quickly ruffled his hair. They'd been a thing ever since homecoming.

"A little," Charlie said. "A little dizzy."

"How do you think it happened?" Jennie asked, munching on a strip of bacon.

"Oh," Charlie said, and I caught his cheeks flush a little. "Well, I..."

"He slipped," Luke said nonchalantly.

"Yes." Charlie snapped his fingers. "Yes, that. I slipped."

"On a banana peel."

"Right, as one does in *Mario Kart*."

"Precisely."

Then the two of them were off to the races, talking at a speed no one could follow. I took a sip of orange juice, but it almost went down the wrong pipe when Reese leaned over, nodded at the boys, and whispered: "Just make out already."

I knew she was joking...but still. *Well, the thing is*, I imagined whispering back. *They already have.*

Charlie had called me after midnight on Saturday, as I was torturing myself in bed, clicking through old pictures of me and Nick on my laptop. Just buddies, just pals, now nothing. "Hey," I'd said into my phone, trying to keep my voice level. "Where'd you go after pizza?"

He didn't respond right away; I could hear him breathing, but he didn't say anything. "Are you alone?" he eventually asked.

I stared at a shot from two summers ago, me on Nick's shoulders at a Dierks Bentley concert. My eyes were shut as I screamed, and he was smiling up at me. I'd never noticed it before. "Yes," I said. "I'm alone."

"I kissed Luke," he said in a rush. "I kissed Luke tonight."

Both my heart and I jumped. "What?! Oh my god, Charlie!" I sucked in a breath. "Was it a good kiss?"

"Good?" His voice sounded different than I'd ever heard it before. I knew he was smiling. "Sage, I can't even..." He sighed again, dreamy and dazed. "I mean, you *know*, you know?"

Yes, I'd thought, my eyes prickling but glancing at the picture of Nick and me again. *Yes, I do know.*

✦✦✦✦✦✦✦✦✦✦✦✦

While we officially deemed Charlie's "concussion" fake news, the second tidbit was nothing but the truth—a confirmation of a rumor that had circulated Saturday night. "Holy crap," Nina said in the middle of *Crazy Rich Asians*. "Guess what Val texted me."

Reese hit pause. "Do tell."

"She says she heard some sophomore saw Emma Brisbane tonight." She paused. "In Mortimer's common room with Nick Carmichael."

My stomach sank, a string of words spilling out: "That means nothing."

"I wouldn't be so sure..." Nina tapped a text back to Val, then smiled. "Because apparently this junior saw them later, walking toward..."

Not the sixth hole, I prayed. *Please not the sixth hole.* Nick wouldn't do that; he wouldn't point out constellations to Emma. Granted, it was way too cold for the golf course, but I couldn't think clearly. Something was snaking around and strangling my heart.

"Sounds like Val was right," Jennie said. "This must be their year."

"Well, I won't believe it until I see it," Reese replied, and resumed the movie—but now, in Addison, we were seeing it. Cody Smith whistled from the boys' hockey table when Nick and Emma walked into the dining hall, hand in hand. He half-smiled and ducked his head, not wanting the attention, while Emma absolutely beamed, loving it.

Nina nudged me. "Pay up," she said. "Twenty bucks, remember?"

I suppressed a sigh. Nina had been so thrilled about the possibility of Nick and Emma that I'd impulsively made a bet with her that it was bullshit. I begrudgingly nodded. "I'll Venmo you later."

She laughed. "Can't wait to see your caption."

"Yeah, it'll be a winner," I mumbled, the line *He's my husband* flashing through my mind. Another quote from *Sweet Home Alabama.* My stomach twisted.

Jack pretend-pounded the table. "Well, all right then," he said. "Now that Nick and Emma are sorted, let's talk about the real deal." He gestured to Charlie and me. "We've been passing the popcorn back and forth for long enough, don't you think?"

The flock went silent.

Had Jack *really* just asked that?

Charlie and I looked at each other. His jaw wasn't tight, exactly, but still *clenched*, and there was a flash of fear in his eyes. I wondered what he saw in mine. A quaver, probably.

Because I was fighting tears.

Our friends stayed quiet. Either waiting for the usual brush-off, or for us to finally profess our love for each other. *I do love him!* I thought about saying, to settle this for once and for all. *Just not like that!*

"You know, Jack," Luke suddenly piped up. "I bet that popcorn's pretty stale by now." He swiped into his phone, shrugging casually. "Might be time to toss it."

◇◇◇◇◇◇◇◇◇◇◇◇◇◇◇◇◇◇◇◇◇◇

Luke and I slid into our usual Pandora's booth around 7:00 p.m. on Wednesday. We'd fallen into a routine of doing homework here after dinner, just the two of us.

"I saw you at practice today," he said as we unloaded our heavy backpacks, books banging onto the table. "You were killing it." He and I were both doing indoor track this term, but while Luke ran long distance, my specialty was pole-vaulting. It was the ultimate rush.

"I know," I said. "I didn't knock the pole once."

I expected Luke to raise an eyebrow at my outward confidence, since that was Charlie's style, not mine. But instead, he cocked his head and said, "I'm guessing you had some rage to release?"

"You guess right."

He stretched his hand across the table, and I took it, squeezing as hard as I could. "I'm sorry," he said. "I would've told you earlier, but we haven't been alone." He paused. "I take it I'm the only one who knows?"

"Yeah." I nodded. "I mean, Charlie knows, but..." I shook my head, as if to shake my fight with him away. *He'd fall fast and hard, and shatter the second you decided things had run their course...* He hadn't apologized, and I honestly didn't think he would. Maybe he'd forgotten it altogether, or he didn't regret a single word. Not that I could completely blame him. I'd said, straight up, that I wasn't looking for a real relationship until I was older.

But that was before Nick happened, before I fell in love with Nick. It was so ironic—Charlie thought I'd shatter his twin's heart, but Nick had shattered *mine*.

The barista called our names a second later. Our drinks were ready.

I volunteered to grab them, but when I got back to the table, Luke wasn't alone. Tristan Andrews and his sky-high hair—styled to look like a shark fin, I thought—stood there talking to him. "I'm so happy I ran into you," he was saying. "Did you have a good Thanksgiving?"

"Yes, it was great," Luke responded. "How about you?"

"Oh, me too. Really good to be home." He laughed. "But good to be back too."

Luke nodded and retrieved the pencil that he'd tucked behind his ear, a polite dismissal. *Time to resume my reading.*

Although I knew their conversation wasn't over yet. "I'm happy I ran into you," Tristan repeated. "Because, I've been wondering..." He reached to fix his hair. "If you wanted to go out sometime?"

"Oh." Luke put down his pencil and stared at it for a second, as if to collect his words. "That's really nice, Tristan, but..." He blushed. "I kind of have someone..."

"You *kind of have someone*?" I asked once Tristan awkwardly shuffled off (especially after discovering I'd overheard the whole thing). "Luke!"

"What?" He sipped his coffee. "I *do* have someone." His lips quirked up in a smile. "And he's not half-bad looking."

I laughed. "I know, but..." I tried not to wince, worried the next part wouldn't come out right. "Are you, um, allowed to say stuff like that?"

Luke's eyebrows knitted together. "*Allowed?*"

My stomach stirred. Yes, I'd said the wrong thing.

"Sorry, no," I fumbled. "I meant that I thought you guys were a secret. That's what Charlie told me. I guess..." I hesitated. "I'm just wondering."

"Well, yes," Luke said. "We agreed to keep things quiet—he wants to, and I understand. But it's only for right now, until he's ready." He shrugged. "But I'm *me*, and everyone knows it, so if people ask, I'm not going to lie about having a boyfriend." His voice dropped. "Because as we both know, keeping secrets doesn't lead to anything good."

My heart lurched.

"I'm sorry, Sage," he said. "As your friend, I want to keep things real with you." He looked at me dead-on. "Charlie claims you're powered by sunshine, but ever since Nick ended things, it's looked like you've lost your light..."

My voice cracked. "Don't, Luke. Please."

"Was it really worth it?" he asked. "Pretending it wasn't real? Just because your parents got divorced doesn't mean it'll happen to you. Mine met when they were eighteen—"

"Luke, stop," I said. "Please stop."

Luke's face reddened. "Okay, sorry," he murmured. "Too far, I'm sorry."

I nodded, my cheeks heated too.

We returned to our homework.

I looked up from my English reading an hour later, and immediately regretted it. Emma and Nick were at the counter, both bundled up in their hockey team jackets. "Jesus Christ," I muttered. "Are they fucking following me?"

A ridiculous question, since Emma was even more of a Pandora's regular than I was. She woke up super early and came here to study every morning. Charlie and I usually saw her when we ran. "Hey, Emma!" a barista shouted now.

"Let's leave," Luke suggested as she ordered hot chocolates for both of them, with plenty of whipped cream.

He likes marshmallows better, I thought. *And then he sprinkles bits of graham cracker on top. "A winter s'more," he calls it. He invented it in my kitchen when we were nine.*

Did he tell you that, Emma?

"Sage?" Luke asked.

"No." I shook my head. "No, let's stay. I'm fine." A lump formed in my throat. "I have to be fine."

"Okay," Luke said, but spoke again when I uncapped my highlighter. "You know I'm here," he whispered. "I'm always here if you can't be."

I nodded and forced myself to continue my chapter, but it was impossible to fully focus. Every couple of seconds my gaze would stray to Nick, sipping his hot chocolate with his new girlfriend at the front window's tiny table. *Does he feel it?* I wondered. *Does he feel me here?*

Our booth was so big that neither of them had so much as glanced in our direction. But a minute later, when Emma excused herself to grab some napkins, I literally jolted to my feet. "I'm going to say hey to Nick," I announced, my voice a squeak. It was like a magnet was pulling me to him.

Luke's look was shaky, but he gave me a thumbs-up.

So I crossed the café, Nick's and my eyes locking after I almost tripped over a random chair. "Hi," I said, trying to play things cool. My pulse pounded. "How's the hot chocolate?"

"Oh, hey," he replied. "Pretty good." He studied his mug. "It could be thicker, but good overall."

I felt a flutter of confidence. Nick always said the best hot chocolate was thick and creamy, like liquid velvet. "No marshmallows, though," I commented.

Nick ignored that. "What're you doing here?" he asked.

"Homework," I said. "Luke and I like to study here..." I gestured to our booth, where the only sign of Luke was the brim of his baseball cap. "Anyway..." I plastered on a smile. "I wondered if you wanted to go for a grind tomorrow? Take Ace and Stinger to one of the cross-country trails?"

Say yes, I thought, awkwardly shifting from one foot to the other. *Say yes, so I know we're still something, that there's* something *between us.*

But Nick shook his head. "Sorry," he said as I heard the *click-clack* of boots behind me. "Emma and I are going—"

"Hey, Sage!" Emma said brightly, my stomach knotting when I turned to see her ever-present smile. She reached to touch my white knitted scarf. "I love this!"

"Thanks." I tried to smile back. "My mom made it."

"It's really cute," she said, then slipped past me to rejoin Nick at their table. I watched her kiss his cheek before snuggling into his side. The corners of my eyes began to sting.

Leave, I thought, but the connection between my mind and legs had been severed.

Nick coughed. "Another time, Sage?" he asked. "Maybe?"

"Okay, yeah." I nodded, blinking tears away. "Maybe another time."

<hr />

Like the mind reader he was, Luke had our backpacks ready to go by the time I made it back to our booth. We wordlessly shrugged them on, then escaped into the night. Neither of us spoke until we stopped at the end of the block, waiting to cross the street. Luke pulled me into his arms, and I cried into his shoulder.

<hr />

Charlie suggested we go to the movies on Saturday. "Just us?" I asked, and was met with a beat of hesitation.

"Well, no," he said. "Luke too."

I nodded. "Sure, of course. What're we seeing?"

Now, we stood in the lobby waiting for Luke. Meet you there, he'd texted us. I'm carrying the team on this group project and can't leave. It'll go to shit.

"I never noticed it before," I said, "but Luke's kinda cocky."

Charlie gave me a look. "You're just figuring that out?" He smiled to himself. "I love it."

I rolled my eyes. "You would."

Grinning, he shrugged, and then we fell into a comfortable

silence. I started thinking about Emma stopping by our table at dinner tonight, annoyingly nice as always. "No concussion?" she asked Charlie.

"Nope." He shook his head. "All clear." After catching wind of his joke, the hockey coaches weren't taking any chances, dragging him to the infirmary for testing. The boys played Ames next weekend, and nobody wanted Charlie sidelined.

It was strange when Charlie broke the silence by saying, "So Nick and Emma, huh?"

My heart stilled. Neither of us had mentioned them yet, and I'd hoped it would stay that way. Luke was the only one I wanted to talk to about them, the only one I wanted to cry to about them. But here Charlie was, bringing it up. "Yes," I heard myself whisper. "Nick and Emma."

Charlie moved close. "I'm sorry, Sage," he said. "The things I said..." He shook his head. "I was a total asshole. I just..." He trailed off. "He's my brother. He's the best of us."

"Yeah, he is." I nodded, eyes prickling. But I mustered up a smile. "No offense."

Charlie laughed and wrapped me in a hug. "I love you, Sage."

I hugged him back. "I love you too, Charlie."

"Hey, that's a good-looking hat!" someone called to us, and I turned to see Luke with his signature smirk on full display.

Charlie reached up to touch the brim of his faded blue baseball cap. "Thanks," he said. "I didn't think hats were my sort of thing, but this one's pretty cool."

"Where'd you get it?" Luke asked, closing the final steps between us. He and Charlie made no moves to embrace each other.

But of course they wouldn't, I thought. *We're in public.*

"Actually, I'm not sure," Charlie said. "Someone gave it to me."

"More like you *stole* it from someone."

"Hey—"

"But either way," Luke continued, "that someone has cool taste."

Charlie smiled. "The coolest."

Luke smiled back and reached out to squeeze Charlie's arm. But he snatched his hand away when Charlie recoiled. "Oh, um, sorry..."

"No, don't be," Charlie murmured. "Just, um, look."

Luke and I followed his gaze to find Reese and Jennie getting their tickets scanned. Jennie waved when she spotted us. I glanced back at the boys: Charlie was staring at the ground, and Luke... looked bummed.

"How did they know we were coming?" he whispered as Charlie took two giant steps away from him. "I thought they were ice skating."

"Yeah, me too..." I agreed. Sometimes in the winter, the rink was kept open late for student skates. Reese and Jack had done a head count this morning so they knew how many pairs of skates to rent, and I'd said I didn't need one...

"Oh, crap," I said to the boys, "I might've mentioned we were going to the movies." I looked at them. "I'm sorry."

Before they could respond, Jennie bounced over, Reese on her tail. "Hey, guys!"

"Why aren't you at the rink?" Charlie asked.

"Too crowded," Jennie answered. "*Way* too crowded."

"And Jack can't stay on his own two feet," Reese added, waving a hand. "I left him in Paddy's care."

The three of us nodded.

"Well," Charlie said, "should we head in, then?"

∞∞∞∞∞∞∞∞∞∞∞∞

Halfway through the movie, I noticed Charlie was no longer watching it. He was watching Luke watch the movie, and when we accidentally made eye contact, he gave me a sheepish smile.

I smiled back, but gestured that I needed to go to the bathroom. Reese and Jennie didn't see me leave, too preoccupied with Chris Hemsworth shirtless on-screen.

After washing and drying my hands, I didn't go back in right away. Instead, I sat on a bench outside the theater and swiped into my phone, pulling up Instagram. Nina had posted a story of the student skate. There was music and chatter in the background. "One foot in front of the other," Paddy was saying as Jack clung to him with both arms, shaking in his skates. "There, there, you got it, dude..."

Then the video panned around the packed rink; Reese and Jennie had been right, it *was* super crowded. There was Val and the soccer girls, and Dove with her junior friends. But it wasn't until Nina zoomed in on two certain people that I shifted in my seat.

Nick and Emma.

They were holding hands and laughing, Emma wearing his hockey jacket. "Stop showing off, Nick!" someone shouted as he spun her around. "We get it! You've got it all!"

You've got it all.

I quickly locked my phone and slipped back into the theater, taking the stairs two at a time. Charlie was no longer gazing at Luke, but now they both had a leg stretched out, feet subtly mingling with each other. I nearly tripped over them.

"Shit," Charlie breathed. "Sage—"

Cheeks flaming, I waved him off and stumbled into my seat, Luke's Wednesday words now haunting me all over again: *Was it really worth it? Pretending it wasn't real?*

No, it hadn't been worth it. *Someday*, I'd been telling myself for so long, but maybe someday was sooner than I'd always imagined. I closed my eyes, remembering Nick and me intertwined together on the golf course that final night, so happy before Charlie's distress call.

But it doesn't matter, I thought. It didn't matter, because I was still trapped between the twins. I wouldn't betray Charlie in order to change Nick's mind. I wouldn't, couldn't. It was Charlie's truth to tell.

It's up to him, I realized. *It's up to Charlie to decide how soon someday comes.*

And I had no choice but to wait.

Wait, and watch Nick and Emma together.

CHAPTER 22
CHARLIE

MOM AND DAD DIDN'T COME TO EVERY HOCKEY game, but they always drove down for the weekend matchups and took a bunch of us to dinner at Bistro afterward. "I made a reservation for ten," Mom told me on Friday. "But maybe we should change it to eleven? In case you want to invite anyone else...?"

I closed my eyes and bit the inside of my cheek. She always did this—baited me, hoping I would bring a girl along.

"No, Mom, ten's fine," I said, glancing over at Luke. He was sitting upside down on the chesterfield, absorbed in some psychological thriller. Up until Mom had called, I'd been reading too. His worn copy of *The Girl with the Dragon Tattoo*. I wasn't really a reader, but Luke laughed when I'd told him that. "I've seen your English grades, C. You can read just fine."

"Oh," Mom replied, disappointed. "Okay. We'll leave it then."

"Ten?" Luke asked after she and I hung up. "For what?"

I rejoined him on the couch, slumping so that I could rest my head back against the cool leather. Luke shifted so his legs were now across my lap. "Just this dinner," I answered, stomach churning a little. "On Saturday, after my game. She and my dad always take Nick and me and some hockey guys to Bistro."

"Ah," Luke said. "So it's a team thing."

I nodded as I swiped into my phone and quickly texted Mom: Actually 11. I'll bring Sage.

Wonderful, she responded with a smiley emoji. I can't wait to see her!

Not only did Bexley love the idea of Sage and me together, but so did my parents. I imagined Mom already having a box of pictures labeled *Wedding Slideshow*.

"Is Emma going?" Luke asked.

"Yeah," I said. Since yes, Emma was coming. Nick had invited her.

"Because she's team manager...?"

"Right," I lied. "Because she's our manager."

Luke was quiet, like he knew I was lying. *I'm sorry*, I wanted to say. *But not yet*. My parents...I could barely control myself around Luke already. I had to mentally straitjacket myself these days, so I didn't fiddle with his fingers during lunch or slide an arm around him as we walked to class. Sometimes I imagined myself actually doing it, but then my heart would clench. *No*, I'd think, scared shitless. *No one can know*.

Because they'd be merciless. Tristan Andrews had been whispered about for weeks when he arrived on campus as a freshman (you just sort of knew with him), and even though Luke had held his head high, he had too. I couldn't do it. I just couldn't.

"Well, that actually reminds me," Luke said, "I don't think I'm gonna make it to the game. I have a history paper due Tuesday."

"What?" I said. "Really?" I liked having Luke in the crowd, liked seeing him airborne after jumping off the bleachers when we scored. That goal was for you, I'd texted him from the locker room last week, in between periods. Bet you said that to all the girls, he'd texted back (but then later in his room, he declared hockey was the best sport and threw himself at me).

"Yup." He lifted his leg and lightly kneed me in the jaw. "I'd like to bang it out this weekend."

"But we'll see each other later?" I asked.

"Sure," he said. "If I make decent progress, sure."

"And if I'm not held captive at dinner," I mumbled.

Luke glanced up from his book. "Then don't be," he said. "If you don't want to be held captive, C, then don't be. It's your life." He kneed me again. "They'll understand."

But would they? I wondered. *Would they understand?*

◇◇◇◇◇◇◇◇◇◇◇◇◇◇◇◇◇◇

Bexley ended up winning the game 4–3, and I felt like a douche-bag by the time our appetizers were served. Sage had steered us away from Nick and Emma, but I caught her sneaking peeks at my brother. *She wasn't just fooling around with him*, I realized once her hand found mine under the table. *Whatever they had, it meant as much to her as it did to Nick.*

I cringed when I remembered what I'd said to her, and worried that it was now too late to fix things between them. Don't center the conversation at dinner around Emma, Nick texted our family group chat today. She gets shy sometimes. Please be cool.

He actually liked her; this was more than just a homecoming date. Nick was trying to move on, and I'd guess it was working based on the way he'd introduced her to our parents, smiling proudly with a hand on her lower back. "Mom, Dad, this is my girlfriend, Emma."

He also wasn't returning any of Sage's stolen looks.

Not that it was easy to keep track—our table was loud and full, Nick and the guys trying to talk over one another. "I'm glad your last slapper went in," Dad told Cody when things calmed down some. "Because, man, those refs..." He let out a low whistle. "Absolutely terrible. I'd say your buddy Jack had the best heckle of the game."

"'Get off your knees, ref!'" Paddy quoted. "'So you can stop blowing the game!'"

They all cracked up, Emma giggling alongside them. Mom shook her head, but even she was fighting a smile. "Really, Jay?" she said as my spine straightened. "Really?"

"And who was that one Ames kid?" Dad asked once we got our entrees. I glanced down at my chicken piccata; my swishing stomach not interested. "Number nineteen?"

"Dan Richards, left wing," Nick said automatically. He knew every prep school player and their stats. "What about him?"

"Nothing," Dad said. "Just that he..."

"Twirls," Paddy said, snorting. "He twirls instead of sprints, like he's figure skating."

"That's because he figure skated growing up," Emma chimed in, her cheeks pinkening a little. She knew her stats too. And did extra research.

More laughter, but it was drowned out by this buzzing noise in my ears. I felt myself slump down in my chair when I saw Dad open his mouth, which was when Sage decided to come to life, straightening her shoulders. "Don't come at men's figure skating, Mr. Carmichael," she said firmly. "If I'm remembering correctly, you *lost it* when Nathan Chen choked in PyeongChang, and cheered the loudest when Adam Rippon won his bronze."

Everyone was silent until Dad chuckled. "I wouldn't dare, Sage." He raised his beer. "To Chen's comeback in 2022!"

Mom toasted her wine. "Hear, hear!"

Meanwhile, I slipped away to the bathroom, sagging back against the door after I'd locked it behind me. It was a one-person sort of deal. "How's it going?" I asked when Luke answered his phone.

"In the library, starting the footnotes," he said. "What's up?"

I swallowed. "We're still seeing each other later?"

"If you hang up and let me finish, yeah."

"Okay, cool," I said, and then asked, "Was it a pain to write?"

"Nah, pretty straightforward. I'm not sure it's my best effort, but it's done."

I shook my head. "I bet it's groundbreaking."

"Well, I'd read it first," Luke said, "before such a sweeping declaration."

I laughed. "I miss you," I murmured, even though that was stupid. Luke and I had seen each other at breakfast. I cleared my throat. "I'm sorry, that probably sounds..."

"Would you like to stay over tonight?" he asked.

Would you like to stay over tonight? I ran a hand through my hair, wishing everyone wasn't right down the hall. But another part of me didn't care, didn't care at all. Just thinking of Luke made my heart ignite. He made everything better. Everything would be better when I saw him.

"I mean, you're allowed to do that, right?" Luke went on. "Sleep over in other houses?"

"Yes." I nodded. "But we need to get permission." I'd done it a few times this year to sleep in Nick's room. All I had to do was text my housemaster, Mr. Fowler.

Luke laughed. "So get permission."

I let out a deep breath. "Should I bring my sleeping bag?"

"Yeah, plus your pillow."

"And you'll handle the snacks?"

"Only if you have a few ghost stories prepared."

I smiled. "They always were my specialty."

◇◇◇◇◇◇◇◇◇◇◇◇◇◇◇◇◇◇

We were all over each other about two seconds after Luke's door slammed shut, once the lock had clicked into place. I was still in my coat and tie from the game, so he helped me shuck off my blazer while I unbuttoned his black peacoat. "That was really impressive," he breathed when it hit the floor.

I kissed him. "Thanks. I'm really good at unbuttoning things."

"I had a hunch." He grinned and unknotted my tie so I could ditch my shirt. I grabbed his hat and flung it in some direction. We started to move backward, toward his bed. "Is this okay?" he asked, our hands everywhere. "Or should we leave and go climb onto the MAC's roof?"

I laughed and kissed him again, remembering what I told him the first night we went up there. Leni Hardcastle and her rite of passage. "Nah," I said, nervous but also feeling this warm burst inside me. Something amazing was about to happen. "Here's great."

Luke tackled me onto the bed. "Yeah?"

"Yeah." I nodded, and we both cracked up while we maneuvered his sweatshirt and T-shirt up and over his head.

"Holy shit, you wear so many layers," I told him.

"Because I get cold easily."

I grinned. "So high maintenance."

Luke broke our kiss. "Says the person who clearly has separation anxiety."

"Undiagnosed," I said after the next one.

He rolled his eyes. "Uh-huh, sure."

I hugged him close. "I just like hearing your voice."

"Me too," he said. "We have really great voices."

"We do," I agreed.

And then we didn't use them for a while.

<hr />

"I love you," I whispered later. "I really fucking love you."

Luke's hand found mine. "That's very cool," he whispered back, entwining our fingers. "Because the feeling's mutual."

He watched me fumble to get dressed after the alarm went off at 7:15. This morning's game was at 9:00 a.m. "Can I borrow a tie?" I asked as I buttoned my wrinkled shirt. It probably wasn't a good idea if I wore mine two days in a row. Someone would notice.

Luke nodded. "Closet."

I opened the door and grabbed the first one I saw, solid gray. I quickly knotted it and turned back to look at him. He was still under the covers, his hair an absolute train wreck. I smiled. "You're adorable."

He smirked. "So I've been told."

"By who?" I pulled on my blazer.

"Well, let's see...my mom, my sisters, my grandmother, Sage, Nina..."

I laughed and flopped down on top of him to say goodbye. "Yeah, I get it. Everyone's in love with you."

Luke shrugged. "Pretty much."

"Must be tough."

"I manage."

"Will you come today?" I asked, sort of quietly. Mom and Dad were going to be there again, but it would be Sage making the introduction, not me. "My dear friend Luke!" was probably how she'd do it, exactly how I needed it to be. I wasn't ready for more than that.

But suddenly I did want them to meet him.

If only for just enough time for a handshake.

"You should be there to see me suck," I added, since I was

exhausted. We hadn't gotten much sleep. "There's a high possibility I'll get benched."

"Of course." Luke grinned. "I'll text Sage, and we'll get coffee first."

I grinned back and hugged him hard.

CHAPTER 23
SAGE

I WAS WITH LUKE WHEN I GOT AN EMAIL FROM Daggett House, saying Charlie had "cordially invited" me to their Tacky Christmas dinner this week. Last year Paddy had asked me, and we'd obnoxiously mimed gagging ourselves while Charlie and his fling-at-the-time canoodled over decorating Christmas cookies.

"I feel kinda bad," I admitted after Luke skimmed the invitation. We were at the bakery in town, waiting to get cupcakes for Reese's birthday. "*You* should be his date, not me."

Luke shrugged. "Better you than someone else."

I laughed, but it felt forced.

"Just don't get too handsy with him," Luke warned. "I hear he's taken."

"Noted," I said as we moved up in line.

"What can I get for you kids?" the friendly-looking woman behind the counter asked.

"We'll take a dozen, please," Luke replied, and I listened as he relayed our Reese-approved selection, ending with: "And one Boston Cream in a separate bag."

My brows knitted together. "Is that last one for you?"

He smiled and rolled his eyes. "Of course not."

We paid for Reese's birthday goodies and then headed back to campus. "Where's Charlie?" I asked after we made room in Brooks' fridge for our white bakery box. I shook the brown paper bag. "You gonna deliver his special treat?"

Luke shook his head. "Nah, I thought you could do that. I have to call Keiko Morrissey, Esquire, about a very important matter."

I sighed. "He's going to be so disappointed."

"He shouldn't be...after all, you're his date to the Christmas thing."

"I thought you said you didn't care."

"I don't."

My eyes narrowed. I couldn't tell if he was bullshitting me or not. "Where is he?"

"Knowles Basement."

I nodded. "You want me to give him a message?"

"Yeah." Luke smirked. "Tell him he has to settle up with me tonight."

∞∞∞∞∞∞∞∞∞∞∞∞∞∞

Daggett's date party was the same day a bunch of early college decisions came out, including Yale, UVA, and *my* first choice. Jennie had gotten into Stanford yesterday (I'd abandoned my math homework and raced down the hall to congratulate her after hearing her happy scream), and at 5:00 p.m. tonight, I could finally find out my own fate. Although it would really be later than that, since I'd decided I wouldn't check until after the party. Charlie was still staying pretty quiet on the college front. All he'd said was that he'd applied to several schools EA, and one ED.

He wouldn't reveal anything else, but after the party, where everyone had been decked out in ugly Christmas sweaters, Charlie suggested we take a campus stroll. We walked in silence for a few minutes, passing by the girls' houses and the library, and then Charlie spoke. "I'm sorry," he said. "I'm sorry for us not getting to hang out lately."

"Oh," I said, somewhat surprised. Yes, he and I hadn't hung out one-on-one for a few weeks, but I wasn't hung up on it or anything. We saw each other all the time at meals, and I'd lost track of how many "dates" to the movies or Pandora's I'd gone on with him and Luke.

"It's totally my fault," he continued. "I spend all my time with him..."

I squeezed his arm. "Hey, relax. It's okay. You really dig him, I get it. I don't feel neglected or anything. I feel like we hang out tons."

"We don't make you feel like a third wheel all the time?"

I shook my head. "No, not usually. In my mind, I'm hanging out with my two best friends."

Charlie nodded. "Okay, good."

"Yeah, good," I echoed, and forced my best smile. I really did love hanging out with Luke and Charlie, but at the same time, it could be so *painful*. Their inside jokes, their laughter, and the way they *looked* at each other...

It was a constant reminder of what I no longer had with Nick.

"So…" I ventured after another beat of silence. "Any news from Nick?" It was almost 8:00 p.m., so odds were he'd found out about Yale by now. I wondered if he'd been nervous…

Probably not, I decided, since Charlie had mentioned his brother getting a "likely letter" several weeks ago. It basically told him that he was guaranteed to get accepted as long as he didn't screw anything up before official decisions were released. He had nothing to worry about.

Charlie laughed. "He's probably ordering Yale-themed Christmas presents as we speak."

He swiped into his phone to show me a text: RIDE OR DIE, BULLDOGS!

"Oh, I knew he would." I let out a sigh of relief, breath visible in the cold air. "I bet the hockey coach would've burned down the admissions building if they didn't accept him. Please tell him I say congratulations."

Even though all I wanted to do was tell him myself.

"I will," Charlie said, and then we randomly slowed to a stop in front of the chapel. "Should we check?" he asked. "You said your school was tonight…" He bit the inside of his cheek. "I have one too. Well, a couple, actually."

I felt a jump of excitement. "Yeah, yeah, let's do it."

We pulled up our emails, Charlie glancing at me. "On three?"

"Yeah," I said. "Okay."

We moved closer together, and Charlie took a deep breath. "One…two…"

And when *three* arrived, I clicked on the link to my decision and watched it slowly load pixel by pixel. Dear Miss Morgan, finally appeared. We are delighted to offer you a place…

Time froze for a second, and I stared at the letter until Charlie elbowed me. "So?"

"I'm in." I turned to look at him, heart pounding. "I got in! To Middlebury!"

"Middlebury?" he exclaimed. "Holy crap, Sage, *yes*! Fire up the confetti cannon!"

I grinned. Middlebury, up in gorgeous Vermont, with kick-ass academics and where I could ski and bike to my heart's content. ("A reach," my college counselor had called it, just like Yale and Bowdoin. "Who cares?" Nick had said when I told him that. "A *reach* doesn't mean *impossible*." He squeezed my hand. "Go for it, Morgan. Don't just play it safe.")

I need to text Nick, I almost said, but then remembered Charlie. "What about you? Thumbs-up?"

He nodded. "Johns Hopkins."

"Oh, wow! Congratulations!"

"Thank you." He smiled. "I got into UNC yesterday too." His rubbed the back of his head. "I sort of want a bigger school..."

"So I've gathered." I laughed and elbowed him. "But tell me where the big kahuna is. What's your ED?"

He shook his head, a slight smile appearing. "I can't, Sage. I want to, but..." He shrugged. "If it doesn't work out, I don't really want to dwell on it, let alone anyone else."

"Yeah, okay." I nodded. "I get that."

After all, I hadn't told him about Middlebury.

We hugged, and when Charlie pulled back, he opened his mouth to say something, but then his phone buzzed. "I need to go see Luke," he said after scanning the message. "I'd like to tell him in person, and Virginia comes out soon, at eight..."

"And then you'll talk about how much you're going to miss each other?" I joked, since winter break started tomorrow. Mrs. Carmichael and my mom were driving down in the morning to bring us back to Darien.

Charlie smirked. "Oh, come on, we're gonna do way more than talk..." He gestured to his tacky red jeans. "Have you *seen* me in these pants?"

"Okay, beat it." I pushed him away. "I don't want to hear any more."

He didn't need to be told twice, but then turned back to look at me. "Thank you," he whispered.

"You're welcome," I said, giving his arm another squeeze. "Johns Hopkins and UNC. I'm so proud of you, Charlie."

"I'm so proud of you too, Sage." He paused. "But no, not that." He shifted on his feet. "Thank you for protecting me."

I tilted my head. "Protecting you?"

"Yeah." He nodded. "I know that's why you kept things with Nick a secret from everyone, to protect me. So they wouldn't suspect..." He trailed off and shook his head. "You should hate me."

Oh, Charlie, I thought, a lump forming in my throat. *Oh, Charlie...*

"I let people believe what they want to believe," he said quietly. "You know they think we're really in love, and I like it that way. I never deny it." His voice wavered. "But that's not fair to you, or Nick. If you wanted to be together again..."

Suddenly hope flared inside me. *You'll tell him?* I came close to blurting. *If Nick and I wanted to be together again, you'll tell him the truth? About us? About you?*

But when he trailed off, I instead heard my stupid self say, "No, no, stop. Stop right there. I could *never* hate you."

"I could never hate you either." Charlie smiled in relief, not noticing my shoulders sag in disappointment. He had no idea how trapped I was, how he was the only person who could rescue me. I still wasn't sure if my *someday* with Nick should be now, but him learning Charlie's secret? I wished it could be.

Charlie opened his arms for a good-night hug, and I stepped into them.

"You're the best, Sage," he whispered in my ear. "The *best*."

No, I'm not, I thought as I wiped my runny nose on his coat. *But I'm trying.*

◇◇◇◇◇◇◇◇◇◇◇◇◇◇◇◇◇

The walk from the chapel to Simmons wasn't that long, but tonight, it seemed to take forever. *Accepted!* kept flashing through my mind as I dodged patches of black ice, but so did my unspoken: *You'll tell him the truth?*

I stopped in my tracks outside my dorm...because two figures were standing out front holding hands, and even though the guy had a hat on, I somehow knew he was Nick. Tears pricked at the corners of my eyes.

His girlfriend spotted me first. "Hey, Sage!" Emma called out. "Did you have fun tonight?"

"Oh hey," I said, and forced myself to start up the pathway.

"Yeah, it was tons of fun. Charlie and I got a standing *O* for karaoke."

"Which song?" she asked.

I shrugged. "'Baby, It's Cold Outside,' but Paddy's 'All I Want for Christmas' was definitely better."

"Oh my gosh." Emma laughed, but Nick kept a straight face.

Then, right as we found ourselves in awkward territory, the front door thankfully opened. "Em, get in here!" Lucy waved her inside. "We're watching the Hallmark channel, and your favorite's on!"

Emma's face lit up. "The one with the Christmas matchmaker?"

Lucy nodded.

So Emma and Nick's goodbye followed. "Have a good break, Nick," she said, moving in for a hug (thank goodness, because I so did not want to see them kiss). Then Emma stretched up and pressed her lips to his. I glanced at the ground, knowing I should've gone inside, but also wanting to wait so I could congratulate Nick.

"You too, Emma," he said after. "Let me know when your flight lands."

Emma touched my arm before she went inside. "Get the girls and come watch with us," she told me. "This movie is the cutest."

I nodded, but at the same time felt my skin crawl. It was ridiculous how nice Emma was. I considered myself a pretty nice person, but I could never even hope to be as nice as her.

"Congratulations!" I blurted after she was gone. "Charlie told me."

Nick smiled, and my heart twisted when his dimple appeared. I hadn't seen it in so long, and he looked so thrilled. "Thank you."

He let out a deep breath. "It's such a relief. I haven't been able to stop thinking about it."

"You completely deserve it," I said. "Are your parents happy?"

Nick nodded. "Yeah, Dad's amped, and Mom was basically sobbing."

"That's amazing," I said, and then it was quiet, except for a few shouts and laughs from inside the house.

"Emma, how is this your *favorite*?" I heard someone say. "I'm cringing! It's so cheesy!"

Nick shifted from one foot to the other. "What about you?" he asked softly. "Any word...?"

"Oh, yeah..." I started, feeling my eyes well up again. "I was..."

Accepted!

Accepted!!

Accepted!!!

"Sage?" I eventually registered Nick saying. "Are you okay? You look..."

I snapped out of my trance. "What?"

"I'm sorry," he said, assuming the worst. "Was it a no?"

"No," I replied. "It was a yes. I got in."

Nick broke into a grin. "See!" he said. "I told you!" He laughed. "I *told* you they would see how epic you are!"

"Yeah, you did," I said, tears now spilling and singeing my cold cheeks. Nick asked why I was crying. "It's stupid," I told him. "But I still can't imagine going to school without you guys." My voice cracked. "I would've liked us to be together."

A blink later, before I knew it, Nick had folded me into his arms, and I was hugging him and crying into his chest. His crimson toggle coat was warm, and he smelled like Humpty Dumplings, but he also smelled like Nick—so perfect and familiar and vaguely like a campfire—and I never wanted him to let go.

But with curfew creeping up, he had to, sending me a signal with one last squeeze. *No, please don't*, I thought. *I want this. I love this. I* miss *this. Don't let go.*

Of course he couldn't read my mind, so he didn't get the message, but before he pulled away he murmured in my ear, "I would've liked us to be together too."

CHAPTER 24
CHARLIE

CHRISTMAS BREAK DRAGGED BY, ALL THREE weeks of it. "The more you pay, the less you go," Dad liked to joke, but I couldn't cross the days off our family calendar fast enough. It was the usual timeline of events: cutting down our Christmas tree followed by the Hardcastles' black-tie Christmas Eve party, a chill Christmas dinner at Granddad and Nana's, and lying around in our pajamas from December 26 to December 30 playing board games. New Year's was spent skiing up at Sugarbush with Sage and her dad, and then *finally* it was time to head back to Bexley.

But soon I had to leave again.

"I don't want to go," I said as I held Luke close. It was a little before 8:00 a.m., the first Saturday classes of the New Year. He had a free period first thing, and I'd been excused from classes so I could get on a bus to Massachusetts at 9:00 a.m. (we were playing Tabor today and tomorrow). I'd spent the night in his room, my backpack and duffel bag for this weekend packed and ready to go. My hockey stuff was waiting at the rink.

Luke rolled over, buried his face in my neck, and mumbled, "So dramatic."

I smiled and ran a hand through his hair. Sleepy Luke was one of my favorite Lukes, all cute and rumpled with his bedhead and pajamas. I had physically ached last night, getting under the covers with him, our legs tangling together—heavenly. *How can I have this every night?* I'd asked myself after Luke fell asleep. *Because I need to have this every night.*

"Okay, come back," Luke groaned when I was up and in my team jacket, and trying to chug a cup of Keurig coffee. He lifted the edge of his comforter. "Please."

"Sorry." I shook my head. We'd hit snooze a couple of times, and the rink was a trek from Brooks. "I'm already going to need to run there."

"But you're a solid runner," he pointed out, smirking hard.

I was in love with him.

"Ticktock..."

"Okay." I put down his new orange-and-blue UVA mug. "But just for a second."

∞∞∞∞∞∞∞∞∞∞∞∞∞∞∞

"Dibs on the window bed," Paddy said as I swiped us into our room for the night, on the third floor of the Hampton Inn near Tabor's campus. He and I always bunked together on away trips.

I tossed Luke's pillow on the closer of the two beds. It was cool and soft and smelled like him, peppermint and soap and whatever else made him smell the way he did. Paddy did the same with his, and then we unzipped our hockey bags to air out our stuff. Skates, shin guards, shoulder pads, elbow pads, gloves—everything came out so it could dry overnight. Nothing was worse than putting on wet equipment in the morning.

After that, the team congregated in Nick's room for about an hour. Tomorrow was an early start, so Coach Meyer informed us that he was coming around at 10:45 p.m. to check that we were all where we were supposed to be. I played with the remote until I found the Rangers-Bruins game on TV, and Cody broke out Cards Against Humanity before some of us went on a field trip to the vending machines up the hall. Things sort of wound down after we epically failed at prank-calling Emma on the fourth floor. "I'm hanging up now, Paddy," she said the last time, after two minutes of him breathing heavily into the hotel phone's mouthpiece. "Sleep tight."

"Well, I don't really know how to say this," Paddy said after our face-to-face with Coach Meyer, "but do you mind if I FaceTime?" His face reddened. "Val, uh, wanted to know how the game went..."

Paddy had invited Val to our Tacky Christmas, and they'd been hanging out ever since (Awkward? A bit). "All right, I'll split," I said, digging around in my backpack for my new iPad. "Gotta make a call myself."

Paddy smirked. "Who?"

My chest tightened, but I pulled off a casual shrug. "Wouldn't you like to know?"

I took the elevator down to the lobby. We'd stayed at this hotel before, so I pretty much knew all the attractions. The business center's door was locked, but with one grand flourish of my room key, I was in. There were four Dell desktops and two printers, and I could hear something humming as I dropped down into one of the swivel chairs. But instead of logging onto a computer, I propped my feet up on the desk and unlocked my iPad, swiping to the FaceTime app.

Luke appeared on-screen after three rings, sitting at his desk, which he referred to as the *command center*. His cheeks were flushed and his breathing heavy, like he'd been running. "Hey there."

"You guys turned on the turf lights tonight," I responded.

And he grinned. "It was *absurd.*"

Sage and the girls had been monitoring the turf's snow situation all week. "Still some patches," Reese had reported on Wednesday, but at dinner yesterday, Nina's recon was way more promising: "Melting as we speak!"

"A shit-ton of people," Luke said, taking off his baseball hat so he could smooth down his hair. *Douchey lax bro flow* the girls had nicknamed it, since he'd avoided getting a haircut over break. I sort of loved it.

"Yeah?" I said. "And?"

"And"—he laughed—"I don't envy them. It doesn't compare to our thing."

"Yeah, we're untouchable," I agreed, since we used my master key on weekends. ("Should we leave her a note?" Luke had joked before we left Jennie's study room one night, and I will admit, it felt different going there for student council meetings now.)

Luke relocated from his chair to his bed, leaning against the wall. "How was the game?" he asked. "The Twitter was blowing up."

I grinned. The Twitter was our team Twitter account: @BexleyBoysPuck. It was Emma's creation; she posted our schedule, any injuries or line-up changes, and live-tweeted all our games. I hope you're hungry, Tabor! was one of today's tweets. Because it's another Carmichael Sandwich! 3–1 #BBVIH.

We ended up losing 5–3.

"It got pretty chippy," I told Luke. "You should've seen Nick wreck this one guy. The boards actually *shook*..."

He nodded along as I recapped the hip-check, then asked, "Was your family there?"

"Yeah," I said. "All the parents were, I think. They had this big tailgate before the game."

"That sounds cool..." Luke said, and it looked like he wanted to say something else, but he didn't. My stomach started to churn a little, so I changed the subject.

"Where's poker tonight?" I asked. There was a midnight poker game every Saturday night in Brooks—PGs only. I'd bought Luke a legit cash box off Amazon because the jar he had for his "winnings" wasn't cutting it anymore.

"Dave Taylor's room," Luke said, and smirked. "And your guy's feeling *good* tonight."

"Is he?" I arched an eyebrow. "Tell me, what will you do with tonight's haul?"

"Buy my boyfriend dinner," he replied right away, no hesitation.

I laughed and rolled my eyes. "Oh, come on, you've footed the bill at Pandora's plenty."

"No." Luke shook his head. "I'm not talking Pandora's. I'm talking a *nice* dinner. Bistro, or the Bluebird."

"But we can't go there," I said, feeling the back of my neck heat up. "It'll seem like we're on a date."

Luke sighed. "Well, that's the point. We should go on a date. A *real* date."

I didn't say anything. Instead, I imagined Paddy or someone showing up at our table. *Ooh, what do we have here?* they'd say, and the rest of Bexley would know within the hour.

"It can't be like this, Charlie," Luke said gently. "It can't be like this forever."

"I know," I told him, heart hammering. "I know, I just need a little more—"

But before I could add *time*, I heard the business center's door open. Nick and Paddy were both standing there when I spun around in my chair. "Aw, how cute," Paddy said, grinning and shaking his head. "I *knew* there was someone."

Meanwhile, Nick looked like he wanted to punch me.

I glanced down at my iPad—Luke was dead silent. His mouth was in a straight line, and he reached up to adjust his glasses. I didn't know what to say. There was this buzzing noise in my ears.

"Come on, Charlie," Paddy came farther into the room, grabbing his own chair. "What's happening? Passionate reunion with Dove?"

"Seriously?" Nick stayed in the doorway. "We need redemption tomorrow, and instead of getting sleep, you're talking to *Dove*?"

"No, it's Sage," I said quickly, then winced. Why was I still doing this? "Sorry, I sort of lost track of time..."

Paddy smirked. "Sure you did."

Now sweating, I ignored him and looked on-screen to see Luke staring at me. "Nick's right," I said, heart so clenched I could barely breathe. "I should go."

◇◇◇◇◇◇◇◇◇◇◇◇◇◇◇◇◇◇◇

You don't have to tell everyone at once, he texted later, after I'd brushed my teeth and gotten into bed. But start with Nick, and soon. Please.

CHAPTER 25
SAGE

IS IT APPROPRIATE, I WONDERED SUNDAY AFTER-noon, *to invite another girl's boyfriend to watch a movie?*

Luke, unfortunately, didn't think so.

"So you wouldn't trust Charlie?" I asked, disappointed. "If someone invited him to get parietals, and he said yes?"

"No, I didn't say that." Luke shook his head. "I meant that I wouldn't trust *you* and *Nick.*" He smirked from over on the therapy couch. "He's been looking at you again."

My heart skipped. "What?"

"Yup, breakfast, lunch, and dinner—he looks over at our table. The old routine has resumed."

Because I've been looking at him too, I thought. Just the other day I'd watched Nick and his sweet tooth seriously contemplate his options at Addison's dessert station. Chocolate cake? Vanilla? Or maybe coconut? I'd only looked away when Emma sidled up to him and pointed to the vanilla, the most classic but also the most boring choice.

Nick served himself a slice, but also a coconut one.

But before I could tell Luke, Charlie slipped through my door. "Hey," I said. "How'd you get in?" I'd had to swipe Luke in with my student ID and then we asked for parietals permission from my housemaster.

In response, he held up an old-fashioned metal key. "Easy." He smiled. "I have the keys to the kingdom." He shucked off his coat. "And snuck up the back stairs."

I rolled my eyes as Luke shifted on the chaise. "Hey there," he said, smirking and patting the spot next to him. "*Mon petit ami.*"

Charlie blushed and joined his *petit ami.* Luke gave him a quick kiss and then grinned when Charlie hid his face in Luke's neck and mumbled something. I kept quiet, letting them have a moment. If I did say so myself, I was the best third wheel ever.

But it kind of sucked.

"You too," Luke replied, then turned to me and gestured to the big white sheet tacked up on my wall. "So, Netflix?"

I nodded and moved to set up our show. Back in October, Nick had announced that my laptop screen wasn't cutting it anymore for our movies. "Then I guess we'll have to switch to your room," I'd replied. "I can't get a TV." I wrinkled my nose. "Prefect privilege."

"But I like yours better," he said. "Your bed is better..." He coughed. "You know, more comfortable, with all your fluffy pillows and stuff..."

The next week, he'd shown up with a cardboard box. Inside were the makings of a movie theater. "Where did you even get that?" I asked, watching as he hooked up the projector. It wasn't ancient-looking, but wasn't brand new either.

"Granddad and Nana," he replied. "They're still decluttering. Nana read some book about it and is obsessed with purging."

We'd watched *To All the Boys I've Loved Before* that night, but right now, with Luke and Charlie, I couldn't pay attention to the crime family drama they'd chosen. My mind instead rewound itself to *The Holiday*. Nick had come over one day during winter break, and we'd watched it again after baking brownies together, the talking and joking somehow so easy again. "You know Iris's cottage isn't even real," he said through a forkful of brownie. "The facade is total CGI."

I'd given him a look, and replied in my best Southern drawl: "'You're shittin' me, right?'"

Nick cracked up at the *Sweet Home Alabama* line. It always came back to *Sweet Home Alabama* for us. "'No,'" he quoted back. "'I'm not *shitting* you.'" He grinned, dimple and all. "Well, a little. It's not CGI, but production did build it for the movie. All the interior shots were filmed on a soundstage in Culver City."

"Way to ruin the fantasy," I joked, but my voice came out breathy—my heart suddenly beating so fast.

Nick noticed, breaking our eye contact to glance down at the already half-eaten brownies. "We should make another batch tomorrow," he said, pointing at the pan. "But take them out early, so they're gooey in the middle."

"Okay, yeah." I nodded quickly. "Good idea."

And then I smiled.

He was coming over again.

◇◇◇◇◇◇◇◇◇◇◇◇◇◇◇◇◇◇◇

By the time the TV show ended, it was dark outside and Luke had fallen asleep with his head against Charlie's shoulder. "Look at him," Charlie said softly, so softly that I wasn't sure if he was talking to me or himself. "He's so cute."

"Yes," I agreed, and snapped a photo. "Absolutely adorable."

"I just had no idea," he continued in a near-whisper, like he hadn't heard me. "I had no idea it was even possible to *feel* this way about a person..."

His words almost knocked the wind out of me. *Who are you?* I almost asked, looking at him. I'd never heard Charlie sound this romantic—this *invested*. My heart twisted, thinking of Nick again. I admired my projector and white sheet, framed with twinkly lights. He'd built me a *movie theater*, in my *dorm* room. Had I even said thank you? "This is so great!" I remembered gushing, but an actual thank you?

Emma would've said thank you.

She deserves him, I thought sadly. *I don't, and might not even someday.*

"Hey, Sage," Charlie said before my eyes could completely well up. His voice was still quiet. "Will you send me that picture?"

◇◇◇◇◇◇◇◇◇◇◇◇◇◇◇◇

Luke left first, moaning and groaning about yet another group project. "It just won't get done," he said as Charlie buttoned up his peacoat for him, then affectionately smoothed its sleeves. "I gave everyone a task, but if I don't go over the Google Doc tonight, who knows what we'll have to turn in tomorrow..."

I laughed. "You're a mad dictator."

"No." He shook his head. "I delegate."

Charlie fake-coughed. "Mad dictator."

Luke gave us the finger on the way out.

"Sneak me downstairs?" Charlie asked a while later, and once safely outside, we joked about Luke probably hunched over his MacBook and grumbling.

"No, I've seen him in action," Charlie said. "If he doesn't like what someone's done, he changes it. He explains why, but he still changes it. Total power move. And by the end of the explanation, they apologize to *him*." We walked across the yard, toward Belmont Way. "It's really impressive."

"Didn't you guys once do an assignment together?" I said, looping my arm through his. It was freezing tonight. "In the fall?"

"Uh-huh." Charlie nodded. "But there was none of that. We literally wrote it together."

"Well, that's because you're top of the class." I zapped his side. "And *possibly* because he was already hypnotized by you."

"No, he wasn't," Charlie said. "And that's the best part." He sighed. "Luke loves me, but he's not hypnotized by me." His eyes were crinkling in the streetlight's glow. "You know what I mean?"

I smiled and squeezed his arm. "Yeah, I get you..." I said at the same time I heard footsteps and a familiar voice calling out: "Are you guys gonna put an announcement in *The Bexleyan*?"

A beat later, Nick became visible in the lamplight. I had no idea where he was coming from or where he was going, but I knew what he *thought*. Charlie and me walking alone, my arm crooked through his, smiling at each other...

"The newspaper?" Charlie asked. "What are you talking about?"

His twin gestured at us, and I quickly unlocked our arms. "You and Sage," he said. "It's happened. Finally. The wait is over. You guys are..." He hesitated. "*Together.*"

"No, we're not," I said the second I felt Charlie stiffen. "We're *friends*, Nick. That's it."

Nick released a frustrated sigh, a sigh that sounded like he'd been suppressing it for ages. "You're unbelievable. Both of you."

My brows knitted together. Where was this coming from? *What about winter break?* I wondered. *What about* The Holiday, *and the barely baked brownies? Things were good, weren't they?*

And he had Emma. Nice, perfect Emma.

"Because this is ridiculous," he continued. "You both aren't with anybody, and it's obvious you're totally head over heels for each other." He took a deep breath. "Just *be* together already. I'm sick of this bullshit, and so is everyone else."

We all stood there in shocked silence. "Nick..." I breathed, mind racing for something to say. But before any brainstorms struck, Charlie stepped in.

"Let's go for a walk, Nick."

"What?"

"A walk," Charlie repeated. "You and me." He took my hand, and I realized what was happening when he squeezed it. I squeezed back as hard as I could.

"I have homework, Charlie," Nick replied. "I'm going back to Mort."

"Then I'll walk you back, but...um, we need to talk."

Nick's brows furrowed, but he nodded his head toward their route home.

Charlie took another deep breath, and when he tried to disentangle his hand from mine, I held on tight. "You're perfect, Charlie," I whispered, feeling him quake with nerves. "Absolutely perfect, and I love you. Always."

CHAPTER 26
CHARLIE

IT TOOK A LOT NOT TO RUN BACK TO SAGE AND ask her to come with us. Nick and I were walking down Belmont Way, but I didn't really know how to start—afraid that if I opened my mouth, my insides would find their way out. So it was my brother who spoke first. "You wanted to talk."

I nodded.

"So talk."

"Okay." I glanced around to make sure no one was within earshot. It was pretty cold out, so most people were probably indoors, but you never knew. I took a long breath. "Nick, there's nothing going on between me and Sage."

"Yeah," he muttered. "If only that were true."

"And there never will be," I added. "Trust me."

Nick picked up his pace, speeding past the chapel. "Why the hell should I? She told me the same thing, but here you guys are, for *four* years now, making it clear to everyone that the only reason you were put on the earth is to be with each other."

Shit, I thought. Suddenly I hated myself, realizing Nick

believed what the rest of Bexley believed about me and Sage. I'd always thought he was immune. Why? Because he was my brother?

God, that made it worse.

I shook my head. "It's not like that. She doesn't love me that way." I felt the back of my neck heat up, but I forced myself to say it: "And I *can't* love her that way. It is *impossible* for me to think of her like that."

"Then you're messed up, Charlie." He gave me a look. His eyes were hard, not like Nick at all. "Because she's the best girl there is."

I stopped walking—heart clenching, and everything else going numb. *Messed up*, I heard again. *You're messed up, Charlie.*

"Are you coming?" he called out, now a few yards ahead of me.

I didn't move. "Do you remember our last soccer game?"

Nick shoved his hands in his pockets and backtracked. "What? Like in eighth grade?"

"Yes."

"I guess." He came to a stop next to me. "The one where you got your yellow card?"

"Yes."

"It should've been a red one. You kicked that kid's ass."

"I know."

"So what about it?"

My throat felt like it was about to close up. "Do you remember *why* I shoved him?"

"Yeah, because he was saying something about you wanting to..." Nick trailed off, working the rest out in his head.

During that game, I'd been told to tail the other team's best player, and unsurprisingly the kid wasn't too thrilled about it.

"Why're you so *obsessed* with me?" he asked all throughout the first half, and I ignored him. But things escalated in the second; he was frustrated because I kept intercepting the passes meant for him. Then I accidentally pushed him, and he grabbed my hand and yelled, "If you want to hold my hand, all you have to do is ask!"

And that's when I *really* pushed him. I remembered Dad asking about it after the game, but I couldn't bring myself to tell him. So it was Nick who answered, saying, "It was stupid, Dad. The kid was making it seem like Charlie wanted to hold hands with him, like Charlie's gay or something."

Our father had had quite the laugh at that one.

Sometimes I could still sort of hear it.

After a minute, I heard Nick whisper, "But you can't be..."

I stared down at the cobblestones. "I am."

Nick was quiet.

I was quiet.

And the whole thing only became unquiet when Paddy and Cody arrived on the scene minutes later. "Carmichaels!" Paddy clapped each of us on the back. "What's the latest?"

I found my voice first. "Just going over our plan of attack." I nodded at Brooks. "Word is there's a pretty impressive sheet cake in your fridge." Yesterday, Jack had made sure everyone and their mother knew it was his birthday.

"Oh, is there?" Paddy asked, at the same time Cody went: "I'll never tell."

They shoved off soon after that, recognizing they'd walked into something. But Nick and I just stood there. It started snowing. The type of snow that Luke loved: feathery flakes. We were lying on the

MAC's roof back in December, letting a layer cover us. "This is my favorite," he'd whispered. "The gods are having a pillow fight."

A car's headlights brought me back to reality, to this silent standoff with Nick. We moved off to the side of the road to let it pass, and all the warmth I felt thinking about Luke cooled until it matched the current temperature outside. After the car was gone, my twin and I looked at each other. *Please say something*, I tried to tell him.

And the message went through, because Nick shifted from one foot to the other, and cleared his throat, getting ready to speak. But then his gaze went to the ground...and it felt like getting kicked in the gut when he murmured, "I don't know what to say."

"Fine." I looked away even though he wasn't looking at me. I fought against the oncoming waterworks, and maybe even shrugged. "I get it."

He sucked in a breath. "Charlie..."

I started walking away. "Sleep tight, Nick."

CHAPTER 27
SAGE

LATER THAT NIGHT, WHEN I WAS TAKING HALF-hearted notes on my Buddhism class reading, my phone began to buzz. *Charlie*, I immediately thought, reaching to grab it from its charger.

But it wasn't him. "Hey." I picked up.

"Hey," Nick said softly, and then nothing else. It was silent for several heartbeats before he spoke again. "You knew, didn't you?"

My eyes were suddenly full of tears. His voice...it was neutral... his tone didn't give me any clues as to how he felt about everything. I was flying blind for now. "Yeah," I admitted, starting to pick at some initials carved in my desk. "I knew...I've known."

He was quiet again. "For how long?"

"Thanksgiving," I told him. "But I've suspected for years."

"Oh."

"You're not mad at me, are you?"

"No," Nick said after another pause. "But I wish you'd told me."

I tilted my head back to stare up at my blank ceiling. "I wanted to...and I was so close a couple of times." I remembered our fall nights together. "But it was Charlie's truth to tell, not mine."

"I know," he agreed, releasing a sigh. "I only wish I'd *known*..."

I shifted in my chair, wondering what he was thinking about. *Charlie? Or maybe us? Would we still be together if he'd known?* I had no idea.

Nick cleared his throat. "I love him just the same," he said. "In case that wasn't clear. He's my brother...my best friend...and I want him to be happy."

I smiled, even though he couldn't see me. Lately I'd been telling Charlie his family would understand, and now here Nick was, doing exactly that. Maybe telling their parents and everyone else would soon follow.

"That's really good to hear, Nick," I said. "He's been wrestling with this for a long time, so I'm glad, you know..." I trailed off, not really knowing what I was trying to say, but hoping he would get it.

He did. "I feel like such a jerk," he said. "You were right. He *was* acting weird in the fall. I saw it, but didn't really think about it because I was so jealous..."

"Hey, it's okay," I assured him. "He's come so far since then." I paused for a beat, hoping I wasn't about to overstate things. "I honestly think these last couple of months have been the happiest of his life."

Silence, and then, "Is he, uh, with someone?"

My eyebrows knitted together. "He didn't tell you?"

Nick sighed. "Well, no. I was so shocked, and we got interrupted by some people..."

I leaned forward and began to pick at the initials again, debating whether or not to tell him. "Um, yeah," I answered, deciding that yes, he deserved to know. "He's with someone. Since Thanksgiving."

Nick was quiet, processing. "It's Morrissey, isn't it? Luke?"

"Yeah," I confirmed, feeling somewhat taken aback. I wasn't certain, but I thought this was the first time I'd ever heard Nick say Luke's name. Even though it was no secret he was one of my best friends, I didn't know why. "How'd you know?"

"I didn't," he replied. "Until just now. I didn't even know he was actually gay...I thought that was only a rumor...and I used to think you guys sort of liked each other..."

And that's why Luke has never come up, I realized, wanting to groan.

"But it makes sense," he added, "because they're together all the time, and Charlie acts different around him...protective."

"Yes," I agreed. "Very inseparable, and very protective." I thought of the quiet, but firm way Charlie stood next to Luke in the out-of-control line at the Tuck Shop, ready to shield him from any accidental jostling, and the way he was quick to back up Luke during any dinner debate. "Yes, if it ever comes to a duel," Luke once said, rolling his eyes, "Charlie's my second."

Again, Nick didn't respond at first. "I think I should go," he said eventually. "I should call him. He took off after we ran into Smith and Clarke, and I want to talk more. Make sure he knows things are good."

I nodded. "Sounds great."

"Thanks." He coughed. "I'm glad we talked."

"Me too," I said, heart speeding up. "Really, really glad."

Nick laughed. "Okay, I'll see you, then."

"Yes." I smiled. "I'll see you."

CHAPTER 28
CHARLIE

NICK TEXTED ME AT 9:00 P.M. ASKING IF I WANTED to crash with him in Mortimer. Coach Meyer said it's cool, he wrote, but I waited a good five minutes before checking with Mr. Fowler and grabbing my sleeping bag. My brother was waiting for me on the front porch, now wearing sweatpants and his god-awful Patagonia, with his big Hudson's Bay blanket draped around his shoulders like a cape. We looked at each other for a few seconds, and then he gestured for us to go inside.

"I'm sorry for earlier," Nick said once we were in his room. I saw that one of his pillows was already on his chesterfield, all ready for me. A box of Murdick's Fudge sat on his desk, along with a bag of Doritos and two sweating ginger beers. My brother was the only person I knew who drank straight ginger beer.

"It's okay," I told him, and dumped my stuff on the couch. I suspected he'd already blown through most of the fudge.

"No, it's not." He took a pull from his bottle. "I was a jerk, and that wasn't cool. I was just...surprised."

I nodded. "I know."

We didn't speak for a minute. "How long have you known?" he asked, and I hesitated—not sure if I wanted to tell him. Part of me wished he could just *know*, and then we could go from there. But when Nick nudged my knee with his, I knew that wasn't happening.

I took a deep breath. "A while," I admitted. "Years." I fiddled with the old rope bracelet on my wrist, remembering when I was twelve: first feeling a flame of something after Cal laughed at one of my jokes. The way my heart had gone in and out. *Charlie, Charlie*, he'd said. *You kill me.*

It wasn't until later that I untangled the truth. The yearning for his approval, the obsessive staring as he and my sister held hands, and the curve of his jawline—so strong and confident. Not to mention the massive meltdown I had when they'd broken up. While Kitsey drowned her sorrows in chocolate, my fourteen-year-old self had full-on sobbed. "Well, Charlie's also taking it pretty hard," I'd overheard Dad on the phone with Uncle Theo, chuckling. "You'd think it was him who's had his heart broken!"

I'd known then, everything in me shuddering. But in bed that night, I stilled the shudder to a clench. *Ignore this*, I told myself. *Forget him and ignore this.*

But I never quite could. That clench became a constant, impossible to ignore.

"Oh, wow," Nick said now. "Years?"

"Yeah." I rubbed my forehead.

"So you were faking with all those girls?"

I sighed. "Pretty much."

"That must've been"—he ran a hand through his hair—"really hard."

I shrugged and sort of smiled. "Just a little."

"But now you have Luke."

"Right..." I raised an eyebrow. "Now I have Luke."

Nick started picking at his bottle's label. "I talked with Sage earlier."

"Ah," I said, feeling a rush of relief. They'd talked, they were talking. Hopefully that meant I hadn't royally screwed things up between them, that they could work their way back to each other. Maybe this was the first step. "You know she's always known too," I added. "Way before I ever told her."

He nodded. "She said that."

"Okay, good."

"Are you going to tell Mom and Dad?" Nick asked.

I sighed. "That's complicated. I sort of wanted to tell them at Christmas, but then..." I trailed off, not knowing what to say.

Nick took another sip of ginger beer. "When do you think it'll become uncomplicated?"

"I'm not sure." I suddenly felt really tired. "I'll figure it out."

My brother nodded. "Now tell me about Luke."

I blinked. "What?"

"Tell me about Luke."

"Uh..." I started, again not sure what he expected me to say. "He's cool...and nice...I really like him..." An understatement, but I didn't want things to get uncomfortable.

"Oh, come on," Nick said. "You've had to listen to us talk about girls for forever, and that must suck. So I'm all ears. What's he *actually* like?"

My heart flickered. "Seriously?"

"Yes, take it away."

"Okay, well, he's pretty epic," I prefaced, and then started telling him random stuff. I told him that Luke drank a minimum of three cups of coffee in the morning, taking it pitch-black. I told him that Clue was Luke's favorite board game, and that he took legit notes whenever he played. I told him that Luke drove his dad's sweet Land Rover Defender back home, and dipped his fries in vinegar. That he was a terrible singer, but could play piano without missing a note. About how he wanted to be in the FBI someday. "And you should see him when he sleeps," I found myself saying. "I can always tell when he's dreaming, because his mouth quirks up in this little smile, and his breathing hitches, and then his eyelids flutter without actually opening—"

Nick coughed. *TMI.*

"He's a really great cook," I said, swinging back around. "You need to try his pancakes; he makes them from scratch and adds cinnamon. His family has two cats, and his Spotify playlist is also totally on point, but One Direction is his guilty pleasure..."

I went on like that for a long time, but Nick didn't cut me off. It was only when I yawned that things wound down. Nick switched off the lights and climbed into bed as I zipped myself into my sleeping bag. "Thank you for telling me," he whispered after we said good night.

"You're welcome," I whispered back.

"I'm happy for you," he added. "You know, happy about you and him."

I smiled to myself. "Thanks."

"You're welcome."

"Good night, Nick."

Nick was quiet, and then, "I love you, Charlie."

"I love you too," I said.

And then we went to sleep.

CHAPTER 29
SAGE

"I THINK LUKE HAS A BOYFRIEND," REESE DECLARED one night, beaming confidence. The four of us were in her room getting ready for Brooks' seniors-only "Wild West" mixer. I stopped braiding Jennie's hair, hoping I'd heard her wrong, because if not...

"Wait, what?" I said.

"I think LM has found himself a boyfriend," she repeated. "Kinda obvious, isn't it?"

"What's obvious?" Nina asked, walking into the room with her phone charger. She hopped up onto Reese's bed and plugged it into the nearby outlet, looking perfect in her orange flannel and brown fringy skirt.

"Luke has a boyfriend," Reese said for the third time.

"Oh my god." Nina nodded quickly. "He totally does! All the texting!"

"And he cuts out early," Jennie chimed in. "He hasn't watched a movie with us in forever."

I wanted to groan. "I'll see you guys tomorrow," was Luke's signature exit line. "My bed won't stop calling me." And then he'd try *not hard enough* to hide his smile as he left to go meet up with Charlie.

"Exactly," Reese agreed. "Don't you think, Sage?"

You have to weigh in, I told myself. *If you don't, they'll think you know something.*

"Sage?"

"I guess it's possible," I finally said, starting over on one of Jennie's braids.

"Okay great." Reese clapped her hands together, and then with a twisted smile, said, "Now *who* do we think it is?"

◇◇◇◇◇◇◇◇◇◇◇◇◇◇◇

"I have to tell you something," I said when Charlie and I reemerged from tonight's "saloon." The kitchen island had been transformed into a bar, with a card game going on at the table and people mingling all around. We'd gone in for a couple of root beers, and now we retreated to a quiet-ish corner of the common room. The girls and Luke were on the far side, caught up in the madness of the mechanical bull. So far Nick had the record for longest ride, but Charlie had made a PSA that he planned on topping it later. ("I thought you were working on his ego," I'd whispered to Luke, who'd sighed and whispered back, "It's been a process.")

Charlie twisted off his bottle cap and took a slug of his soda. I reached up and adjusted his cowboy hat. Tonight he belonged in a John Wayne movie. "What is it?" he asked.

"Okay, so..." I took a deep breath. "The girls are pretty sure that Luke has a boyfriend...and are, um, trying to figure out who it is." And they'd been warmer rather than colder, suspecting it was someone in the closet since Luke told us last month that Tristan Andrews wasn't his type.

I wasn't sure how I expected Charlie to react, but he rolled his eyes à la his better half. "Of course they are," he said. "Can't anyone mind their own freaking business at this school?"

I didn't answer, thinking, *Why can't you tell them? They're your friends.*

"I can't wait for this weekend," he added under his breath. "To just get out of here."

My ears pricked up at that. "Where're you going?" Bexley was giving us a long weekend in honor of MLK Day. My mom was picking me up tomorrow so we could go skiing in the Pocono Mountains. Mr. and Mrs. Carmichael were away right now, so the twins were staying on campus.

Charlie glanced around to make sure no one was eavesdropping. "Charlottesville, Virginia."

"Charlottesville?" I asked. "What's in Charlottesville?"

"UVA."

I raised an eyebrow. "UVA?"

Charlie shrugged. "Luke wants to visit."

I smiled, and launched into my version of the *Gilmore Girls* theme song: "And where Luke leads, you will follow..."

"Dear god, Sage..."

"...anywhere..."

Charlie groaned and pulled down the brim of his cowboy hat. I resisted the urge to ask him about college, assuming he was still choosing a school. He'd mentioned nothing about his ED choice, so something told me it hadn't worked out. I didn't want to rub salt in the wound.

"How do you plan on pulling this off?" I asked, since leaving campus was far from a piece of cake. If we weren't just going into town, Bexley housemasters required permission from parents before allowing us to go anywhere.

"Simple," Charlie replied. "JCarmichael@gmail.com."

"But of course!" I exclaimed. JCarmichael@gmail.com was Mr. Carmichael's secondary email account. Apparently, he'd created it a few years ago, saying that he wanted to "separate" work stuff from home stuff, but ended up neglecting it completely. However, it took less than three seconds for Charlie to hack into the account—Mr. Carmichael was notorious for using the same password for *everything*—and he proceeded to take full advantage of it whenever a situation arose. He'd given himself countless permissions.

"So basically, the school thinks I'm going home for the weekend, and that..." He trailed off, plastering on a smile. "Oh hey, you two."

I turned to see Nick and Emma—in their own flannels and cowboy hats, with Nick also wearing a gold sheriff's badge—approaching us. Emma was smiling brightly, but Nick looked stressed, rubbing his forehead.

"Do you want to get a drink, Emma?" Charlie asked after a few minutes of mechanical bull chitchat. He gestured his empty root beer toward the saloon. Once they were gone, Nick's tense shoulders unwound.

"So..." he said. "Skiing this weekend, right?"

"Yup." I nodded. "Cross your fingers it doesn't rain."

Nick chuckled and held up a finger-crossed hand.

"What are you doing this weekend?" I asked, even though I already knew. Staying here.

"Oh." He rolled his eyes, but I detected a slight smile. "Charlie's put me on dispatch. I'm fielding any parental calls while he and Morrissey go off the grid."

I laughed. "You're a wonderful brother."

Nick reached up and ran his fingers through his hair. "I almost wish I could go with them, though." He coughed. "I mean, not really. Because obviously they'll be...uh..."

"You'd be third-wheeling so hard." I smiled.

"Yeah," he sighed. "I just don't want to be here."

"So come skiing," I blurted, heart suddenly fluttering. "Come to the Poconos. My mom won't mind. She has your garage code, to get your stuff..."

Nick shook his head. "Sage, I can't," he whispered, stepping closer. "I have to stay here." He nodded at Charlie and Emma, returning with sodas. "I need to do something here." He glanced at the floor, then looked back up so we made eye contact. His were so very blue.

Hope sparked. He was going to do it; he was going to break up with Emma. I reached for his hand. Not to hold, but to squeeze in support. My feelings aside, I would always support Nick.

"Okay, guys," Emma said as I snatched my hand away from her boyfriend. "Charlie has *officially* challenged the bull. He's up in a couple of rounds."

"She speaks the truth," Charlie confirmed. He began rolling up his sleeves. "Wish me luck."

"I hope you get knocked all the way into next week," Nick said blankly.

I nodded, a swirling in my stomach. "Or the week after."

"Oh, come on." Charlie flashed us a smile. "That's poor sportsmanship."

We both gave him middle fingers.

He rolled his eyes.

Emma laughed.

CHAPTER 30
CHARLIE

THE TRAIN LUKE AND I CAUGHT WASN'T AS EARLY as I would've liked, but we found an empty section and stuffed our duffels in the overhead compartment before flopping down into our seats. The plan was to do homework on the ride, so I was surprised when Luke unzipped his backpack and pulled out his Ray-Bans. He silently offered them to me.

"What're those for?" I asked.

"To complete the disguise," he replied drily, gesturing to my outfit: my wool coat overtop his Adidas sweatshirt. Its hood was pulled up over a black hat Mrs. Morgan had knitted me.

"Oh," I said, biting the inside of my cheek. Our train had a changeover in DC, and a bunch of Bexley kids lived there. We hadn't been the only ones waiting on the station platform. "Sorry."

Luke gave me a long look. "Is it going to be like this the whole weekend?"

"No." I shook my head. "No, I promise."

Then I tugged down the hood.

⋄⋄⋄⋄⋄⋄⋄⋄⋄⋄⋄⋄⋄⋄⋄⋄⋄⋄

We got to Charlottesville after dark, and took an Uber to our Airbnb. It was an apartment just a few streets over from UVA's campus, courtesy of Luke's Keiko Morrissey–tracked American Express card. Unlike me, Luke had real parental permission to leave school. "Does she know I'm with you?" I asked, to which he responded, "You mean with me *here*? Or *with me*, with me?"

Both, I guessed. She knew both.

That rattled me a little. What if she told my aunt and uncle?

The apartment was a studio, with hardwood floors and each corner serving as a different room. The kitchenette was against the far brick wall, complete with a tiny Ikea table and two aluminum chairs. Taller than the fridge, Luke opened it to find only a bottle of ketchup.

A small sectional couch sat atop a cool ropey rug and faced a flat-screen, and I checked out the bathroom only to almost walk into the sink. Very compact.

"Should we flip a coin?" Luke joked as we eyed the bed. "To see who has to rough it?"

"No way," I said, falling back against the mattress. After a long day on the train, it was the most comfortable thing ever—a queen with a soft striped bedspread and simple white pillows. "I will happily rough it here," I told him. "You can have the couch."

Luke laughed, and then he was on top of me and kissing me. "Such a gentleman," he whispered. "Thank you for coming."

"Why wouldn't I?" I asked, a hand now in his hair. "I mean, I'm also—"

Luke's stomach rumbled.

I tipped my head back and laughed. "Should we go find dinner?"

"Eh, not yet," Luke said. "Maybe later. Right now I just want to..."

I didn't let him finish the sentence.

◇◇◇◇◇◇◇◇◇◇◇◇◇◇◇

Both our stomachs were grumbling by morning, since *maybe later* never came to fruition. So we walked over to The Corner, one of UVA's main social hubs, a street lined with everything from Starbucks to a student center and plenty of stores and restaurants. Pretty much postcard-worthy. There were also a handful of side streets that I knew Luke and I would explore at some point. But first was a trip to Bodo's Bagels before a campus tour. "I did some research," Luke admitted as we pushed through the doors. "And this is *the* place to come for breakfast."

"Sounds about right." I nodded. "If this..." I gestured to the winding line of students, most of them looking pretty hungover from a wild Friday night. "Is any indication."

Luke smirked and pressed closer to me, and two cups of coffee and sausage-egg-and-cheeses later, we crossed the street to the school. I'd downloaded a map, but Luke already seemed to know his way around. "My dad took me to one of his reunions," I remembered him once saying, but it was still hard to believe. He'd been so young then.

We started with The Lawn. "Good, similar jargon," I joked, but unlike Bexley's circular Meadow, UVA's lawn was rectangular and rambling, a historical court outlined with neoclassical brick pavilions and rows of individual rooms. "Our founder Thomas Jefferson called this the 'Academical Village,'" I overheard a nearby tour guide saying, a group of parents and prospective students trailing behind him. "It's the symbolic center of campus, and for their final year, forty-seven students are selected to live in its dorm rooms—a true honor."

"Follow me," my own personal tour guide then said, leading me off the grass and onto the stone walkway. Luke stopped in front of a black door whose gold placard read: SYDNEY BLAIR. Outside sat a rocking chair, along with a small trough full of wood. I too had done some research, learning that each lawn room had a fireplace. "This is it," Luke said. "This was my dad's room." His throat bobbed. "He was a Jefferson Scholar."

GRAHAM MORRISSEY, I imagined embossed on the nameplate, and four years from now: LUKE MORRISSEY. It seemed inevitable.

We stood there in silence for a minute. "How do you remember this?" I asked eventually. "Weren't you only ten the last time you were here?"

One side of Luke's mouth quirked up. "Charlie, I remember everything," he said, knocking his hip against mine. "*Everything.*"

I waited a second, but then leaned over to quickly kiss his cheek, not bothering to check if people were watching. *You can do it,* I'd realized earlier, at breakfast surrounded by strangers. *You can be anyone here, nobody knows you here. You can be* you *here. This is what college is for, and you can start right now.*

I *wanted* to start right now.

So I took Luke's hand and threaded our fingers together.

Luke grinned. "Let's go," he said, tugging me. "Plenty to see."

And he was right—there *was* plenty to see, and we somehow

saw it all. We roamed through the various buildings, ran whooping through the outdoor amphitheater (the students passing by looked at us like we were nuts), found the football stadium, and spiraled down the library steps to see the school's Hogwarts-esque reading room. Lights dimmed, it looked exactly like the Gryffindor common room, with its warm oriental rugs and furniture, old-fashioned lamps and bookcases everywhere. Some students were studying, some stretched out and sleeping.

"You go ahead," Luke whispered, the two of us standing in the doorway. "I don't think I should." He shrugged. "Being a Ravenclaw and all."

"Well then, Nick's the only one allowed in," I whispered back. "Because Sage is a Hufflepuff, and I'm pretty sure I'm a Slytherin."

"What?" Luke shook his head. "C, no." He reached to ruffle my hair. "*Both* Weasley twins are Gryffindors, remember?"

I rolled my eyes, and he cracked up. A few people looked up from their laptops to shoot us glares. Which only made Luke laugh harder, so I crooked my arm around his neck to hide his face in my shoulder. "Stay cool, Ravenclaw," I whispered. "Or else we can't trespass..."

Our final campus destination was the famous rotunda, The Lawn's beacon of light. It was modeled after Rome's Pantheon, standing strong with its brick exterior, white Corinthian columns, and domed roof. "Will you take a picture of me?" Luke asked. "I promised my mom."

He handed over his phone, but after snapping the shot, I pulled mine from my back pocket and took another one. Here we are, UVA, I captioned the photo and Snapchatted it to Sage...and, after some hesitation, also Nick.

He was the first to respond, Sage probably still on the slopes. There was no picture, only a message: Shouldn't you be in that picture too?

◇◇◇◇◇◇◇◇◇◇◇◇◇◇◇◇

Dinner was downtown, at an upscale steakhouse in the open-air mall. "We should go on a date," I hadn't forgotten Luke saying that night on FaceTime, right before Paddy and Nick had barged into the business center. "A *real* date."

But instead of it being funded by his poker winnings, this dinner was all me. He had the Airbnb, I had the food. "Carmichael," I told the hostess. "It's under 'Carmichael,' for two."

This is better than Bistro, I knew as soon as we were seated. *And the Bluebird, no question. So much better.*

Luke looked so handsome in dark jeans and a forest-green sweater, with the collar of his white T-shirt peeking out, and his hair perfectly imperfect. "What?" he said when he noticed me staring, glancing up from his menu. "You good?"

"Yeah, yeah." I nodded, feeling my face warm. I took a sip from my water glass. "It's just not fair how handsome you are."

"Thanks," Luke said, and tilted his head with a half-smile. "You're not so bad yourself." He laughed. "Even if I've seen a version of this look *hyaku* times already."

I sighed. I didn't know Japanese, but my guess was *hyaku* translated to something like a hundred. Since I was wearing my usual: blue blazer and striped tie. "Well, sorry," I said. "Not my fault that I was raised in America's preppiest state."

Luke smirked and stretched out his hand, palm faceup.

I met him halfway, putting mine on top of his for a second before shifting so that our fingers could lock together.

"I like this," he whispered.

"Me too," I whispered back.

We didn't let go until our food came.

⟨⟨◇◇◇◇◇◇◇◇◇◇◇◇◇◇◇◇◇⟩⟩

"Okay, okay," Luke said into the darkness. We were back in the apartment, under the covers in bed. "First crush, go."

"First crush?" I asked, sort of smiling. We did this most nights—told each other things or stories about ourselves, sometimes from when we were kids, and sometimes from only a few years ago. "Really?"

"Mm-hmm," he said. "I wanna know."

"Well, you," I told him. "You, of course."

Luke snorted. "Liar."

"What?" I said, and stopped tracing figure eights on his shoulder blades.

"I know it was your sister's boyfriend," he said. "Cal, right? The guy in that photo on your wall?"

I was quiet for a second. The picture of Cal and me, licking ice cream cones together on the Vineyard. "Yeah," I murmured. "It was him. He was pretty cool."

"Good-looking too," Luke added. "Very good-looking."

I shrugged. "I guess."

"You guess?" Luke nestled in closer, tangled our legs together. I felt him kiss my neck. Everything went hazy.

"Your turn," I said when I could speak again. "Who was your first crush?"

He didn't hesitate. "You."

This time it was me who snorted. "Very funny."

"I was ten," Luke went on as I resumed the figure eights. "It was at this neighborhood party, during a game of hide-and-seek. We hid together, then hung out the rest of the time. He had these great blue eyes, and my face got really hot when he laughed..."

"How do you remember stuff from when you were ten?"

Luke laugh-yawned. "I told you, C. I remember everything."

We fell asleep not long after that. He drifted off first, then me. And the last thing I remembered was making a mental note to ask him what he'd been dreaming about, because just as my eyes shut for good, I heard him mumble, "You were wearing alligator pants."

◇◇◇◇◇◇◇◇◇◇◇◇◇◇◇◇◇◇

Our train back to Bexley was at 10:00 a.m. on Monday, but I asked our Uber driver to make a detour on the way to the station. "What are we doing here?" Luke asked as I popped open the car door, UVA's rotunda shining in the sun. "We already..."

I ignored him, instead asking some early-bird tourists to take our picture. Luke straightened his new *VIRGINIA* hat before I draped my arm around his neck, and he reached up to twine our fingers together. Our photographers looked a little taken aback, but then the woman told us to smile.

I already was.

CHAPTER 31
SAGE

I KNEW SOMETHING WAS UP WHEN I NOTICED Luke eating Cheerios for breakfast on Tuesday. I'd gotten back to school just before curfew last night, so this was my first time seeing everyone since before the weekend. Charlie sprung up from the table to give me a hug, but Luke didn't.

"What's this?" I asked as I sat down with my buttered bagel and gestured to his breakfast. "No omelet or pancakes? I thought cereal was beneath you."

We made eye contact, and I wasn't going to lie...he looked sort of sad. "Chef's block," he replied, and gave me a smile. But it wasn't genuine. Something was definitely wrong. I debated shooting him a quick text, but a familiar voice interrupted my thoughts.

"Hey, you mind if I join?"

I looked up to see the newly single Nicholas Carmichael standing there, waiting for us to say yes before taking a seat. It was bad, Nina had texted our group chat this weekend. He took her to Captain Smitty's and she started crying. Then Reese had chimed in with: And apparently she'd already bought a dress for Mort's Valentine's thing...

"By all means." I smiled, heart beating faster, and the flock nodded in agreement.

"Thanks," he replied, and sat next to me. Our shoulders brushed before he sliced into his stack of pancakes. "Oh man, you're so right, Luke," he said after swallowing. "These are epic with cinnamon!"

∞∞∞∞∞∞∞∞∞∞∞∞∞∞∞

"So it was good?" I whispered during architecture. "You guys had fun?" Charlie and I were in the middle of sketching out our latest project: a town building that incorporated elements from the Victorian style. It was due at the end of the week.

"I'd say that's an accurate statement," he whispered back, flipping his pencil over to erase a crooked line. "Considering Luke said he never wanted to leave."

I smiled and rolled my eyes. "Well, lucky for him, he's about to spend four years there."

Charlie stayed silent and then admitted that he hadn't wanted to leave either before returning to our blueprint. But I caught a hint of a smile, the curling of his lips—a secretly proud smile that out of nowhere, made me think of Nick.

Who I found myself walking with to Addison for lunch. "How was dispatch this weekend?" I asked after telling him about the Poconos. "Did your parents check in at all?"

"Yeah," he replied, zipping up his hockey jacket. "But it was me who called them. Mom, actually. I wanted to talk to her about..." He trailed off.

Emma, I figured. He wanted to tell his mom about Emma.

Ouch. I started fiddling with my mittens, feeling awkward. Not that their breakup had anything to do with me, but...

Did it?

Maybe?

Just a little?

Nick changed the subject before I could ask any follow-up questions. "Did Charlie send you that other rotunda picture?" he asked. "Of him and Luke together?"

"Yes." I nodded, trying to seem upbeat—even though my initial reaction to Charlie's second Snapchat had been pure jealousy. Seeing him smile so widely and openly with his arms around Luke...well, it made me wish for a picture like that, of me and Nick. *If he came with us*, I'd thought, sitting on my hotel bed. *If he'd come skiing with me...*

He wouldn't have ended things with Emma, I reminded myself, a bounce back in my step. *If I'd convinced him to come, Emma would still be in the picture.*

But she wasn't. Not anymore.

"It's an epic shot," Nick said as I snuck a peek at him, heart twisting at his handsome face. He dug his iPhone out of his pocket and tapped its screen. "Isn't it?"

"Oh my god, Nick!" I gasped at Luke and Charlie's matching grins. "That *cannot* be your wallpaper!"

"Why not?" he asked. "I ship them."

I gave him a look. "You ship them?"

"Of course. Luke's cool and I've never seen Charlie that amped..." He paused to gauge my face. "I mean, don't you?"

"Well, duh!" I glanced around, to see if anyone was

eavesdropping. "They're adorable, but you still have to change it. Charlie would *freak the fuck* out." I imagined Nick getting a text notification and someone catching sight of his wallpaper. One of the things I loved about him was that he wasn't a guy who casually passed his phone around, but you could never be too sure.

We walked wordlessly for the next few yards, past Knowles. "Has he said anything to you?" Nick asked, adjusting his backpack straps. "About telling everyone?"

"No," I said, and sighed. "No, he hasn't."

Nick nodded then swiped into his phone. I stared straight ahead at the dining hall, remembering Luke's slumped shoulders this morning, until I felt Nick elbow me. "This better?" he asked, and showed me his new wallpaper: the two of us at a Vineyard bonfire, years and years before spin the bottle. Sixth grade, maybe—we both had braces. Wearing fluorescent orange necklaces, we were smiling and holding up freshly toasted marshmallows.

A wave of something suddenly rocked me. *I ship them*, I thought. *I ship those two so much.*

"Yes," I told Nick. "Way better."

He smiled, white teeth now perfectly straight.

◇◇◇◇◇◇◇◇◇◇◇◇◇◇◇◇◇◇

The next day, I texted a still-subdued Luke asking if he wanted to get Pandora's after track practice. You read my mind, he replied, and was already in our favorite booth when I arrived at the café later. A few open notebooks and his MacBook were keeping him company.

"Hey." I smiled, taking off my backpack and putting it down on the bench opposite him. "You want anything?"

"Regular coffee, please."

So after getting him his coffee and me my usual latte, I cut right to the chase: "Did you not have a good time this weekend?"

"What?" Luke's eyes went wide. "Why would you think that?"

"Because you've seemed kinda out of it lately."

Luke straightened his glasses. "Yeah, I know," he said. "But it's not because I didn't have a good time. This weekend..." He looked at me and smiled. "It was the *best* weekend of my *life*."

"Then what's wrong?"

He glanced away. "It's just, I wish things could be like that all the time."

"You mean you two being on vacation?"

"No, not that." He shook his head. "I mean, how things *were* between us while we were there."

My stomach sank, suspicions confirmed.

"I'm so mad at myself," he murmured. "I told myself it was fine, that I didn't mind keeping things a secret." He sighed. "But that was before I realized what it would be like if we *weren't* one."

I fumbled for something to say, but he kept going.

"He held my hand, Sage. Everywhere we went, walking through town, walking across campus, he held my hand the entire time—kissed me on the cheek, even." He smiled. "There were people everywhere, and they *knew* we were together, and I *liked* that. I liked walking down the street and knowing that the people we passed knew that we were *us*. I'm trying to be patient...God,

I'm trying *so hard*...but suddenly it's impossible. He means so much to me, and I want people to know that."

I took a breath. There it was: Luke Morrissey was human. He'd been such a saint in only being with Charlie behind closed doors, but now he wanted more. Which made me wonder... Would Charlie give it to him? Or would he run away?

Or would Luke be like Nick and *walk* away?

"So what does this mean?" I asked gently.

Luke reached up to run a hand through his hair, and his sweater sleeve pulled up just enough for me to see Charlie's bracelets on his wrist: one was a black-and-red striped tie bracelet, and the other a faded green-and-white knotted rope one. A lump formed in my throat, since it was another testament of how much he loved Luke. Those bracelets were Charlie's, and Charlie's alone. He never let anyone else wear them.

"I don't know," Luke said, looking more disappointed than I'd seen him in months. "I don't know."

<hr />

The vibe at Pandora's was pretty low-key that night, so we studied without distraction until the door's bell rung, signaling someone's entry. Luke looked up from his laptop and raised an eyebrow. "My, my," he said, and I turned to see Nick at the counter, backpack slung over his shoulder and hair matted from hockey practice. "What a coincidence."

Before I could stop myself, I jumped up and was waving at him.

"Subtle, Sage," Luke whispered. "Real subtle."

"Shut up," I whispered back as Nick jokingly glanced over his shoulder, as if thinking I meant someone else. Then he cocked his head, smirked, pointed to himself, and mouthed:

Who, me?

My heart cartwheeled for the first time in a long time. "He's flirting, right?" I asked Luke, to make sure I wasn't losing it.

"Yeah." Luke nodded. "Not very well, but yeah."

I grinned. Nick had never been the best flirt, but I loved flirting with him. I'd forgotten how fun it was.

He joined us after ordering one of Pandora's bottomless pasta bowls. *Chicken alfredo*, I knew without having to ask. "Addison didn't step up tonight," he explained, sliding into the booth next to me. "Something resembling meatloaf?"

"But do they *ever* step up?" I joked.

"That's why I always do the make-your-own stations," Luke said, then shook his head. "I really don't understand how you guys have survived four years on Bexley food." He gave us a look. "You know our food provider also stocks a bunch of prisons?"

"What?" I exclaimed.

He nodded. "The term *institutional food* doesn't just include schools."

Nick chuckled. "Don't tell my dad that! He and my uncle Theo always talk about how much they miss the food here..." His phone chimed. "Charlie," he announced, skimming the message. "He tweaked his ankle at practice and went to the trainer's for ice, and now wants to know if he should swing by?" He glanced at Luke. "You haven't answered his texts?"

Luke ignored the second question. "No, that's okay," he said.

"Tell him to meet me in my room." He began packing up his stuff, and I caught him roll his eyes. "Provided he can make it upstairs on his ankle."

"They sure don't call it 'deadpan' for nothing," Nick commented once Luke was gone. "His sarcasm is deadly."

"Extremely," I agreed as his pasta was served.

Although soon the bowl was halfway between us. "Can I ask you something?" Nick said as we shared, his fork battling my fork for a juicy chunk of chicken.

"Only if I get this piece," I said.

He conceded.

I smiled and popped it in my mouth. "Go."

But Nick hesitated. "How long do you think she's going to be upset?" he eventually asked, putting down his fork. "I feel really bad..."

I felt something inside me jolt.

"Sage, how long do you think?"

I opened my mouth, although nothing came out. How long did I think it would take Emma Brisbane to get over Nick?

"I don't know." I half-shrugged. "I don't know her that well." I bit my lip, not wanting to think about my own breakup with him. "But she's definitely hurting. She really liked you, Nick."

From the way he winced, it was obvious Emma had *more* than really liked Nick, and told him that. And as much as it killed me, I assumed he'd reciprocated, too nice not to say those words back.

Those words...

Tell him! a voice inside me said. *Tell him you love him!*

But I couldn't. I couldn't, because even though Nick now

knew about Charlie, and had broken up with Emma, there was still that part of me...that part of me that worried...

"I'm sorry," I said instead, to fill the silence. "I'm sorry for everything."

"Thanks," Nick replied, then sighed. "It just blows that this place is so small." He looked out the window, toward campus. "I have stuff to do, but don't want her to have to watch." His voice dropped to a mumble. "I still feel awful that you had to watch..."

A ripple went through me. "Stuff?" I asked. "What stuff?"

"Don't worry about it."

"Nick, seriously."

He laughed. "Yeah, seriously," he said, one side of his mouth curling up in a smile. "Don't worry about it, Morgan."

CHAPTER 32

CHARLIE

THE END OF JANUARY GOT WEIRDLY WARM, SO Sage and I started running again. "I think you may have a problem." She shook her head as Dag's door clicked shut behind me. "You have *zero* chill with college stuff." She smirked. "And it's not even your college."

Not even your college.

"True, it's not," I replied, zipping up the navy-and-orange windbreaker. "Because UVA is technically a *university*." I yawned. "Plus, you're one to talk..."

She grinned and rolled her eyes. Sage was really pumped about being a Middlebury Panther next year. "The mountains!" she kept saying. "Skiing! Biking! Hiking!"

"And school," I'd reminded her. "Don't forget about school..."

That comment had earned me a punch in the arm.

"Okay, look." I gestured to the windbreaker. "I couldn't resist. I'm excited and want to support."

"Right..." Sage said slowly, cocking her head. "You're excited for *Luke* and want to support *Luke*."

A yawn saved me from answering.

"Are you even awake?" she asked.

"Barely." I blinked a couple times. We started jogging around Portnoy Circle, toward Darby Road. "I only got three hours of sleep."

"And why's that?"

I didn't answer right away, not sure I wanted to tell her. But then I swallowed hard and mumbled, "Dove asked me to her date party."

Sage laughed. "Oh my god, why? That's ridiculous! *You* dumped *her*. Not the other way around. No offense, but why would she ever ask you?"

I sighed. "Because remember what I said when I broke up with her? I really like you, but I don't think we should be together..."

"Right now," she finished. The series of Valentine's Day date parties were staggered between now and the actual holiday, and Hardcastle was kicking things off this weekend. Dove had found me after hockey yesterday, carrying a box of macarons from Pandora's, and I hadn't really comprehended what was happening at first. Practice had been seriously grueling, and all I wanted to do was tangle myself with Luke and watch *Survivor*. But the vision vanished when Dove smiled sweetly and held out the macarons. "Will you be my plus one?" she'd asked.

"Exactly," I told Sage.

She sighed. "That was such a stupid idea, Charlie."

"Very half-baked," I agreed.

"Well," Sage said, "that sucks, but at least she got the message when you said no."

My stomach churned as she and I made eye contact.

She shoved me. "Charles Christopher Carmichael, *please* tell me you turned her down. Tell me you didn't say yes."

I was quiet.

Another shove. "What the fuck, Charlie?"

"Hey, I didn't really have a choice." I picked up my pace. Sage did too. "I mean, what was I supposed to do? Nobody says no to these things. You get invited, you *go.*"

"Yeah, but you have a boyfriend." Sage's brows were furrowed. "What happens when she starts flirting?"

"Then it'll be one-sided," I said. "I told her it would just be as friends."

She gave me a look. "You should've asked Luke first."

I stared straight ahead, clenched. "I know."

"Have you told him?"

"Not yet." I shook my head. "Later today."

"Okay, good."

"Yeah, everything will be fine." I nodded, hoping she didn't catch the hitch in my voice. "He'll understand."

Sage bit her lip. "Fingers crossed."

◇◇◇◇◇◇◇◇◇◇◇◇◇◇◇◇

It stayed warm the rest of the week, so everyone started dressing like it was Red Hot American Summer. Reese wasn't impressed as we walked to Friday's school meeting, passing guys in shorts and pastel polos and girls in short dresses and flip-flops. "Just because the temperature goes up," she muttered, "doesn't mean you should dress out of *season.*"

Ten minutes later, I was reviewing my notes for the meeting (as student council's Arts Representative, I had to go over the logistics for Bexley's Winter Dance Expo, its performances next week) when Nick sat down next to me in his PAC seat. "Hey, how's it going?"

"Good," he said. "I visited the mail room."

I put down my notes. "And...?"

"Got the goods."

"The lanterns came?"

"Yup." He grinned. "And the paint *and* the glow sticks."

I laughed. "Right, we can't forget the glow sticks."

Nick elbowed me. "Fuck off. The glow sticks are *key*."

He was right, they were. Sage always brought a mess of green and purple and orange glow sticks with her when she visited the Vineyard. One of the photos on my collage was of her and Nick back in middle school. Both with braces, they were decked out in fluorescent necklaces and bracelets and holding up toasted marshmallows. It was the summer I'd realized Nick had feelings for Sage. She was smiling at the camera, but he was smiling at her.

This summer, I thought. *This summer the glow sticks and bonfires and s'mores will be back and better than ever, and maybe it won't be just the three of us...*

"You've got this," I told him. "It's going to happen."

Nick sighed. "I hope so."

I nudged his knee. "No, you *know* so. She..." I trailed off, not quite sure how to put it. I thought of Sage these past few weeks, the way she acted whenever Nick hung out with us, sat with us at meals. "She glows, Nick," I murmured. "She glows around you."

My brother didn't say anything; he just watched the stage, where Sage sat on the edge with Luke and some other seniors.

"What about you?" he asked eventually, and I saw him nod toward Luke. He didn't need to voice the next part: *Are you going to ask him to yours?*

Yes, I thought as I tried to catch Luke's eye, feeling a twinge when he ignored me—because Luke always knew when I was looking at him. "Stop staring," he would sometimes say as we studied, not even glancing up from his homework. "Your econ notes might get jealous."

"Charlie?" Nick said, but I didn't respond until the lights went down and Jennie assumed her post behind the podium.

"I want to," I told him. "I *really* want to."

∞∞∞∞∞∞∞∞∞∞∞∞∞∞∞

Luke was on the phone when I slipped into his room on Saturday. "Yeah, I'm not really hungry yet," he was saying, "so I'm thinking dinner around seven?"

He was sitting at his command center, studying his laptop screen.

I shut the door and watched as Luke reached up and rubbed his forehead—listening to whatever Sage was saying on the other end—and I sort of smiled when I noticed his Arsenal jersey. He'd been really getting into Premier League soccer lately, now the newest recruit in Nick's fan club. A bunch of guys always crowded into my brother's room so they could watch the Sunday games together.

"Cool, see you then." Luke nodded and looked over at me once he'd hung up.

"Was that Sage?"

"Affirmative," he responded, and then his computer claimed his attention.

I wrapped my arms around him from behind. "Where're you guys doing dinner?"

Luke leaned forward to break away. "Humpty Dumplings."

"Yum."

"Indeed." He cleared his throat, still focused on his screen. "You should probably go."

I ran a hand through his hair. "Nah, there's time."

"It's 5:27."

"Yeah, then I guess I should," I agreed, the party at 6:00. "You want to come? Tie my tie for me?"

"Nope," he said. "I'm good."

"Okay." My stomach suddenly felt off. "I guess I'll see you later, then."

"Tell Puffin I send my best wishes."

I just stood there, not sure what to do—but then I grabbed the back of his swivel chair to spin him around, so we were looking each other. Luke's mouth was in a straight line and his eyes were razor-sharp. "I get it," I whispered, heart going in and out. "You're pissed."

Luke rolled his eyes.

I sighed. "Then why did you say you were fine with it?" Because when I told him right after my run with Sage, I convinced myself he was. He hadn't said anything at first. Instead, he got up and left to take a shower, but when he came back, I asked point-blank if it was okay, and he'd nodded. So I believed him...or rather, my conscious and subconscious decided to blow off all reason and rationale to believe him.

"Because you already fucking told her yes," Luke said now. "It wasn't like you asked how I felt about it." He stood. "You made your decision *before* telling me, so clearly my opinion didn't matter."

"I know." I reached for his hand. "I'm sorry, but she caught me off guard. I didn't know what to do."

Luke's face didn't thaw. "I don't want you to go. I know that's not really fair to say, but I don't want you to go. I don't want my boyfriend going to some romantic Valentine's Day thing with one of his ex-girlfriends."

Neither of us said anything for a couple of seconds. He was eyeing the floor, while I just held his unresponsive hand, but then I squeezed it. "Do you want me to tell her I can't come?"

"It's in less than an hour," he mumbled.

"So?" I shrugged. "If you don't want me to go, I won't."

Luke shook his head. "Charlie, please don't make this my decision. That isn't fair. You should go. She's a good person and shouldn't get hurt. Don't ruin her night." He shook me off and sat back down in his chair, spinning around to face his MacBook again.

I bit the inside of my cheek. "Luke—"

"You should go," he cut me off. "Don't want to be late."

"Okay." I nodded. "I'm sorry I didn't ask you."

He was quiet, but as I turned his doorknob to leave, I caught, "Yeah, I would've liked that."

◇◇◇◇◇◇◇◇◇◇◇◇◇◇◇◇◇

I called home when I was sure Luke was comatose, his body completely relaxed against mine. After two hours of fending off Dove's advances, I'd walked out of Hardcastle to see him waiting at the end of the front walk, looking so slick in his new bomber jacket, hands in his pockets. *That's your guy*, the voice inside me said. *Here to pick you up.*

I moved toward him. "Where's Sage?"

Luke shrugged. "After dinner, she bumped me to hang with Nick. He said something about an air hockey tournament?"

"Sounds about right." The weather had been iffy today—misty rain—so Nick had decided to postpone tonight's original plan until next weekend. "Because the stars are pivotal," he'd said. "It needs to be the *apex* of night skies."

"Can we go?" Luke asked after a few moments of us just standing in Hardcastle's front yard. His voice dropped low. "Because you look really hot." He gestured at me—I'd forgone the coat and tie tonight, instead wearing a casual black blazer over a gray sweater. "Very Euro."

I smiled as we headed away from the girls' houses. "It's all for you."

He glanced at the ground. "I hope so."

"Hey." I touched his arm. "Tell me you're kidding."

But he wasn't, face looking pretty miserable when we made eye contact again. I tried to swallow the lump in my throat. *I'm sorry.*

"Stay in Dag tonight," I murmured, looking around to see if

anyone was nearby. Then I tucked a hand in his jacket pocket. Our fingers found each other. "It's brutal sleeping without you."

Luke sort of laughed. "Why?" he asked. "Do you have nightmares or something?"

"No." I shook my head, chest aching. "Just self-diagnosed separation issues."

"Well, that works out." He smirked, and something in me burst when he winked. "Because so do I."

⬦⬦⬦⬦⬦⬦⬦⬦⬦⬦⬦

It was late, past 2:00 a.m. when I snuck out, and no one was around to see me shut myself in the obsolete hallway phone booth that had been there for countless years. I ignored its phone, using my own. "Hello?" Mom answered, sounding sort of panicked. Clearly I'd woken her up. "Charlie?"

"That's me," I said.

She let out a long breath. "Is everything all right?"

I shut my eyes and leaned back against the wall. "Yeah."

"Can't sleep?"

"Something like that," I whispered, when I should've said, *I need to tell you something.*

But I didn't, so Mom did what she always did when one of us couldn't sleep—she started talking, as if we were at the dinner table. "Nicky mentioned that your Valentine's parties are coming up," she said. "Have you asked anyone yet?"

"No." I stared up at the ceiling. "Not yet."

"Well, why don't you ask Sage?"

Sage—I needed to end this white-wedding vision of us once and for all. "Because I don't think she'd say yes," I mumbled. "My competition's pretty stiff."

Mom caught the hint and laughed, like she'd known all along. "He's our romantic."

"Yeah," I agreed, relieved but then suddenly feeling my insides clench up again. I wondered if she thought of me as one too. Probably not, since I was with girls for five minutes and talked about them even less. The evidence wasn't in my favor.

But there's this person, I shut my eyes. *There's this person I love with everything I've got. And right now he's asleep in my bed, because my voice is the last thing he wants to hear before going to sleep, and my favorite thing on earth is waking up to see him smiling at me.*

We talked for about ten more minutes before the conversation wound down. "I need to tell you something," finally slipped out when I sensed a goodbye coming.

"What is it?" she asked.

I opened my mouth, but said jack shit. I was distracted—someone was twisting a corkscrew into my heart.

"Charlie? Are you still there?"

I forced myself to speak. "Does it matter to you?"

"Does what matter to me?"

I sighed. "Who I take to this thing?"

She laughed. "Oh, Charlie, please don't tell me it's your economics teacher. Yes, she's very pretty, but—"

"Mom," I said. "I'm not kidding."

She stopped laughing. "Relax, honey. No, of course it doesn't matter. Ask whatever girl you want. Your dad and I understand."

No, my eyes burned. *You don't.*

I wished she would just ask, ask instead of me out-and-out telling her. It would be so simple to be questioned and then respond with a yes. But Mom didn't know to do that, since again, the evidence wasn't there. Which made things even worse.

"Charlie, you should get some sleep," I heard her say. "Midterms are coming up. I don't want you getting run-down and sick."

"Yeah," I murmured. "Okay."

"I love you."

"I love you too."

And we hung up after that, but I didn't move.

I just sat there.

CHAPTER 33
SAGE

A WEEK AFTER TAKING THE GOLD IN MORTIMER'S annual air hockey tournament, I reported to detention, because I'd thought it was a good idea to ignore my alarm and sleep through English on Friday. It was always in the CSC's lecture hall from 7:00 to 9:00 p.m., and you were supposed to do your homework, but I couldn't focus. It sucked being stuck in here. I'd still have three hours until curfew once detention ended, but I didn't want to miss out on a Saturday night with my friends. Someday, they were going to be what I remembered most about Bexley.

But of all the nights to be put in a time-out, this was definitely the best one. The girls were at the dance, while Luke and Charlie were hitting the movies and then going on an "expedition" together. Back in December, they'd stolen a campus map from Admissions and had since been drawing big X's over certain places, like the library and college counseling building ("There's this great couch in the lounge," I'd overheard Charlie say before that one). Apparently, they wanted to conquer the ropes course tonight.

I slipped in and out of daydreams for the rest of detention. I was so beyond lost in my head that it felt like someone snapped me out of a trance when Dr. Latham announced we were free to leave, that detention was over. There was a text from Nick waiting for me: Meet me @ boathouse when you're released. Something to show you!

Excited, I biked back to Simmons to ditch my backpack before pedaling like my life depended on it in the direction of Perry Lake. The bright stars sprinkled across the sky seemed to light my way. But as I peeled off Ludlow Lane and onto Lake Road, the weirdness of it all registered. *Why the boathouse?* I wondered. Sure, the weather was still springlike, but it was strange. The boathouse was so out of the way, and there was literally nothing to do. Plus, we weren't technically allowed there at night. I upped my pace.

What's the plan, Nicholas?

<><><><><><><><><><><>

The boathouse was dark when I got there, but I almost wiped out—because the dock was *not*. I quickly jumped off Stinger and hit my kickstand, still unsteady on my feet.

It was glowing. The dock was *glowing*, completely decked out: Coleman lanterns lining the edges and probably *hundreds* of green glow sticks scattered across the walkway. Nick was sitting at the end, wearing a few illuminated necklaces and his beautifully hideous Patagonia.

"Hey!" he called when a creaky board announced my arrival. "Come make a s'more!" He beckoned me over, and that's when I noticed he was attempting to toast a marshmallow over the mini Weber grill he'd gotten for Christmas.

"What is all this?" I asked as I dropped down next to him. He gifted me with my own necklace and a roasting stick. A marshmallow was already impaled on its tip.

"This," he said, "is what Nick Carmichael does when he breaks the rules."

I laughed. "Go big or go home?"

"Exactly," he agreed. "I thought we'd do s'mores first, then go kayaking. It's a great night, right?"

Kayaking. Whenever I visited Martha's Vineyard, Nick and I went night kayaking on the Oyster Pond. It felt like a different world out there: just us and starlight.

"What do you say?" Nick asked.

"But where's the kayak?" I wondered.

"In the water," he said like it was obvious, so I leaned over to see for myself.

My heart stopped, because sure enough, there it was, tied to the dock and bobbing along contently, but that wasn't all. Written on the side in yellow glow-paint was:

MORGAN, VALENTINE'S?

The letters were kind of dripping, and soon my eyes followed suit...because I'd been *hoping*. Secretly, but hoping so much that it lately took me hours to fall asleep at night. More than anything, I wanted to go with Nick to his party but thought there was no chance. While we'd been flirting a little, nothing had truly changed between us since he'd broken up with Emma, and I figured Charlie would ask me to Daggett's soon. They were the same night.

"Sage?" Nick asked quietly. "What do you think?"

"Yes," I said, laughing away my tears as our eyes locked. "Hell, yes!"

Nick's dimple popped before he leaned in to kiss my cheek.

But I made sure our lips met instead. Nick pulled me into his arms, and I hugged him tight. We were both breathing heavily when we broke apart. "Kayaking?" I suggested, and just like that, we were out on the water. I grinned. "Okay, now remind me where Ursa Major is. Because I see the Big Dipper..."

So Nick the Astronomer pointed out the gigantic constellation whose nickname was the "Greater She-Bear" and then I felt a hand on my arm. "Sage..."

I turned back to look at him. "Yeah?"

He sighed. "I don't want it to be just Valentine's Day."

"What?"

"Us," Nick rephrased. "I want us to try again. For real this time." He shifted in his seat, shifting the kayak. "I love you."

His hand was still on my arm, and a garden of goose bumps bloomed underneath it. I grabbed it and tangled our fingers together. "I love you too," I whispered against his knuckles.

"But what are you so afraid of?" he asked when I didn't say more.

"I love you," I said again. "I love you, and I have such a *crush* on you."

He chuckled. "I do too," he replied. "I've always had a crush on you, to be honest. You're my first."

"Right, exactly." I squeezed my eyes shut. "And I don't want anything getting in the way of you being my *last*."

"Hey—" he started, but I kept going, all of it finally spilling out.

"I'm scared that if we do this now, we're going to mess something up. You'll be at Yale, and I'll be at Middlebury, and long-distance almost never works. We're too young and there's too much going on, and I want us to be fanatic hockey parents together someday. I want us to throw our neighborhood's annual Fourth of July cookout someday." I swallowed, having no control over myself. "So I don't think we should chance it. I don't want to end up like my parents. I don't want to ruin us before we've even begun. We should wait, until it's right, until we've experienced life away from each other."

Nick was quiet for a while, but then he resumed paddling, directing us toward the shore. I climbed back up on the dock first, and then helped him drag the kayak out of the water. It was only when I started cleaning up the s'mores setup that Nick finally spoke. "That's the dumbest thing I've ever heard," he said.

I swallowed the marshmallow I was chewing. "Huh?"

"What you said, about how we shouldn't be together yet. That's a load of crap and sounds like an *epic* waste of time. Why can't it be 'right' right now? I want you, and you want me, so why wait? Let's be together. It doesn't matter how young we are, or that we'll be at different schools." He moved to wrap me in a hug. "Yeah, it might be hard. It might even be *really* hard, but I want us to try."

My heart was pounding. I did too—really, truly did. Honestly, I didn't think I could do another week, much less another few years, of us not being together. Of him being with someone else. It was too hard now that I knew how good it could be.

Nick smiled and tugged on my ponytail. "So come on, what do you say?"

◇◇◇◇◇◇◇◇◇◇◇◇◇◇◇◇◇◇◇

We rode Ace and Stinger back to main campus together, after hiding Nick's stuff behind the boathouse. "Charlie will help me deal with it tomorrow," he said. I spotted Reese and Jack out on Simmons' patio when we parked our bikes in the rack. They waved.

Nick waved back, but I didn't. I just grinned and threw my arms around him so we could kiss for all to see. I heard Reese say to Jack, "I fucking knew it."

Unfortunately, Nick didn't stay on the patio for long. "I don't want Emma to find out like this," he whispered after politely booting me from his lap, ex-girlfriend now in sight. "I'll see you tomorrow?"

"You better." I smiled, and not fifteen minutes later, Charlie was calling me. "Fantastic news!" I greeted him. "Now we *both* have boyfriends!"

But the line was silent for five long seconds, before I heard my best friend say in this trembling voice, "Please come, Sage." He let out a choking sob. "I really need you."

My heart dropped about ten million stories. "Charlie, where's Luke?"

More uneven breathing and hiccups, and then, "Just please come."

"I will." I nodded quickly. "Where are you?"

"My room."

"Okay, I'm on my way. Calm down. I'm coming as fast as I can."

CHAPTER 34
SAGE

I DIDN'T USUALLY WAKE UP UNTIL 11:00 A.M. ON Sundays, but that morning, I rolled out of bed at 9:53, when my phone buzzed with a new text. Passing on brunch today, Luke had written. Really tired.

Well, I thought, shifting into protective-best-friend mode, *"really tired" or not, we need to have a chat.*

I was at his door by 10:13, after creeping through Brooks' eerily deserted common room and up to the top floor. I hesitated at first, thinking that maybe I shouldn't wake him, but knocked on the door anyway. "Yeah?" I heard Luke call, and I jumped. He sounded *very* awake.

"Hey," I said when I walked in. "We need..."

But I trailed off, suddenly speechless. Luke's room was a colossal *mess*. His bed was a wreck—an explosion of pillows and blankets—and all his dresser drawers were open, clothes spilling out of them. "What are you doing?"

"Purging," Luke answered, rifling through his closet and emerging with two checked button-downs. And he too, I saw, was a mess. His jaw was locked and his eyes red-rimmed. I stood there like a dumbstruck idiot while he crossed his tiny room and carelessly folded the shirts before tossing them in the box on his desk. My pulse pounded, realizing what he was doing.

"Luke, no," I began. "Don't—"

"I want it all gone," he said, voice ice-cold. "I don't want to look at any of it." He turned away and dropped to his knees to ransack the drawers under his bed. I moved forward to see that the box was over half full: the two Vineyard Vines shirts, Charlie's blue EDGARTOWN YACHT CLUB quarter-zip, the Prince Charming crown, a black-and-white ribbon belt, and at the very bottom, Charlie's bracelets.

"You can't do this," I said, fingering the tie bracelet. "You guys are—"

"Done," Luke finished, brushing past me. He picked up a pen and quickly jotted something down on a notepad before going over to his dresser.

My eyes welled up, remembering Charlie last night. I'd left him on his bed, wrapped up like a burrito in his comforter and bawling his eyes out. "He broke up with me," he kept repeating, over and over, while I'd tried so hard to calm him down...but to no avail. Curfew had then called, and I hated knowing he cried himself to sleep.

"What went wrong?" I asked, a little nervous that Luke would snap at me for being nosy. But I needed to know.

I heard him sigh, and then he was next to me again, adding Charlie's noise-canceling headphones to the mix of stuff. "We went to the movies," he said, "and things were great. The seats were great, the movie was great, and *he* was great. Literally no one was there, so he held my hand the whole time." He sighed again. "But later, we went to the ropes course, to"—he shrugged—"you know, and that's when I realized I couldn't do it anymore, this thing with him. I'm done."

"Did something happen?" I asked quietly.

Luke nodded. His voice was quiet too, but *angry*-quiet. "On the way back," he said, "we heard someone, and what does Charlie do?" Luke pointed to a scrape on his cheek. "He *pushes* me into the goddamn woods. I took a branch in the face and tripped over a rock, all so Paddy fucking Clarke and Val didn't catch us *walking* together."

Suddenly dizzy, I sank down into Luke's desk chair.

"Which makes it crystal clear," he continued. "He's not comfortable with who he is."

My heart twisted. "Luke..."

Luke shook his head. "He's not, Sage. Yes, he's told you and Nick, but his parents *still* don't know anything, after three whole months. He hasn't told them about me. He said he would, but he hasn't. The only reason I met them was because of you. He hasn't done anything. He's fine with them just thinking of me as 'Luke from down the street.'" He sighed. "And it's not even their street."

"No, you're not..." I tried.

He ignored me. "So I can't do it anymore. I love him." His voice wavered. "It's probably unhealthy how much I *love* him, but I can't go on like this. I've tried so hard to be patient, but I'm tired. I want to be with him for *real*. I want to hold his hand in public and for people to know that he won't flirt with them because he's with me. I want him to introduce me as his boyfriend, and I want everything we've talked about to actually happen. I want *Virginia* to happen."

My stomach swirled with a feeling that he wasn't just referring to their Charlottesville getaway. Charlie's blue-and-orange windbreaker flashed through my mind.

"See?" Luke fell back on his bed. "He hasn't even told you *that*." He groaned. "Charlie Carmichael gets into one of the best schools in the country and tells *no one*."

Suddenly I was crying. "No, Luke, he has." I blinked, and remembered. Here we are, UVA! the Snapchat had read, but I really hadn't picked up on the *we*. It was so subtle. But Charlie had said something, in his own way. I told Luke as much.

"That hardly qualifies," he said, then smiled sadly. "I mean, now we're *stuck* together. You know, since it was early decision." He took off his glasses. "Binding."

"Please don't do this," I whispered. "Don't give up on him. He loves you. So much."

"I know he loves me," Luke said. "But it's not enough." He rubbed his eyes. "I can't wait until college, Sage...and I don't think he should either. It's like he keeps telling himself that once he's somewhere new, where nobody knows him, the switch will be magically flipped. I want to believe him, but I'm not sure he truly believes that himself. If Charlie is really going to accept himself, and *be* himself, it needs to be now, among all the people who love him."

◇◇◇◇◇◇◇◇◇◇◇◇◇◇◇◇◇◇◇

I really didn't want to, but I agreed to be Luke's courier. I'd return Charlie's things and get Luke's back. "This is a comprehensive list of everything he has," he said before I left, handing over a piece of paper. "Make sure you get it all." And all I did was nod and say okay. I didn't tell him I thought he was being harsh, maybe even cruel.

Then I set off for Daggett.

"Charlie?" I said, knocking on his door. "It's me. Can I come in?"

No answer.

I pushed the door open anyway and found Charlie wearing faded sweatpants and Luke's gray Adidas sweatshirt. My shoulders slumped; I didn't need to check the list to know it was number one with a bullet. Charlie was curled up on his couch, and I saw his eyes were even worse than Luke's—not just red, but bloodshot.

"Hey," I said gently, tucking the breakup box behind his desk. "Did you sleep?"

His voice was a croak. "No."

I joined him on the couch and took his hand. "Why didn't you tell me?" I asked. "Why didn't you tell me about UVA?"

Charlie didn't answer.

I squeezed his fingers.

"I didn't *not* tell you," he said quietly.

"No, I know," I said, eyes prickling as I noticed the blue-and-orange *VIRGINIA* pennant tacked up by his house flag. "But, why? Why there?"

"Because it's exactly what I want," he replied. "I told you: I want to get out of here, I want somewhere big, I want..."

"Him," I guessed. "You want him."

There was a beat of hesitation, but then Charlie nodded.

Oh, Charlie, I thought.

Right on cue, his head dropped into his hands. "I know I

shouldn't have done it, Sage, but..." His voice quavered. "I just found him, he just found me, and we don't want to be apart."

We don't want to be apart.

I remembered thinking that back in eighth grade, when first hearing that the twins were applying to Bexley, and again this fall, during college application season. Now, I couldn't help but feel a small burst of pride, knowing that even though my friends and I would be at different schools next year, nothing could truly separate us. We would be fine.

No, better than fine, I decided, thinking of Nick. *We'll be epic.*

"But you know what's happened." Charlie looked up, tears streaming down his face. "He says that unless I get it together, we're over."

I sucked in a deep breath. "Then get it together, Charlie."

He shook his head. "I can't."

"Why not?" I asked. "Yes, you're gay, and that's far from the easiest thing to tell your family, but you've come so far! I know, Nick knows, and nothing has changed. Absolutely *nothing*. We still love you, and your parents will too. There's no reason to keep putting this off. If you want to be with Luke, you *need* to tell everyone the truth. Why are you so scared?"

"Because it's too late," he said. "Because I'm already *him*."

I gave him a look, confused. "Because you're *him*?"

"Yes." His voice flatlined. "Because I'm him—I'm *that guy*. Bexley's big man on campus. People think I'm that guy, my parents think I'm that guy, and I've worked so hard to make that happen." He raked a hand through his hair. "I've known for years, Sage. I've known for *years* that I'm...the way I am. I'd notice some random kid's eyes through his hockey helmet...or another's smile on the soccer field. And Cal, of course. There was Cal." He swallowed. "Girls are nice...all those girls were nice, but that's it. *Nice.* The only reason I hooked up with them was to shield myself, to hide myself." He shook his head. "To be the guy everyone wants me to be, expects me to be..."

"Well, not me," I said when he trailed off, a lump in my throat. "I don't want you to be that guy." I hugged him. "And neither does Luke, and neither does Nick. We want you to be happy. We want you to be *you*."

Charlie buried his face in my shoulder. "People will talk." He shuddered. "It'll be a shitstorm. I don't understand why Luke can't just wait for UVA. I'll be better, then. I can't handle it all right now."

"Yes, you can," I said. "Be brave, Charlie. You shouldn't keep hiding, you shouldn't wait any longer to be yourself." I paused, uneasy but unable to lie to him. Everybody talked, and he had a reputation. "I mean, yeah, they'll be shocked, but you can count on me to hold any shitstorm's umbrella."

I waited for a laugh, even for the ghost of one, but Charlie didn't chuckle.

"It'll pass, Charlie," I added. "Everyone loves you, no matter who you are. It'll pass."

Again, Charlie didn't respond. He just cried harder.

CHAPTER 35
CHARLIE

MONDAY MORNING, I STARED INTO MY WATERY scrambled eggs, wishing they were one of Luke's omelets. "Hey, are you going to eat that?" Matt Gallant pointed his fork at my plate. I glanced up to see that he'd already demolished his waffles. My stomach twisted, regretting not blowing off class to stay in bed. *Maybe I'll go to the infirmary*, I thought. *Sleep the day away.*

"All yours," I told Matt, right as Paddy joined us and let out a long sigh.

"Well, it was a good fight, gents," he offered Cody his hand to shake. "But it seems a choice has been made."

Matt spoke through a mouthful of eggs. "What're you talking about?"

Paddy nodded toward one of Addison's window tables: the flock's table, where Nick sat in my seat. He was laughing and eating while Sage held one of his hands, hugging it to her chest. She looked extra-awake today. And yeah, I was happy for them, but it was hard to show it. I felt Paddy clap me on the shoulder. "You and Nick gonna be okay, Charlie?"

I didn't respond, because Luke was there now. He dropped down next to Nina with only a mug of coffee. *Look at me*, I willed him. *God, please look at me.*

He didn't, but I kept looking at him until I saw Nina reach out and touch his cheek. *What happened?* I knew she was asking, and my heart lurched—back to Saturday night, in the woods. It was like someone else had taken over my body. "Sorry," I'd blurted after shoving him off the trail, clumsily switching on my phone flashlight while I glanced over my shoulder to make sure Paddy and Val hadn't heard anything. "It was an accident."

Luke had silently picked himself up off the ground. "I'm bleeding," he said, voice devoid of anything. It made the hair on my neck stand up.

"I'm sorry," I repeated, moving close to see how badly the branch had swiped him. "It was an accident."

"No, it wasn't." He backed away from me. "No, it fucking *wasn't*."

"You're right," I whispered an excruciatingly long second later, because Luke and I didn't lie to each other. "I'm really sorry."

And it had been all downhill from there.

◇◇◇◇◇◇◇◇◇◇◇◇◇◇◇

For the next week, and the one after that, I didn't hang out with anyone after sports and dinner. I shut myself in my room and tried to dare myself to do it—call Mom and Dad and tell them. Some nights I practiced first, after pacing for an hour. "I have something to tell you guys," I said to a family photo on my wall. "You've probably noticed I've been acting weird, and that's because I'm..."

But I could never actually say it—my ears started ringing before the buzzword, like they always did. "Now that's Charlie, right?" I'd overheard Party Guest #1 ask Party Guest #2 at this year's Hardcastle Christmas party, while I waited for a drink at the living room bar. They were a few yards away, sipping glasses of wine.

"Yes." The first woman nodded. "He is personality-plus and apparently always has a girlfriend, but for some reason, Whitney suspects he's gay."

"Oh," the second woman said as I leaned against the bar, the ringing noise overwhelming. "Well, I wonder how Jay and Allison feel about that..."

That was what scared me shitless—I had no idea how they felt, or *would* feel. Because I couldn't remember them doing anything but laughing off Aunt Whit's probing questions, and we weren't friends with anyone like me. Sage's uncle, but not really. We'd never met. I knew they weren't *against* it, but I figured it was different when it was their own son. *Would I still have to call Luke my friend?* I wondered. *Even if they knew?*

It was a total shot in the dark.

◇◇◇◇◇◇◇◇◇◇◇◇◇◇◇◇◇◇

"So does the condo sound good to you?" Dad asked. It was around 10:00 p.m., and he'd picked up before I bailed on the call. First, we'd talked about his Valentine's plans with Mom, and then about Granddad needing a hip replacement.

"What?" I jumped a little, Post-it Notes scattering. I usually hid them in my desk, but tonight I'd spread them out on my bed—all in Luke's handwriting, from whenever he'd been in my room. The one I was holding said: *You are my entire heart.*

I loved how sappy Luke got on paper.

"Turks and Caicos," Dad said. "Theo's invited us down for your spring break."

"Oh, cool." I bit the inside of my cheek.

"Yup, we're thinking deep-sea fishing."

"Awesome." My voice caught.

Because last month Luke had asked me to come to Grosse Pointe for break. "Come home with me," he'd said after we opened a chocolate chip cookie-filled care package from his mom. "I want you to meet my family."

But obviously, it wasn't an option now. I collapsed back against my pillow—I missed him so much, it was crippling. We hadn't talked in two weeks. Every night I fell asleep by holding my own hand, pretending it was his.

"Oh, listen," Dad said, "I've gotta run. Mom wants to watch *Top Chef.* Anything you need me to tell her?"

My chest clenched. *Yeah, there is, Dad. I can't go fishing because I want to meet my boyfriend's family. And you didn't hear wrong: boy-friend. Because I'm—*

"No, nothing," I said before the ringing could start.

◇◇◇◇◇◇◇◇◇◇◇◇◇◇◇◇◇◇◇

My body was in knots when I woke up the morning of Valentine's Day. 5:15 a.m., my phone read. *Why can't you do it?* I tossed and turned. *Why can't you just fucking do it?*

So maybe because I knew he was still asleep, or maybe because I was aching for him, I texted Luke: I'm not as strong as you.

Ten seconds after I hit send, my phone buzzed:

Yes, you are.

CHAPTER 36
SAGE

"SO HOW'D IT GO?" I ASKED NICK WHILE WE danced. It was officially Valentine's Day, and Mortimer had reserved the music hall for their date party. In truth, the streamers and balloons weren't the most elegant (the guys had decorated the place themselves), but they looked chaotically beautiful with the lights dimmed, and you could always count on Ed Sheeran to set the mood. Anyway, I didn't really care...I was dancing with my boyfriend. *He looks so adorable*, I thought, gently running a hand through Nick's flaming hair as he focused super hard on not stepping on my feet. *He's handsome in the daytime and adorable at night.*

I couldn't stop smiling.

Nick pretended to groan. "Do we have to talk about Charlie?"

I stretched up to kiss him. "Yes."

He nodded, because he knew we did. This afternoon, he'd dragged his heartbroken twin out of Daggett for dinner at Humpty Dumplings. For the past couple of weeks, Charlie had been acting like we'd banished him from the kingdom, now eating with the hockey guys and locking himself in his room at night. "What happened?" the girls had asked, but when Luke and I stayed quiet, they'd dropped it. The one time I'd seen Charlie today was this morning, when he'd been heading into Knowles for French. He was wearing his headphones, which said it all. Charlie almost never shut Bexley out.

We will hold that umbrella for you, I kept thinking. *You won't brave the storm alone.*

Nick sighed heavily. "Not the best. He didn't eat anything until I basically forced him, and he barely spoke. Pretty much catatonic. And then we got that email for the..."

"The superlative nominations," I finished for him. Today the *Annual* editors had emailed the senior class a list of fifty yearbook superlatives, with five nominees for each one.

"Right," Nick said. "So that didn't exactly help the cause."

"Best Bromance," I whispered, hardly feeling him stomp on my foot. CHARLIE CARMICHAEL & LUKE MORRISSEY were the first two names in the category.

"He needs to go home," Nick said after apologizing and hugging me closer, my back humming with his hand resting on it. "I told him I would buy the train ticket..."

"And?" I said when he trailed off.

But Nick didn't answer, his eyes now wide. I twisted around to see Charlie stalking across the dance floor. "Holy crap," I breathed.

He stuck out like a sore thumb thanks to tonight's semiformal attire: red-gold hair extremely sleep-rumpled, L.L.Bean moccasins on his feet, and still wearing the Adidas sweatshirt that he'd *refused* to give back to Luke. I tried to catch his eye, but the only person he was looking at was his twin, determined as ever.

"3:08 tomorrow afternoon," he said when he came up to us.

"Okay," Nick said back. "I'll book it."

Charlie nodded and then left.

∞∞∞∞∞∞∞∞∞∞∞∞

Nick walked me home after the party. "Tell me it's going to be okay," he'd said when we reached Simmons' back door. "Tell me he'll be okay."

"It's going to be okay," I said. "And he's going to be *more* than okay."

He nodded a few times. Instead of an exasperated mom, he was now a full-on helicopter parent. Suddenly I didn't think there was anyone in the world who loved their brother as much as Nick loved Charlie. "You're right, he will." He sighed. "But do you think—"

"No." I shook my head. "You cannot go with him."

Nick laughed and put his hands on my waist. "I had fun tonight," he said. "Did you?"

"Yes," I told him. "I had a lot of fun tonight. Thank you for inviting me."

"You're welcome," he said, spinning me around once.

I grinned. "I love you, Nicholas Carmichael."

Which made Nick grin back, dimple and all. "I love you too, Sage Morgan," he murmured and leaned close, so close his lips brushed mine. "And now I'm gonna kiss you good night."

CHAPTER 37
CHARLIE

NICK TRIED TO GIVE ME A PEP TALK BEFORE I left. "It's going to be *fine*," he told me, then amended, "No, it's going to be *great*. You're going to do it, and then you're going to come back here and fix it all with him, and then things will be good again."

I gripped my backpack straps and just looked at him. *Come with me.*

He shook his head. *I can't.*

"Yeah, I know." I shut my eyes and nodded.

"But I've got you," Nick said, trapping me in a hug before pretty much pushing me onto the train. "I've *always* got you."

∞∞∞∞∞∞∞∞∞∞∞∞∞∞∞∞

I wondered if Mom and Dad knew something was up. "What do you mean you're coming home?" they'd said when I called them. "Aren't you studying for midterms?"

It had taken a lot to keep my voice steady. "Yes," I told them.

"But it's no big deal, and I just"—I hunted for the best words— "want to come home for a night."

I looked at the *Annual* email again on the ride. Everyone loved the yearbook's superlatives and I *knew* it was time when I saw the nominees. Because amid all the stupidity of MOST LIKELY TO WIN IN A STREET FIGHT (Val Palacios, was my vote) and FIRST TO MARRY A MILLIONAIRE (Jack Healy, hands down), there they were: Luke's and my names, next to BEST BROMANCE, and I hated that. *The ultimate typo,* I thought. We weren't just a bromance, and everyone needed to know it. I *wanted* them to know it. The *B* needed to be dropped. *But that's later,* I reminded myself before my chest tightened. *Mom and Dad are first. Don't think about Bexley now.*

Just like back in October, Mom was waiting at the end of the platform when my train pulled in. It was almost dinnertime. "Hi, honey." She wrapped me in a hug. "How are you?"

"Hungry," I said.

She touched my cheek. "Me too. Should we go to the club for dinner? Your dad and I still haven't used up this month's minimum."

But instead of growling, my stomach started to churn. Everyone at Darien Country Club knew my family. We could never get through a dinner without people stopping by our table. "Actually"—I swallowed the lump in my throat—"can we eat at home?"

"Sure." Mom nodded. We left the station in pursuit of the parking lot. The Jeep beeped in response to Mom's keys. I threw my stuff in the back and climbed into the passenger seat, leaning my head against the window as she turned over the ignition. I'd just shut my eyes when I heard her add, "Dad's excited to see you."

I looked at her. "What?"

She smiled. "He's happy you called, that you're here for the night." She laughed. "He's really missed you lately. We both have."

"I've missed you too," I said, and we were quiet for the rest of the drive. When we got home, Dad thumped me hard on the back before I went upstairs to unpack my stuff. Then I lay on my bed while my parents figured out food, trying to collect my thoughts.

⬦⬦⬦⬦⬦⬦⬦⬦⬦⬦⬦⬦⬦⬦⬦

Mom ended up reheating leftover chili, but the clenching inside me made it hard to eat as Dad asked, "Would you like to go first?"

I shook my head. We did this every night when Nick and I weren't at school, went around the table and said something we wanted to "get off our chest." Dad's go-to was always complaining about the fact that Nana called him about ten times a week for TV tech support. "I love her," he'd say, "but sometimes it's so exasperating. She can never understand that all she needs to do is press *source*!"

Now, Mom went ahead and vented about her latest listing. "It's been the biggest nightmare," she said. "The deal is contingent upon the buyers selling their house, and we just found water in the crawl space..." She trailed off and her eyebrows furrowed. "Charlie, are you all right?"

I didn't respond. I could hear the blood pumping through my ears and feel the sweat beading on my forehead. And it wasn't because the chili was too spicy.

"Charlie—"

"I'm gay," I blurted.

Her eyes widened. "What?"

"I'm gay," I repeated, lungs threatening to give out if I didn't exhale. "That's what I'm getting off my chest."

Mom blinked—once, twice, three times before she nodded slowly. She opened her mouth to say something, but I wasn't done yet, seeing Dad's blank expression. Just staring at me.

"It's not a joke," I told him.

"No," he murmured, face paling. "I didn't think it was." He cleared his throat and pushed back his chair. "Excuse me a minute."

"Jay," Mom said as he walked out of the kitchen, not looking back. My eyes were stinging, ears ringing. "Jay..."

Neither of us said anything for a few seconds, but then she took one of my hands and started massaging my palm. That's when the stinging shifted to a full-on spill of hot tears.

"Did you know?" I asked softly.

Mom shook her head. "No, but it answers a lot of questions." She squeezed my hand. "We've been worried about you. You haven't been our Charlie for the past five months...perpetually preoccupied, and so *thin* at Thanksgiving..." She wrapped an arm around me, and I put my head on her shoulder.

"I'm not the person everyone thinks I am," I whispered.

She hugged me tighter. "Yes, you are. This is only one part

of you, and it won't change how we feel about you. We love you. We'll *always* love you."

I shuddered. "You have no idea what I'm like at school."

I waited for her to ask me, but she didn't. She just started to comb her fingers through my hair. "Does Nicky know?"

"Yeah," I admitted, "and Sage."

"Okay." She let out a deep breath. "Okay."

We sat there in silence again. Mom kept finger-brushing my hair like when I was little, but eventually she murmured, "Dad is just surprised."

More tears spilled. "Never would've guessed," I mumbled, unable to stop shaking. He'd left—*left*. He didn't even let me explain or try to understand.

"Give him some time." She kissed my forehead. "He's surprised now, but I think he'll soon realize he's relieved. Believe it or not, it really hurt his feelings that you never invited any girls to dinner or back here for a weekend. He thinks you're embarrassed of us."

I shrugged. "None of them were him."

Mom tilted her head. "There's a him?"

"Yeah," I said. "He's not very happy with me right now, but yeah. There is."

"Does he have a name?"

"Luke."

"Luke? Luke Morrissey? The Hoppers' neighbor?"

I nodded.

"We met him," Mom said. "He was with Sage at the second Ames game. Only for a few minutes, but your dad complimented his handshake, and I liked how well-spoken he was, and that he didn't quite catch all his bedhead." She sort of smiled. "He's adorable."

"Yeah, he is." I sort of smiled back. "But also a major smart-ass." My heart flickered, then flamed. I took a deep breath. "I love him."

She smiled more and wiped her eyes. "Dad's probably in the study."

◇◇◇◇◇◇◇◇◇◇◇◇◇◇◇◇◇◇◇

Dad was really quiet after I got up the guts to open the study door. There was no point in knocking, since the doors had glass panes. He'd seen me outside. My body stiffened as I joined him by the fireplace, sitting in the one of the leather club chairs. Neither of us spoke. "Are you sure?" was what he eventually settled on.

"Yes," I said, almost adding, *You would know if you'd stayed at the table.*

He nodded, then rose from his seat and crossed the room to the bar cart. I watched him grab a bottle of scotch and two tumblers before locating a pair of cigars. The ones from Uncle Theo that he'd been saving for a special occasion. "Mom won't let us smoke these in the house," he said, "so we'll go out on the deck later." He poured us each a couple of fingers of whiskey, handed me my glass, and then held up his own. "To you," he said. "To you, my son. You are a stronger man than I will ever be."

We clinked glasses.

"I love you, Charlie," he told me. "I love you very much."

⬦⬦⬦⬦⬦⬦⬦⬦⬦⬦⬦⬦⬦⬦

My train on Sunday was obnoxiously early, but I needed to get back to Bexley. Mom and Dad hugged me long and hard before Mom handed me an unsealed envelope. "I found this in one of the albums last night."

I waited until I'd found a seat before checking out the mystery photo. But everything turned to white noise when I did...because in Mom's perfect handwriting, the caption on the back read: *Charlie (10) and a (sleepy!) new friend at Cousin Banks's christening party!*

And there we were: Luke and me. *You've met,* my mind nudged me as I soaked in the picture. *You've met before.* We were such little kids, but it was unmistakably, undeniably, even eerily *us*. I was wearing these navy pants with green alligators embroidered on them, and Luke had on a blue-and-white sweater vest and his glasses. We were sitting on the Hoppers' big red couch, and while I had my arms crossed over my chest and sported my jaw-aching grin, Luke wasn't even aware the picture was being taken, because he was asleep with his head on my shoulder. I reached for my phone and went to my camera roll.

Pretty soon my eyes prickled. Without even knowing it, we'd reenacted this photo a thousand times, and Sage had documented them all: me smiling with Luke passed out against my shoulder. My favorite was from a while ago, Luke and me together on Sage's chaise. I wasn't really looking at the camera, instead, grinning down at a dreaming Luke. Our legs were entwined, and he held one of my hands.

I leaned back against my seat and shut my eyes.

I really wanted to be holding his hand right now.

∞∞∞∞∞∞∞∞∞∞∞∞

Sage hadn't said anything, but I knew she and Nick would be waiting for me at the station. What time do you get back? she'd texted last night, so when the conductor came over the loudspeaker and announced we were running behind schedule, I sent: Probably going to be a couple of minutes late.

Sure enough, she replied: Okay!

I released a deep breath, already picturing them on the platform: hand in hand, with Sage waving and wearing Nick's Patagonia, and my brother glowing next to her. *Hercules*, I mused to myself. *He'll look like Hercules.*

Which was good—I sort of needed them to be there. I needed Sage to smother me in a hug and for Nick to suggest we grab food from Pandora's. They'd get me to laugh and relax before I went back to Daggett and figured out what to say to Luke. How to tell him about this weekend at home and how sorry I was and show him the picture. *Look at that*, I would say. *That's us.*

∞∞∞∞∞∞∞∞∞∞∞∞

The train ended up slowing to a stop ten minutes after it was supposed to, and since it was Sunday morning, there weren't many people aboard. I shrugged on my backpack and pulled down the hood of Luke's sweatshirt before standing up and heading toward the front of the car to the exit. "Have a nice day, young man," the conductor said as I stepped down onto the platform. My pulse quickened when I didn't see Nick's hideous Patagonia or Sage's swinging ponytail. They weren't waiting for me on the platform or over by the benches. *No*, I felt like a forgotten child. *Where are you?*

But then I felt it—a hand on my shoulder, right as I heard: "Hey there."

I pivoted around to see Luke, in a faded sweatshirt and plaid pajama bottoms with his UVA baseball hat. Behind his glasses, there were violet half-moons under his eyes. Sleepy Luke.

I am in love with him, I thought.

"Sage texted me at the crack of dawn," he explained as my heart hammered. "And told me to be here, like some type of sketchy hazing—"

I didn't let him finish. Instead, I hugged him, burying my face in his warm neck and slumping against him. It was the same sort of hug I'd given him back in November, the night we decided to be together, and later, the same sort of hug I gave him after a long day. "A Collapsing Charlie," Luke had dubbed it, and now I heard myself groan as his arms tightened around me.

"Me too," he murmured.

"I have something for you," I told him once we broke apart. My fingers fumbled to unzip my backpack, but I somehow pulled out Mom's photo and handed it to him. Then I held on to his sweatshirt cuff and stayed quiet, letting him look at it.

"Yes." Luke glanced up at me after a few seconds, his lips quirking into a kind of bittersweet smile. "I remember that day well."

"Why didn't you ever say anything?" I asked, voice catching.

"Didn't I?" He cocked his head, and suddenly that night in Charlottesville came to mind. Our first crushes. He *had* said something; I just hadn't believed it. "But," he added now, as he took my hand and threaded our fingers together, "there are some things you needed to figure out yourself."

Eyes stinging, I nodded. "I know."

Luke squeezed my hand.

I squeezed his back.

"I'm proud of you, C," he whispered. "Really fucking proud."

"Thank you."

"How do you feel?"

"Looser." I pointed to my chest. "But still sort of clenched." I released a deep breath. "You know, about Bexley."

"It's going to be okay," Luke told me. "It's all going to be okay."

I nodded again.

A few beats, and then: "So, what shall we do now?"

"Be us," I said.

"Well yes, that was implied." His eyes glinted, and I ached when he laughed. "But I meant should we get breakfast?"

All I could do was respond with another Collapsing Charlie. "I'm so tired, Luke," I told him, breathing in his Luke-ness: peppermint and soap and *him*. "I really want to take a nap."

Because truthfully, I hadn't slept in ages—even last night. I'd stared at my ceiling as I listened to unintelligible snippets of Mom and Dad's conversation down the hall.

Luke raised an eyebrow. "With me?"

"Yeah, with you," I said, smiling. "I'm yours, Luke."

"Well, that's very cool," he replied. "Because the feeling's mutual." He grinned. "You're mine, C."

"And everyone's gonna know it," I told him.

Then I kissed him with everything I had.

CHAPTER 38
SAGE

Three Months Later

NICHOLAS LAWRENCE CARMICHAEL WAS THE first person I saw when the girls and I got to The Meadow, the four of us decked out in variations of the classic white dress. Before the ceremony, it was tradition for all the seniors to gather outside Knowles so we could head over to the grove together. "We're one long line of overgrown kindergarteners," was Luke's assessment during this morning's 7:00 a.m. rehearsal.

"Oh my god," Nina breathed now. "Are they *serious*?"

Because Nick was standing underneath one of the nearby maple trees with our valedictorian, and they were playing their "twin card" for all its worth. Yes, most of the guys were matching—blue blazers, white button-downs, and striped Bexley School ties— but the Carmichaels had never looked more identical. They both had on their Wayfarer sunglasses with the most *in-your-face* pair of pants in existence. I smiled, unable to believe they'd actually gone through with it. "They're Lilly Pulitzer," Nick explained when he first showed me the electric-green-blue-and-yellow patchwork pants. "From the eighties. Dad and Uncle Theo wore them to their graduation, so Charlie and I are doing the same. How epic are they?"

I remembered begging him to model them for me, but he blushed and shook his head. "You gotta be patient, Morgan."

"Those two..." Jennie began, right as someone else said, "Good morning, girlfriends."

I spun around to see Luke approaching, also looking pretty sharp. We hugged, and then Reese kissed his cheek and left behind a mark from her lipstick.

"Come on, Reese," he groaned, doing his best to wipe it off. "My mom's bad enough."

We laughed. "Are your sisters here?" Jennie asked.

Luke nodded. "Of course. This is my..."

"Victory lap!" we finished for him.

He smirked. "Exactly."

◇◇◇◇◇◇◇◇◇◇◇◇◇◇◇◇◇◇◇◇◇◇◇

The sun was high in the cloudless blue sky, but it wasn't beating down on us in the shady grove, every single folding chair filled. Reverend Chambers welcomed everyone, and when he remarked what a "sensational day" it was, I leaned over and whispered to Luke, "He says that every year. Even sophomore year, when it was overcast and thundering in the distance!"

Dean Wheaton was next, speaking about our class as a whole, and then he invited Jennie onstage to pass on the torch to next year's school president. "That guy has one tough act to follow," Luke said under his breath as we watched Jennie drape the ceremonial cape over her successor's shoulders.

After that, it was Headmaster Griswold, still rocking his handlebar moustache, behind the podium. I took a deep breath and reached over to take Luke's hand.

Headmaster Griswold introduced my best friend by speaking about Charlie's many achievements, from his "effervescent" performances, like flying up and down the ice or onstage in a musical, to his "exemplary" transcript. He hadn't gotten anything less than an A on any assignment ever, and I saw some people roll their eyes at that...and also caught Luke roll his back. *You have no idea*, I read his mind. *You have no idea how hard he works, because he makes everything look so easy.*

When our headmaster started in on Charlie's "illuminating personality," I squeezed Luke's hand and felt a burst of something inside me.

"He's amazing," I whispered.

"He's taken," Luke whispered back.

"We are all especially grateful for the boundless enthusiasm and myriad talents Charlie has shared with us," Headmaster Griswold continued, "and I have no doubt he will bring the same joy for life and learning to the University of Virginia next year." He chuckled. "In fact, I'm not certain they know *just* what they're in for..." He cleared his throat. "So it is with much pride and admiration that I congratulate Charlie Carmichael on being selected as this year's Bexley School valedictorian."

The applause was deafening. Half the audience stood, and Luke and I craned our necks to see Charlie make his way up the graduation grandstand. "That's my boyfriend," Luke remarked, beaming as Charlie bounded up the steps in that slick way of his.

"Thank you, Headmaster Griswold, for that kind introduction," Charlie said once he was behind the podium. "And thank you, parents, families, faculty, and fellow Bexleyans, for granting me the honor to speak to you on this"—he smiled, and then his quick wit made its first appearance—"*sensational* day."

All the students laughed, catching the reference, but I got closer and closer to tears as the speech went on. First from laughing too hard, and then from feeling just plain sentimental. Because Charlie had written a thank-you note to Bexley...or more accurately, *multiple* thank-you notes to Bexley, since his speech was based off *The Tonight Show*, with most of it being his take on the "Thank You Note Friday" bit. Everyone cracked up when he said, "Thank you, Turn-It-In, for doing your best to teach me that procrastination is not the best course of action. The 'Always Crashing Whenever Charlie Tries to Submit an Assignment Three Minutes Before a Deadline' approach is both effective and cathartic," and there was another round of laughter when he added, "Thank you, Mrs. Collings and Bexley Campus Safety, for helping me understand what it's like to be a fugitive from the law. I now feel adequately prepared for when I actually am one."

I got goose bumps at that. "But what about your shirt?!" I'd shouted just the other night, as Nick and I ran for our lives, Mrs. Collings and her bloodhound on the pursuit. Nick was shirtless, blue MURDICK'S FUDGE T-shirt left behind on the sixth hole's putting green. "It doesn't matter!" he'd said, and scooped me up into his arms. "We need to go!"

After "Thank you, Mr. Magnusson, for your immeasurable wit and wisdom. I hope I learn what half of it means someday," Charlie paused, like he'd lost his train of thought.

"Finally," Luke tried to prompt him from afar, "a huge thank-you to my fellow graduates, for letting me spend the last four years with the likes of you..."

Charlie glanced up and scanned the audience before continuing. "Thank you, to that person"—he smiled—"who has been with me since before I can even remember. Your endless support and eye rolls mean more to me than I can say, and I consider myself so lucky to know you."

When he moved on to the address's final remarks, I felt eyes... *lots* of eyes, but I knew they weren't focused on me. "Did you hear that?" I asked Luke.

"Yes." He nodded, unable to suppress a smile as he folded his arms over his chest. "And it was not in the original version."

<hr/>

The grove was a CFS afterward (Luke-speak for "Clusterfuck Situation"). I kept ahold of Luke as I basically elbowed my way through the madness, scouting out the flock. People were laughing and taking pictures, and some called my name, but I only slowed down when I heard Nick's voice.

"Morgan!"

He was by the grove's ivy-covered brick wall, waving some celebratory cigars and holding the gold Prescott Cup, the award for best senior athlete, like it was the Stanley Cup. And the next thing

I knew, I'd dropped Luke's hand and was flying into Nick's arms. He laughed and spun me around. "You're beautiful," he whispered after, tugging on my ponytail.

I grinned and reached to straighten his tie. "You're beautiful too."

Jack and Reese found us a few minutes later, and so did the others. The cigars were a Bexley tradition dating back to when the school was all-guys, but I lit up along with the rest of them. "Oh, Sage." Reese sighed and shook her head.

"What?" I said, feeling Nick start playing with my hair again. "I've earned this cigar fair and square!" I took another puff and looked at Luke. "Where's Charming?"

Because Charlie had yet to make his appearance.

"Probably big-shotting," Luke said, at the same time we heard, "Relax guys, the traffic's been heavy."

Charlie brushed past me and went to slip an arm around Luke's shoulders. Totally grinning, Luke leaned into him and reached up to entwine their fingers. I laughed and told Nina to snap a picture. *The stance*, the girls and I called it, since Luke and Charlie stood like this all the time.

"Here's proof!" Reese had said the other day, when we were sifting through prom photos. There was one of the boys in their tuxes, out on the balcony: a perfect shot. Twinkly lights were strung around the riverboat's railing and an American flag waved in the background. Neither of them was looking at the camera; Charlie had an arm hooked around Luke's neck and was busy whispering in his boyfriend's ear, while Luke was smiling at the ground. ("What was he saying?" I'd asked later, but Luke just shrugged and said, "That's classified.")

"You went off-script," Luke said once Nina had moved on to paparazzi-ing Reese and Jack, who were recently named Bexley's cutest couple. Every time I saw Charlie sign an *Annual* this week, the first thing he did was flip to the superlative spread and scribble out the *B* on his and Luke's, so that it now read BEST ROMANCE.

Charlie laughed. "I thought it was pretty subtle."

Luke shook his head. "Not that subtle."

And I did a double take when Charlie kissed him. They never kissed in public; it was a lot of walking really close together at first, which morphed into hand-holding, and now, the stance.

"Okay, Chluke, break it up," Paddy said as Nick whistled, coming up to us with his own cigar in hand. *Chluke* was his nickname for the boys. Luke claimed he hated it, but Charlie's face rivaled the sun whenever Paddy said it, eyes crinkling so hard.

"Clarke." Charlie saluted him, hand then finding Luke's again.

Paddy saluted him back. He'd already unknotted his tie, and his black eye was long gone now. Back in February, Charlie hadn't made an announcement or anything; he just gave Luke his hockey jacket to wear and let people put it together themselves. There was no true shitstorm. No one really said anything, and I wasn't surprised...because no one went up against Charlie Carmichael. But Paddy had intercepted us in the library that first day, prepping for midterms. Chluke and I were holding down a study room, while Nick was outside paying for our Chinese takeout. "Well, I guess this makes sense." Paddy smirked and gestured to Charlie fiddling with Luke's fingers. "Considering you've run out of girls, Carmichael..."

Then Charlie had stood and literally dragged Paddy out of the room and into the stacks nearby. He came back about a minute later, right hand shaking. "Ice," he told us. "I'm going to find some ice."

They were good from then on, and Paddy had since joked about officiating Luke and Charlie's wedding someday.

Reese called for a flock group photo before everyone scattered to locate their parents and migrate over to The Meadow for the graduation luncheon (allegedly when Bexley brought out the good food). "Squad picture," Nick declared later, after we'd tracked down our own families. Because within the flock, there was now *the squad*, the four of us. Charlie and Luke and Nick and Sage.

"I'm going to seriously miss you," I whispered to Luke once we had our arms around one another. "July's so far away."

"I already have a countdown going," he whispered back, and I smiled. This summer we were going to spend three weeks on the Vineyard with the Carmichaels. "It's going to be epic," Nick kept telling Luke. "You haven't lived until you've gone night kayaking."

At the thought, I quickly turned and kissed Nick's cheek before the flash went off. "Nicky, over here!" Mrs. Carmichael called out after a few clicks. "Look at the camera!"

Everyone laughed, but my heart rippled.

Because I could feel him looking at me.

⬦⬦⬦⬦⬦⬦⬦⬦⬦⬦⬦⬦⬦⬦⬦⬦

We said goodbye on the MAC's roof, of all places. "I can't believe you guys," Nick said as we took in the view, big and blue and beautiful. "Why didn't you ever tell us about this place?" He gave Luke a look. "I thought we were bros, Q."

I laughed. Nick had been calling Luke *Q* since we all went home to Darien one April weekend. We'd been in the Carmichaels' basement watching *Skyfall* together. "Holy shit." Nick had paused the movie and pointed the remote at the screen, at Agent 007's quartermaster. "That's *you*, Luke."

"So if Luke's Q," Charlie said now, "that means I'm Bond."

Luke and I exchanged an eye roll from our beach chairs; he and Charlie had brought them up here earlier in the spring. There might've been *X* after *X* on their secret campus map, but I suspected this was truly their spot. They hadn't forgotten to leave their mark: *CCC* + *LGM* was tastefully written on a skylight (meanwhile, Nick and I'd stolen the sixth hole's flag).

"No." Nick shoved his twin. "Bond and Q aren't a couple."

Charlie shoved him back. "Yeah, they are."

"Says who?"

"Certain people on the internet. You should see the GIFs."

"Okay, you wish," Nick said, and trapped Charlie in a headlock. I heard Luke release a deep sigh as they wrestled.

"You know, Sage," he said. "I've discovered something."

"Oh yeah?" I turned to look at him, an eyebrow raised. "What's that?"

Then Luke Morrissey smirked at me, and in that deadpan delivery of his, said: "We have terrible taste in boyfriends."

ACKNOWLEDGMENTS

My hands are shaking, I am smiling, and my heart is beating so fast. There are so many people who helped make this book happen, and I am so excited to give them the thanks they deserve. Hopefully no music plays me off the stage...

Thank you to my agent extraordinaire, Eva Scalzo. I know we always joke about our partnership being meant to be (usually with Harry Styles GIFs), but I profoundly believe it was written in the stars. I can't imagine anyone but you responding to my rambling emails with such care, composure, and insight. You are, without a doubt, the coolest. Should Nick suddenly become available, I will let you have him.

To Annie Berger, my editor: After submitting this book to you, I crossed my fingers and toes that you would fall in love with it. Thank you for doing just that, and more. Your thoughtful suggestions and comments both stretched me as a writer and made the story even better.

And to the rest of the Sourcebooks squad, particularly Sarah Kasman, Cassie Gutman, Jackie Douglass, Beth Oleniczak, Christa

Désir, Ashley Holstrom, Nicole Hower, and cover artist Kat Goodloe. All of you must have slipped into my dreams to create such beautiful concepts for this book. It is everything I could've hoped for, and I'm still in awe.

I am so grateful to Liz Denton, whose office feels like being wrapped in a hug, and to Sydney Blair: I will never forget the afternoon you kept me after class and told me I had the stamina to someday write a novel, and the way you grinned and said "Good" when I told you I already was. You will always be in my thoughts. I miss you.

My girls, my beta readers! Madeline Fouts, Emily Kovalenko, Erica Brandbergh, Stacy Brandbergh, Kelly Townsend, Hannah Latham, and Margaret Rawls. Thank you for reading and swooning. A special shout-out to Mikayla Woodley, my library study buddy. "How'd the *Hamlet* essay go?" you asked at the end of the night, and laughed when I replied, "*Hamlet?* Hamlet, who? I wrote Luke and Charlie's first kiss!"

Michael Atkins, did I ever truly tell you what this book was about while writing it? I don't think so, but your friendship and "premonitions" helped get me to today. You passed your bar, I passed mine.

Thank you to House Schenker for letting me camp out in your kitchen last summer. The change of scenery and an endless supply of seltzer did wonders for my writer's block. I'll water the geraniums anytime. Delaney, I love how much you love my characters' humor and heart. Madison, I love that you always want to hear my word-vomited thoughts and don't sugarcoat your well-articulated ones afterward. If I have a problem, you and Oishi have the answer.

To Trip Stowell, the most epic godfather in the galaxy. Sarah DePietro, I trust your creative eye more than my own, and cannot imagine where this book would be without your input. Kathleen Webber, thank you for writing about me when I'm too modest to write about myself. Josh Walther, for being there when I needed you most. Grandparents, you bring the hype. Thank you for all your enthusiasm and encouragement!

Hats off to my siblings: Hardy, I don't care if you think releasing your name is a security risk. You contributed to this story, and I think you're pretty great. Emily, I know I talk about Bexley a lot (like, *a lot*), but thank you for bearing with me and reading every word. Your light is so bright, and I love seeing it shine. You inspire me every day.

Mom and Dad: Thank you. Thank you for building me that dollhouse, for tying my skates, and letting me stay up late to read another chapter. Thank you for filling so many photo albums, for all the Rangers games, and for picking me up when I've fallen down. For your unconditional love and support. I know I've written so many letters to you over the years, but I am so blessed to be in our family, to call you my parents. I love you both very, very much.

And finally, to my high school alma mater. This book is not about you, but you are everywhere in it. You made me laugh, you made me cry, and you gave me a collection of memories that will last a lifetime. Bexley may be cobalt blue, but I will always bleed Big Red.

ABOUT THE AUTHOR

K. L. Walther was born and raised in the rolling hills of Bucks County, Pennsylvania, surrounded by family, dogs, and books. Her childhood was spent traveling the northeastern seaboard to play ice hockey. She attended a boarding school in New Jersey and went on to earn a BA in English from the University of Virginia. She is happiest on the beach with a book, cheering for the New York Rangers, or enjoying a rom-com while digging into a big bowl of popcorn and M&M's. Visit her online at klwalther.com.

FIREreads

#getbooklit

Your hub for the hottest young adult books!

Visit us online and sign up for our
newsletter at FIREreads.com

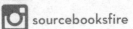 @sourcebooksfire

 sourcebooksfire

firereads.tumblr.com